The
Fearful

The Fearful

KEITH GRAY

Definitions

THE FEARFUL
A DEFINITIONS BOOK : 9780099456568

First published in Great Britain by The Bodley Head,
an imprint of Random House Children's Publishers UK

The Bodley Head edition published 2005
Definitions edition published 2006

7 9 10 8 6

Set in 12/15pt Garamond by Palimpsest Book Production Limited,
Polmont, Stirlingshire

Definitions are published by Random House Children's Publishers UK,
61–63 Uxbridge Road, London W5 5SA,
a division of The Random House Group Ltd

Addresses for companies within The Random House Group Limited
can be found at:
www.randomhouse.co.uk/offices.htm

THE RANDOM HOUSE GROUP Limited Reg. No. 954009

www.**randomhousechildrens**.co.uk

A CIP catalogue record for this book is available from the British Library.

Penguin Random House is committed to a sustainable future for
our business, our readers and our planet. This book is made from
Forest Stewardship Council® certified paper.

Printed and bound in Great Britain by Clays Ltd, Elcograf S.p.A.

*Biggest thanks must go to the effulgent Charlie
Sheppard, who fights very hard for me, and to
Carolyn Whitaker. They both deserve medals:
For tolerance in the face of extreme adversity.*

*Thank you to Miriam Hodgson for helping shape
the idea in the beginning, and to Harriet and Lucy
for eleventh-hour inspiration; to the Scottish Arts
Council for their support; and to Andy Briggs and
Steve – for being Andy Briggs and Steve.*

*But I'd like to dedicate this book,
with all my love, to Jasmine.*

Contents

Part One

Tim Milmullen's Monster

Whatever it was, it could only have been dead for a couple of hours. But in those couple of hours it had obviously been re-run over at least half a dozen times. Animal pancake. Either a fox or a cat, way too big for a squirrel. It took a lot of elbow grease to get it up from the road, the spade's metal blade ringing harshly against the tarmac in the early morning hush. And even then there were sticky bits of fur or something still left there.

Tim grimaced as he dumped it into the sack.

He stood in the lamppost light; even the sun wasn't up yet. It was six-thirty in the morning of what looked like turning out to be a particularly miserable November day. The tail end of last night's storm still whipped its chill wind around the tall elms and horse chestnuts lining either side of Park Avenue. It rattled the branches high above Tim's head and bit right through his cagoule and all four of his jumpers. On his I-hate-this-job scale of 1 to 10, he rated this at a 9, easily. Maybe even a 9½. He refused to give it a 10. Not that he knew a job worthy of a full 10; he just hated the thought that he could be doing *the worst job in the world*.

A car passed by on the road, kicking up leaves. He turned his back on its headlights in case it was someone who might recognize him.

Last night's storm had ripped the last of the leaves from the trees and they covered the avenue like a soggy blanket, making his task even more difficult. He slushed through the thick drifts in the gutter with his wellies, spotted the stiff, crooked body of a blackbird amongst all that brown, and tossed it quickly into the sack to join the fox or cat or whatever it was. He hated these mornings when he was forced into helping his father with the collecting; he tried not to think about having to do it for the rest of his life.

But he was determined *not* to have to do this for the rest of his life – that was the point. He'd do anything to stop it from happening. Anything. He'd change his name; he'd leave home if he had to. He just had to do it soon, because in only a few days he'd be sixteen and then, for what it was worth, the rest of his life would be over.

His father appeared from out of the darkness of the bushes at the edge of the park and Tim immediately felt guilty, worried his father would be able to tell what he was thinking. But the man didn't show any sign of it if he did. He was carrying a spade and a sack of his own. He stopped to kick around in the leaves by the roots of an old elm, aiming his torch, but didn't see anything interesting so walked over to where Tim was standing shivering in the road.

Bill Milmullen was a couple of centimetres taller than his son, with a black beard and slightly scruffy-looking hair that came down over his ears. He grew it long because he'd always

4

been self-conscious about the hearing aid in his left ear, something he'd had to wear since he was a child. He wasn't a man who usually drew attention to himself, but he looked conspicuous enough today in his yellow waterproofs.

'Any luck?' He took Tim's sack to feel the weight.

'Not much,' Tim said.

Bill shook his head, tugging gently on his beard. 'Not a good day,' he said. 'Not a good day at all, eh?' He turned to Tim, who simply shrugged.

He looked back across the park, tapping the toe of his boot gently with his spade, deciding what to do next. Tim watched him, wanting to force a decision on him; thinking, *Let's go home. Just say, 'Let's call it a day,' and head for home.*

But his father was no mind reader. And Tim didn't have the courage to voice his thoughts. The wind stirred the leaves at their feet.

'Didn't you manage to find anything?' Tim asked.

'Half a hedgehog,' his father said with a sigh. He took his spade up again. 'Well, the way I see it, we've got a choice. I checked the freezer before we came out, and it's full enough for tomorrow as it is, so we could always head home now. It's next week that worries me – if things are still no better we could end up with only half a feed for your Carving.' He raised his eyebrows at Tim, who was looking at his feet. 'So maybe it'd be best to head for the playing fields and hope we're luckier there. What do you think?' He checked his watch. 'We've got plenty of time before breakfast. It's not even seven yet. What do you reckon? See what we can find at the playing fields? That's going to be the best bet, isn't it?'

Tim didn't say a word as he trudged after his father back towards the van. He knew it wasn't as if he'd really had a choice anyway.

I'm going to leave home, he thought. *I'm going to have to get away*. And the thought shocked him a little. Not because it was a new thought – he'd been thinking it for months. It shocked him because he suddenly realized he could; he really and truly, honestly *could*. He trembled slightly inside his thin cagoule and four jumpers. If push came to shove, he had to get away.

'Mr Milmullen. Hello! Mr Milmullen.'

Both Tim and his father turned at the sound of the voice. Mrs Kirkwooding was standing at the top of the driveway of her large, austere house that overlooked the park. The elderly lady waved again, clutching a purple dressing gown around her skinny frame. Bill hurried over and Tim was quick to follow. At last, this was a stroke of luck. He realized her appearance could mean he got to go home early, so he put a spring in his step to catch up with his dad.

'Mrs Kirkwooding; how are you this morning?'

'Ah, Mr Milmullen, good. I'm so pleased to have caught you.' The old lady fought with the wind for the hem of her dressing gown. 'I'm afraid I've lost Marshal,' she said. 'I was hoping you could help.' Tim's father looked dubious. But the old lady was already walking away up her long driveway, expecting the pair of them to follow.

Mrs Kirkwooding was a friend of the Milmullens, a regular on Saturday mornings: one of the Fearful. She lived alone in her grand house, had done ever since Dr Kirkwooding died. She kept the house itself spotless, even had a girl from Tim's year at school help her with all the dusting and polishing, but she refused to touch the garden. She'd left it to grow and sprawl exactly as it wanted to over the years, saying that it had always been her husband's passion and she had no right to interfere even now. But she sometimes prowled through the unruly bushes and overhanging trees, searching for small dead things – frogs, or birds, or mice. And of course anything she found was saved for Saturday mornings.

They left their sacks and spades outside when she ushered them through the back door into the kitchen. She shivered and closed the door behind them to keep the weather in its place. Tim's father nudged him with a discreet elbow to remind him to wipe his feet on the mat. He shuffled them quickly, glancing around the kitchen. It looked almost as old-fashioned as theirs back home, but he got the feeling the pipes under Mrs Kirkwooding's sink didn't leak, and he reckoned the toaster probably popped up without the help of a fork jammed in its side.

'He passed away in his sleep,' the elderly lady was telling his father. Her dark, permed hair was wind-blown and showing its steely roots. 'I'm sure it was peaceful enough.'

Tim stepped up behind them. The dead golden retriever was in his basket in front of the washing machine.

Bill knelt down and gently stroked the dog's ear. 'Yes,'

he said quietly. 'He certainly looks peaceful enough, doesn't he?' Without turning to look at the old lady he asked, 'Are you sure you want Tim and me to take him?'

Mrs Kirkwooding nodded. 'Oh, yes. It's what I decided a long time ago.'

'Maybe burying him – or cremation maybe? – would seem more respectful.'

'No, I'd like you to take him.'

'It's just a thought, Mrs Kirkwooding, but in the past when anyone's allowed a family pet to be eaten—'

The old lady folded her arms and stood her ground. 'If you are anxious about what my neighbours may think, Mr Milmullen, then thank you for your concern. But my family has lived in Moutonby just as long as yours, and my sisters and I were all brought up to believe in the legend just the same as *you* and *your* brother were. We have always been proud to be Fearful.'

Tim's father rose to his feet, nodding quickly, smiling widely, trying to placate her. 'Yes, I understand that – of course I do. It's just that with times being like they are, certain people may see feeding Marshal to the Mourn as, well, a rather callous thing to do.' He turned to Tim. 'Wouldn't you agree?'

Tim didn't get the chance to answer.

'No, I would not.' The old lady simply refused to back down. 'I would see it as doing my duty. And if "certain people" would also do theirs, then you would not be outside my house at the crack of dawn collecting roadkill, would you?'

Bill slowly shook his head, looking at the dead dog. 'No,

Mrs Kirkwooding, I don't think we would.' He tugged on his beard, as was his habit, and sighed heavily. 'I don't think we would.' Then to Tim: 'I'll bring the van round. We'll have to carry him between us.'

Tim nodded, not exactly sure what to say. His father left and he stared down at the dead Marshal. Okay, at least this meant they had enough for the Feed and could go home now, so he guessed he was pleased. But Marshal certainly wasn't their usual kind of collection. And for some reason it made Tim feel peculiar inside.

'The lake was one of his favourite places to be walked,' Mrs Kirkwooding was saying.

Tim nodded and murmured a kind of 'um' sound. He had often seen the two of them. Maybe that was what was so strange about it.

The old lady smiled at him. 'Maybe you'd like to include him in the Feed next Saturday? It would certainly be an honour on your special day. I'd like to feel I'd made a contribution to your Carving celebration.'

Tim stayed quiet; he wouldn't look at her.

'I'm sure your school friends are all very envious.' She was standing at his shoulder, beaming down at both him and Marshal. 'You're going to be the most important person in Moutonby.'

And with a bit of effort he managed to hold his tongue.

Ten minutes later they had Marshal covered by a blanket in the back of the van and were heading home. Bill had been right: it had taken the two of them to carry him. Tim

9

couldn't stop himself from turning round every so often and staring at the hump of the dirty, brown blanket. The tip of the dog's tail poked out at one side.

'We'll get complaints about this,' his father said. 'Somebody's bound to say something, just you wait. Somebody'll complain.'

'Are you really going to use him as feed?'

'I don't suppose I have much of a choice, really. Mrs Kirkwooding can be very specific when she wants to be.' He smiled, albeit briefly. 'I'm just not looking forward to having to fend off the phone calls from outraged animal-lovers in the middle of the night. It'd be nice if these people would realize that we're doing it for their own good. I know it's unpleasant, but if it wasn't for our family, well . . .' He sighed, looking tired; looking like a man with the weight of the whole town on his shoulders. Which is exactly what he believed he was, of course.

Tim didn't say anything in reply, but he managed to turn round and face forward again.

They drove home in silence along the streets of the small northern town. People were just beginning to wake up; you could almost hear the hundreds of alarm clocks ringing. They'd be sitting down to breakfast and beginning to psych themselves up ready for another day at work or school. In the old days, or so Tim had been told, everyone would have waved or shouted greetings to his father as he passed by, just as they had done to his grandfather, and great-grandfather, and great-great-grandfather. And so on. Everybody in those days had been Fearful.

10

The Milmullen family history had been a proud one in Moutonby. As the Mourner his father would have been one of the most respected men in the town. People would have asked for his opinion and advice. But times had changed – or so Tim had been told – because nowadays his family were the butt of every joke these people told. Not that his father seemed to notice. He still followed the old traditions; he still talked about duty and commitment; he still held dearly to the legend. He spent two mornings a week scraping roadkill out of the gutter to protect these people. These people who no longer waved or shouted greetings, but laughed as soon as his back was turned.

Tim hated these people sometimes. And then other times . . .

He watched his father behind the wheel of the ancient, crappy van. He looked older than he should, with deep lines across his brow, and more than one bag under each eye. Recently he'd acquired a few silver threads in his beard. Tim had been told a hundred times or more by the other kids at school that his father was crazy. To Tim he just looked tired. And he knew that one day he would be just as tired, just as talked about.

Just as crazy?

The Milmullen family tradition says that the son will take over the father's role when he turns sixteen, which was exactly what his father had done before him. And his grandfather, and his great-grandfather. And so on.

Tim was sixteen in only eight days' time – next Saturday,

the 25th. He'd have his Carving and then his future would quite literally be set in stone.

The road ran around the tip of the lake and the houses fell away. Bill swung the van off the road onto the muddy track that led across the waste ground towards the water's edge. The van bounced and groaned in the ruts. Their house stood alone on the shore and Tim had once asked his father why no one else had a house next to the lake. 'Because the town likes to keep its distance,' had been the simple reply.

Built over the year 1699 to 1700 by Old William Milmullen, it no longer looked like the sentinel or ever-watchful guard it had originally been intended as. But neither did it look like the welcoming guesthouse it was meant to be now.

From the outside it was a tall, spiny, grey, angular building – remarkable for its ugliness. There was a patchy wall of conifers on one side, and a garage on the other – a very twentieth-century addition and pebble-dashed to prove it – but no lawn as such. There was the attempt at a gravel driveway with room enough for several guests' cars. No doorway faced the town, but an arched entrance opened out onto the lake shore (and Tim's mother's 'garden', consisting of two much-fussed-over flowerbeds on either side). Above the door, carved into the weathered stone of the arch, were the words MOURN HOME.

A side door led from the kitchen onto the driveway. Bill pulled up beside it. 'You go get changed and ready to help with the breakfasts,' he said. 'I'll be okay getting everything to the freezer.'

'Don't you want me to give you a hand with Marshal?'

'No, no; I'll manage.' He smiled at his son, but looked slightly distracted as he did so. 'He's big enough to make two feeds, and I'd rather sort that out myself.'

Tim nodded, but couldn't help sneaking one last glance at the hump of the brown blanket (and the tip of the tail) as he climbed out of the van.

He headed straight upstairs. He could hear his mother and sister starting breakfast in the kitchen but decided he wanted to leave the job of talking about Marshal to his father as well.

His bedroom was at the top of the house, third floor up; it used to be the attic. He dumped his cagoule on the floor in front of his wardrobe and set to work getting rid of the four jumpers he'd stuffed himself inside.

The room was messy, but massive; he didn't have enough posters to cover the walls. The floor was wooden, which looked nice, but was way too cold first thing in the morning at this time of year. A scattering of threadbare rugs made a well-trodden path from his bed to the washbasin in the far corner. He had a bulky, almost-antique bookcase that wasn't as full as he'd like it to be, and an old dressing table that he used as a desk, with last week's homework still unfinished somewhere in among the chaos of papers scattered on top.

There was also a second-hand electric typewriter from when he'd wanted to be a journalist. Leaning against the wall next to his wardrobe was an acoustic guitar because he'd wanted to learn how to play at one time. It was covered in dust and had two broken strings. There was a pile of photography books that needed to go back to the library because he'd never been able to save up enough to buy himself a camera. Over and over he'd tried to find something he could be that would take him far away.

The most remarkable feature of his room was the three huge windows looking east, south and west. Moutonby and Lake Mou are buried in the heart of Yorkshire, and Yorkshire is renowned for being the largest county in England. Which was why he couldn't see too much of it, even from up here. The imposing lake filled the valley and the view – to walk its circumference would take at least half a day and over nine miles worth of anybody's stamina.

Tim often stood at his windows. To the east he could see the deep, dark waters of Lake Mou. And to the south he could see the dark, deep waters of Lake Mou. While the view out of the west window was, well, pretty much the same really.

No, that's not strictly true. To the west the shore was uneven and ragged, with the pine woods tumbling over the hills and rushing all the way down to the water, and the slow blue of the river Hurry threading its way down between them towards the town and its lake. Pure picture-postcard scenery. South was just water – water for as far as he could see. But stretching out seventy metres or so from the shore was the gangplank feeding pier Great-Grandfather Thomas had built when he'd realized he was scared of boats.

For Tim, looking east had always been the most interesting view, because the WetFun water-sports club sat on the gentle curve of shoreline – just off the main road which would take you to Lancaster, Leeds, York, wherever you wanted to escape to. The club was an endless source of fascination for him. He enjoyed watching the windsurfers and water-skiers doing their stuff. The night-time bar was usually loud and lively.

He often wished he had a fourth window, one to look north with a view of the town. The water could be beautiful, especially on summer days with the million golden camera-flashes winking in the sun, but he sometimes thought it would be nice to look at something solid for once, something which wasn't constantly rippling and shifting and changing. It could make your eyes go funny if you stared at the lake for too long.

He freed himself from the last jumper and moved over to the south-facing window. The wind chopped and stirred the surface of the water, making waves. He certainly had the best view in town of Lake Mou; there was no denying that. And he'd watched the water every day of his life for as long as he could remember. So if anyone was going to see the creature that supposedly lived there, it'd be him, right?

Yet so far . . .

Mourn Home

'Have they been told?'

Bill Milmullen couldn't stop a sneaky draught of cold air from squeezing past him into the kitchen. He hurried the door closed and set to removing his waterproofs and heavy boots.

Like the rest of Mourn Home the kitchen had been built with a stately scale of ambition. But, like the rest of Mourn Home, it hadn't aged well. The stone floor was dangerously worn and uneven, and required concentration when carrying stacked crockery. The slab-like wooden table in the centre could easily seat ten, so to be able to hold a conversation without shouting during meal times the Milmullens all huddled around one end. And while the oven was probably great at roasting wild boar, it could certainly be a little heavy-handed when it came to fish fingers.

Bill glanced over his shoulder at his wife and Tim, but nodded at Tim's twin sister, Jenny, in particular. 'The students,' he said. 'Has anyone told them?'

Jenny was carrying two plates full of Full English. She shrugged. 'I haven't said anything.' She tried to catch Tim's eye but he was determined to keep out of it as long as he could – because he knew what was coming. He concentrated on the washing-up like it meant life or death or something.

Bill turned to their mother. 'Annie?'

'Let them eat first, love.' She was cracking fresh eggs into the frying pan.

It was sometimes difficult to tell with Bill whether he was honestly having trouble with his hearing aid, or simply wasn't listening. 'They'll be wanting to get out there as soon as they've had their breakfast.'

'I'm not sure if it's the kind of thing your guests want to hear about while they're eating,' Anne said, raising her voice just a little.

Jenny stood in the middle of the kitchen looking from one parent to the other, still holding the two plates. Tim scrubbed harder than was necessary at the cereal bowls, adding yet another generous squirt of Fairy.

'I don't want them going out there without being told,' Bill said.

His wife smiled at him reassuringly. 'I'll catch them before they leave.'

Anne Milmullen was a beautiful woman. Tim knew this. It couldn't be denied when you compared her to other Moutonby mothers. She wasn't drab, or grey, or gloomy. She'd been born here, lived all her life in this small town, yet he and Jenny reckoned their dad was lucky to have met her. And although they were twins, it was Jenny who was growing up to look like her. Whereas Tim worried he was getting more and more like their father every day.

17

Bill took over from Anne at the stove so she could get her own breakfast. Jenny was still standing there with the students' meals, unsure whether to serve them just yet. 'Mum?' she asked.

Anne nodded. 'Don't let them get too cold.'

But Bill was insistent. 'I think Tim should tell them.'

Even though Tim could have guessed this was going to happen he still flinched at the sound of his name. He buried himself up to his elbows in suds and pretended he hadn't heard. He did not, *not*, want to have to talk to the students about the Mourn. They'd laugh in his face.

Jenny had been halted mid-stride yet again and clicked her tongue with audible annoyance. Nobody spoke. Anne was pouring herself a cup of coffee; Bill was pushing the spitting, popping eggs around in the pan. So Jenny sighed as loudly as she could.

Anne glanced across at her husband before making up her own mind. 'Come on then, Tim. Their stomachs will be thinking their throats have been cut.'

He was still washing up. 'I'm still washing up.'

'Your father's right. The boys need to be told before they go out on the lake.'

'Can't Jenny tell them?'

'I don't mind telling them,' Jenny said. Tim had known she would. He knew her so well. It was obvious she fancied the one who called himself Gully – any more obvious and she'd have a neon sign flashing on her head. She was wearing a T-shirt usually regarded as far too cool for serving breakfast – make-up too.

The battery in Bill's hearing aid must have been on the blink. He still had his back to everyone when he said, 'It's your responsibility now, Tim.'

'And it'll be your neck as well,' Anne told him, 'if they complain about their breakfasts being cold. Jenny, you can take Mr Spicer his, please.'

Tim had plenty more arguments left in him, but knew now was not the time. Reluctantly he dried his hands, then when he tried to take the plates from Jenny she held on and pulled a face at him. But it wasn't his fault, was it? They silently tussled for a second or two. It wasn't like he wanted to serve her darling Gully.

And he felt resentful towards her. He said, 'These breakfasts are massive. Have you been giving them extra portions on purpose, Jenny?'

She went red – instantly. And leaped away from him, letting go of the plates.

'Tim . . .' his mother warned.

'But look at the size of them!' he said, holding out the plates for all to see.

Jenny spun on her heel to face the sink as if something in there desperately required her attention.

Tim said, 'What happens if they think we're trying to fatten them up for tomorrow's feed?'

Bill turned round sharply. But before he could say anything Tim was pushing backwards through the door into the guest dining room.

'I'm going, I'm going,' he muttered.

* * *

19

Anne took pride in making the dining room as bright and welcoming as she could. There were always fresh flowers on the sideboard and at the tables. She did her best to hide the fact that it was over three centuries old with a contemporary, but still warm, decorating touch.

Three of the eight tables were occupied. Jack Spicer sat looking out at the lake from the table everyone had come to think of as his for the past thirty years, an unread newspaper in front of him. He was their most regular guest, spending maybe two or three months here each year. Tim's father regarded him as an old family friend and he often accompanied Bill around the lake. Tim and Jenny had always thought of him as a little severe, chilly – not at all the grandfatherly type. Even as youngsters they'd found themselves becoming quiet and polite and respectful in his company, which Tim knew had always been an effort for his sister. The old man nodded good morning to him now and he smiled quickly in reply.

The annoyingly friendly American couple, Mike and Sylvie, were in front of the fireplace at the table Anne considered the most pleasant. They were already eating but found time to smile hello as well. They'd only been here a couple of days, weren't planning on staying much longer. The two university students who'd arrived yesterday afternoon were at the smaller table just behind them. Gully sat up straight, rubbing his hands in expectation when he saw the huge pile of bacon and eggs and sausage and tomato and black pudding that Tim was carrying. Scott, on the other hand, looked half asleep.

'Brilliant, brilliant, brilliant.' Gully was generous with the brown sauce the second Tim put the plate down in front of him. He was tall, blond, with a pop-star-perfect face – which was why Jenny liked him so much, Tim guessed.

Scott was darker and a lot broader. Maybe he played rugby or something. His face was pale this morning, however, and he seemed reluctant to move. Tim realized he must be hung over, remembering they'd both spent a late night in the bar at WetFun, coming back loud and drunk after midnight.

He stood at their table, watching Gully shovel the food down while Scott summoned the courage to start. He felt small and young and embarrassed. And he hated it. The familiar resentment towards his father was soaking up into him, feet first, as though he were a sponge for it.

Scott was looking at him and Tim shrugged quickly to hide his awkwardness at hovering there. He said, 'You look like you could do with an aspirin or something.' It was just so he had something – anything – to say.

Gully grinned and jabbed his fork at his friend. 'You look like shit.'

Scott nodded as though it hurt. 'Yeah. Déjà vu.'

Gully laughed through a mouthful of sausage, louder than Tim thought was necessary, but he tried to join in on the joke by laughing as well because he wanted to be liked by them. He'd heard Gully say 'Who cares?' at least half a dozen times when they arrived yesterday afternoon. Tim could easily imagine being one of them himself some day.

The kitchen door swung open and Jenny appeared with

Jack Spicer's breakfast. Gully, Scott and Tim all watched her. And it was obvious she knew she was being watched because colour rose up her neck to her cheeks. She served Mr Spicer quickly but politely, and still without once looking at the students' table she asked the American couple if everything was okay for them ('We're fine, honey. Just fine,' Sylvie beamed); only then did she turn and scowl at Tim. All he could do was scowl back as she disappeared into the kitchen again.

He continued to hover, not wanting to say anything more, but knowing he couldn't escape back into the kitchen until he did.

Scott broke the yolk of his egg with his knife and let it ooze across his plate. He looked up at Tim as if he'd forgotten he was there and raised his eyebrow by way of a question.

'Aspirin?' Tim asked. 'Can I get you one?'

Scott shook his head. 'I'll survive.'

But Tim couldn't go anywhere just yet. Gully was also watching him now, so he said, 'You're windsurfing then?'

'That's the plan.'

He nodded. 'Great.' The awkwardness was making him hot. 'So . . . How did you know about this place? It's a bit out of the way.'

'I've been here before,' Scott said. 'Came here when I was in my first year.'

'Yeah? Why?' Maybe he wouldn't have to explain things after all.

'I was doing a Geology degree, before it got too boring. But it's a weird shape or something – weird rock formations along the shore? – and we had to discover why it happened thousands of years ago. Big waste of time, really, if you ask me. But isn't it meant to be deeper than anywhere else around here too?'

'That's right, yeah. It's really deep.'

'So they said. Weird shape, but deep. A bit like Gully.'

His friend grinned at him but didn't stop chewing.

Tim was smiling furiously, wanting desperately to ingratiate himself. 'Yeah, yeah. It used to be called the Hundredwaters, because it was so deep. You know, people say, "It's as deep as one hundred waters." Nobody's ever seen what's at the bottom.'

Scott shrugged. 'I just remember that it rained all the time, and it was ridiculously cold, freezing, so half of us went to the pub anyway. Geology wasn't for me. But that's how I knew about the water-sports club.'

Gully suddenly joined in. 'Last night the guy who runs the place said we could use a couple of the jet-skis if we wanted. I'm up for that.'

Tim nodded as if it was the most interesting fact he'd ever heard. 'Great.'

'You must have been a few times,' Scott said. 'You any good?'

Tim's smile slipped a little. 'Jet-skiing?' He shook his head. 'No. Never tried.'

Both Gully and Scott looked as surprised as their attitudes would allow.

And Tim took the plunge. 'Well, you know, it's meant to be dangerous.'

23

He let his words hang there; hoping one of them would jump in and say, 'Yeah, we know all about *that*,' and save him the embarrassment. Unfortunately they simply stared at him.

So with a shrug he said, 'What with the monster and everything . . .'

Gully's chewing slowly came to a halt. 'What?'

Tim felt like he was wading through deep water. 'Hasn't anybody told you?' He tried to look shocked. 'It's the local legend, you see. The Mourn. It's called the Mourn.' He was nodding his head like it was on a quick spring. 'Yeah. It lives in the lake. It eats people . . .' He coughed, shuffled his feet. 'Sometimes.'

Gully's mouth hung open wide enough for Tim to be able to see the mush of bacon and beans in there. He had a real urge to laugh and shout, 'Nah! Just kidding!' But couldn't. He realized the elderly American couple were listening in, and guessed Mr Spicer might well be too. He said quietly, 'It's the local legend.'

Scott narrowed his eyes dubiously. 'You've got a monster? In the lake?'

Tim nodded. 'Yeah. It's called the Mourn. It—'

'Like the Loch Ness Monster or something?'

'Erm . . . Not really.'

'Like a leftover dinosaur or something?'

'No. Not really,' Tim repeated.

Gully swallowed hard. 'This is *so* cool!' He looked to Scott for confirmation of just how cool it was.

'I've never heard of it,' Scott said. His narrowed eyes watched Tim carefully.

24

'It's just local,' Tim tried to explain. 'But, you know . . . I thought you'd better know before you go out on the lake.' He said, 'Be careful,' and felt stupid the second the words were out of his mouth.

Gully was ploughing through his breakfast even quicker now, desperate to get it down him. 'I want to go out there. Water-skiing with a big, massive monster snapping at my arse. Fantastic! You ever seen *Jaws*?'

Scott laughed at him before asking Tim: 'So who's it eaten, then?'

'Some kids; years ago.'

'When? I didn't see anything on the news.'

'No, no, you wouldn't have. It was three hundred years ago.' He was being forced into saying far more than he'd planned to. He wanted to be back in the kitchen where they could take the piss without his knowing or seeing them do it. 'Well, just over. 1699.' But he couldn't shut himself up now. 'There were five of them and it—'

'Come on,' Gully was telling Scott. 'We've got to get out there.'

Scott wasn't moving, however. '1699? So it's just a legend, then?'

Thinking, *How many times do you need telling?* he said, 'Yeah.'

Sylvie turned round in her seat to face them. 'It's a real interesting story,' she said to Scott. 'There's a little piece about it in my guidebook. I'll let you read it if you like.'

Her husband leaned forward and waved his fork at them. 'It's barely more than a paragraph – blink and you'd miss it. But we've come out of our way because she liked the story so much.'

'But it's so interesting, Mike.'

Mike murmured that he guessed it was.

Scott raised an eyebrow. 'Sounds like I missed the best part of the lecture when I was here.'

'I want to look for it,' Gully said. 'I was up at Loch Ness as a kid once and had a *riot*.' He was grinning hugely. 'I made my sister cack her pants when I pushed her in.'

Tim felt overwhelmed by the sudden interest everybody was showing. 'Nobody's seen it for ages,' he blurted out.

'Is that why this place is called Mourn Home?' Scott asked. 'Because of your legend?'

Tim didn't get chance to answer, Mike jumped in there for him. 'That's right,' he said. 'It was built so the town could be protected if the monster ever attacked again. Sonny, here – his pop's its guardian or keeper or something.'

'Its keeper,' Sylvie said. 'They call him the *Mourner*. It's all in the guidebook. I'll get it for you.'

'Have you seen it, then?' Gully asked Tim. 'Or is it just a load of bollocks like Nessie?'

'No one's seen it for ages,' he said, feeling their stares and questions as if they were physical blows.

Scott was nodding. 'Just another tourist trap,' he said.

Tim frowned. 'No, it's not . . .' But he didn't know how to explain it. 'It's just my dad's job. It's tradition.' He was struggling to defend something which deep down he didn't really want to.

And then Mr Spicer said: 'I've seen it.'

Tim was thankful to be able to duck back through into the kitchen while Jack Spicer told his story. He wanted to act up and stamp his feet and declare how embarrassing and stupid it had been, but he couldn't, because Sarah was there.

She was sitting at the table next to his mother with a cup of tea, chatting away quite happily. Anne said, 'Sarah's here,' as if he couldn't tell.

His girlfriend smiled widely. 'I thought we could walk to school together.' Her cheeks were rosy with having just come in from the cold, her long hair pleasantly wind-blown. She was as nice-girl pretty as ever. And Tim managed a decent smile in return, but struggled to feel honestly pleased about her visit.

Bill was cooking his own breakfast now. He'd recently become concerned about his cholesterol so he didn't fry his sausages and bacon; these days he used one of those mini grilling machines instead. 'Did you tell them?'

'Yes. I told them.' He felt like he needed some kind of victory of his own so he added, 'Not that it did any good. It just made the idiot one that Jenny fancies want to go out there more.'

Jenny pulled a face at him. 'You're not *funny*, Tim.'

'But it's true, isn't it?' he asked with fake innocence. 'I saw all the extra tomato and bacon piled up on his plate and—'

'Just shush, the pair of you,' Anne told them, sounding like she'd said it a million times before – which she probably had. 'The last thing our guests want to hear is you two bickering.'

Bill tutted, whether at the students or his children it wasn't clear. Tim and Jenny sneered at each other. Then both turned to Sarah to win her support against the other. Sarah looked uncomfortable and stared at her teacup, hiding her face behind the fall of her tightly curled brown hair.

Her father was the Underbearer, the Mourner's right-hand man. And she was also in Jenny's class at school; they'd been best friends since they were little. She'd become Tim's girlfriend last of all, and that had been by accident. It was true he liked her a lot – she was pretty and clever and interesting, and they'd done more than just kiss. But the problem was, she was part of everything Tim wanted to get away from.

'My dad asked if you'd call round to see him sometime today, Mr Milmullen,' she said to Bill, filling the awkward silence.

'I can do that,' he said. 'Everything okay?'

'I think so. He was just saying he's not sure about every-thing that happens next week. If he has to do anything special when he becomes Tim's Underbearer.'

'No problem. I'll talk to him.'

Sarah gave Tim an uncertain smile. 'It'll be kind of weird having you as my dad's boss.'

Quite honestly, the thought frightened and appalled him in equal measure. 'It's not really a *boss*,' he said. Only a couple of weeks ago Mr Gregory had gone mad when he'd discovered a love-bite the size of a 20p piece on his daughter's neck. He'd given Tim hell. He'd banned him from Sarah's bedroom, threatened to tell Bill, but Tim had practically begged him not to. And a week tomorrow Tim was meant to be his boss? It made him shiver inside.

He met Sarah's eye and reckoned she was thinking something similar. She seemed to find it funny, however, and forced a cough, covering her mouth to stifle a giggle.

Jenny was watching her curiously, and Sarah recovered herself quickly to ask, 'Have you seen what's happening at WetFun?'

'What's Vic Stones up to now?' Bill grumbled.

'I'm not sure,' Sarah said. 'But when I passed on the way here I could see all these trucks and bulldozers there. Is he building a house?'

'Not that I know of.' Bill caught his wife's eye.

'He can't be,' Anne said. 'We signed all of the forms making it clear we were against giving him planning permission.'

Bill didn't look happy. He abandoned his breakfast and headed outside to see what he could see.

Tim was quick to follow him. Anything that happened at the water-sports club had always been of the utmost importance to him.

'You've got a guest, Tim,' Anne said reprovingly as he shoved his shoes on without untying the laces first.

'I'm only looking. She can come too if she wants.'

He followed his father around the front of the house. It wasn't quite full light just yet – the sun was still climbing from cloud to cloud – but they could make out the buildings across the way.

There was a kind of love/hate relationship between Bill Milmullen and Victor Stones, who owned WetFun. Stones didn't like the idea of the Milmullen family tradition because it wasn't always clever to tell his water-worshipping customers that a man-eating creature lived in the lake where they played. But many of those customers travelled a fair distance and needed somewhere to stay, and Mourn Home was the closest guesthouse to the club. So, on the other side of the coin, although Bill certainly couldn't approve of people being out on the lake and putting themselves in constant danger, he needed their custom. But it didn't mean he and Vic Stones had to be friends or anything.

The water-sports club itself was little more than a modern blot on the landscape. The main clubhouse was a lot of glass and neon, looking like a large aquarium to Tim's eye. Late at night there were often private parties in the bar, and from his bedroom he could see everybody drinking inside, having a good time. There were three grey metal sheds to the side of the flashy main building – storage sheds for the boats and equipment. Two narrow jetties shot out over the lake with dinghies and sailing boats moored close together. More small boats were pulled up on trailers on the shore.

It was in front of the storage sheds that the trucks Sarah had talked about were standing; construction trucks with breeze blocks and sand, a cement mixer and even a small JCB. There were workmen milling around. While Bill and Tim watched, Vic Stones himself arrived in his new silver BMW. He was a big man and the car rocked as he climbed out.

'What's he building?'

Bill took several long seconds to reply. Then with a growl he said, 'Bad news for us, that's what.'

Monster Boy I

There was a fine rain on Tim's high window at the top of the house. Peering out he could see the two students making their way along the footpath that skirted the shoreline, heading for the water-sports club. Gully was tall and animated, enthusiastically waving his arms out at the lake as he spoke. Scott's hands were shoved deep in his pockets and he walked slightly hunched, as if up a steep slope, but his head was turned, his eyes watching the water. They followed the path all the way onto WetFun property, passed the trucks and the workmen, walking through the spaces where the walls of Vic Stones's brand-new hotel would soon stand.

Bill was on the phone downstairs, trying to get an answer to just why Stones had been granted planning permission for something that could spell the end of Mourn Home, even when he had so vehemently opposed it? Tim had heard the angry accusations of money greasing greedy palms as he disappeared up to his room. He watched the JCB lumbering into position and wondered how long it would take to build a whole hotel from scratch.

Longer than a week, probably. Because that's all the time Tim felt he had left.

Jenny shouted from the bottom of his stairs for him to hurry up.

'Yeah, yeah,' he muttered under his breath, finally turning away from the window to face his immediate problem this morning.

He sighed even louder at the sight of his desk. The mess was quite staggering. He didn't honestly think he could find what he was looking for, did he? He was frustrated with himself for letting everything get into such a state – again.

He insisted that it was *his* room, *his* space, and his parents respected the fact (albeit his mother rather reluctantly). But he could retreat here. It was up a different staircase to his parents' and Jenny's rooms, making him feel cut off from everything else that went on downstairs. Exactly the way he liked it.

He did try to be neat and tidy and organized, but stuff just seemed to *accumulate*. Most of it was crap, he'd admit that. There was age-old schoolwork buried amongst piles of comics and magazines. Half a dozen half-read books. Pages of stories he'd half written. There was a mug of cold tea and a dirty breakfast bowl; a couple of CDs out of their cases smeared with fingerprints; one empty can of deodorant and two still half-full.

He heard footsteps coming up the stairs and guessed his sister was wanting to chivvy him along a little. But it was Sarah who poked her head round the bedroom door.

'Jenny says you've got to get a move on. She says she's fed up always being late because of you . . .'

He caught the look on his girlfriend's face when she saw the state of his room and cringed inwardly. 'Tell her I've just got to find my homework.' He did his best to block her view – but it was a big room. Usually he managed to shove things under the bed or into the bottom of his wardrobe when he knew she was coming round. 'Say I'll be down in a minute, will you?'

Unfortunately Sarah didn't leave. She stepped over to him carefully, not treading on the dirty clothes strewn here, there and everywhere, obviously in awe of the mess.

'I know it's a tip,' he said, embarrassed. 'But you've got to admit, it's an impressive tip.'

'How do you manage to find *anything* in here?'

'Luck,' he told her with a straight face. He kicked a jumper and a dirty pair of jeans under his bed, picked up one of the piles of stuff to put it on top of another – as if that helped to make things look a little more respectable. 'And patience.'

She laughed and took hold of his hand, squeezing it. She stood on her tiptoes to kiss him quickly. 'I've been wanting to do that all morning.'

'Me too,' he said without meeting her eye.

More and more these days he felt strangely awkward around her, as though it was getting more and more difficult to find things to say to her. Talking hadn't mattered much at first; kissing and stuff had easily filled the silences – who needed to talk? Nowadays, however, he was seeing her less and less because even the kisses felt forced. He wished he could put into words what had happened. Being with her had lost its shine – was that it? He wasn't meaning to string her along – he knew he must be going mad because

33

she was beautiful and clever and cared for him. And maybe it was just a phase, maybe the 'shine' would come back. He'd felt it once, so maybe he could feel it again.

He didn't have the guts to say anything to her about it, obviously. She was Jenny's best friend; her father was the Underbearer; she was pretty much a part of the family already. If he stopped going out with her everybody would want to know why and he didn't think he could admit the truth. It would be opening a far bigger can of worms than he reckoned he could cope with.

He'd thought about it often enough and decided that his perfect girlfriend would probably not even live in Moutonby. His perfect girlfriend would agree that being the Mourner was a crappy job and would want to escape with him to live on the other side of the world somewhere. It wasn't Sarah's fault, but she seemed happy here.

'What homework is it?' she asked, ignoring the fact that he was tugging on her hand, trying to pull her towards the door.

'Nothing much. Just some English for Mr Wing.'

She tugged back gently, slipping her hand free. 'And it's definitely in here somewhere?'

'Think so.'

She surveyed the disaster site in front of her. 'Come on. I'll help you look.'

But the thought of having her rooting through his mess was too much. 'No! No, don't worry. May as well just forget it.' He took hold of her wrist to drag her away this time. 'Let's just go.'

'You can't not hand it in. You know what Mr Wing's like.'

Jenny shouted from the bottom of the stairs again, threatening to leave without them, but only got halfway through what she was saying before suddenly falling silent. Tim guessed Bill must have snapped at her to quieten down.

'Is my dad still on the phone?'

Sarah nodded. Then asked, 'How bad will it be if Mr Stones builds a hotel?'

'Are you kidding? My mum and dad are always going on about not having enough guests, and if everybody goes to Stones's hotel we won't have any at all. You can't run a guesthouse without guests, can you?'

'Do you think you'd have to move?'

'I don't know,' Tim admitted. There was a small part of him that wondered if this was how he avoided becoming the Mourner. *No Mourn Home, no Mourner.* Guiltily he forced the idea right to the back of his mind. Sarah was watching him closely; he avoided meeting her eyes. 'Come on,' he said, pulling her towards the door. 'Better get moving before Jenny—'

'What about your homework?'

He shook his head. 'Who cares? It'll just be a detention or something. But it's not as if it matters, is it?'

Sarah didn't answer.

'What are they going to do? Kick me out?' He laughed quickly, tried to make it sound like he couldn't care less either way. 'The teachers know I don't need to pass my exams to get a job or anything. I could drop out of school after my Carving next Saturday if I really wanted to, and I doubt any of them would notice. It's not like I'm their star pupil or anything.' He didn't mean this to come out quite as sharply as it did, because they both knew Sarah *was* that star pupil. 'You know what I mean,' he said.

She pulled a tiny smile.

'I'm *Monster Boy*,' he told her, using the hated nickname lightly in an attempt to make her believe his false levity. 'Who's going to argue with me?'

She smiled fully now, putting her arms around his neck. 'You're *my* Monster Boy.' She put her head on his shoulder. 'And I love you.'

He squirmed – just a little, not so she'd notice. He knew what she wanted to hear in return. But . . . He grinned his cheesiest grin. 'I love me too.'

She didn't find it funny. She blinked quickly but wasn't quite able to hide the disappointment in her eyes.

He wrestled for something to say that would please her. He squeezed her hand and said the first thing that came to mind. 'When are we going to get some time alone? You know, just me and you?'

'Any time *you* have time, I suppose.'

The moment was uncomfortable. He said, 'Why don't you come and stay over this weekend? Like we've said about before?'

'My parents would never let me.'

'Tell them you and Jenny are doing homework or something.' He felt it was a safe suggestion to make, didn't believe she'd actually go through with it. 'I'll get a key for one of

36

the rooms, yeah? And we can spend the night together. Like we've always said we would.'

She nodded slowly. 'I'll try. But you know what my dad's like . . .'

He hugged her briefly, pleased he'd kept her happy without actually committing to anything in his own mind. 'Great. It'll be great.'

Sarah's mobile rang briefly. She dug it out of her pocket. 'Jenny's sent a text.'

'What's she say?'

'"Bye."'

'We'd better go.' He reached for his coat.

'Just one last kiss.'

He pecked her and ran.

It wasn't a long walk to Moutonby High, but it was uphill all the way. There was a cracking view of the small town from the playing fields.

Sarah was lively with chatter and gossip as they walked. Did you know about this, this, this? Have you heard about that, that, that? And Jenny did her fair share of joining in: Gully, Gully, Gully. Tim tuned most of it out. He reckoned he'd hear it all again on the downhill journey anyway. What concerned him more was the fact that the black holdall he had slung over his shoulder was empty of English homework. No matter what he'd said to Sarah he knew he'd have to hand something in, and was frustrated and angry with himself because it meant wasting break or lunch time having to do it all over again.

The sun looked about as bright as it was going to manage today, but the streets were busier now, people were moving about; the town had pretty much woken up. Tim, however, felt like he could quite happily crawl back into bed. He'd been up since before six and his body-clock kept insisting the day should be half over already.

There were a few kids hanging around outside the school gates. It was a Friday so the usual dawdlers were dawdling even more, reserving their energy for being lazy at the weekend. Parents' cars pulled up to drop off sons and daughters who pretended they didn't have a clue who those irritating adults were from the very second they slammed the passenger door closed. Bikes darted and weaved onto the pavements and flew up the footpath between the tall gates. Everyone knew Tim and Jenny – of course they did, who in Moutonby didn't? Few acknowledged them. If anyone managed a smile or a 'Hiya' it was probably aimed at Jenny, so Tim didn't even bother to look up. He avoided eye contact, walked with his head down. Keeping himself to himself usually worked well. But not today.

'Hey! Monster Boy!'

There were some days – the good days – when he managed to survive all seven periods undisturbed and unmolested. Good days meant he remained hassle-free. Today wasn't going to be one of those days.

'Monster Boy!'

He glanced back over his shoulder at the school gates. He measured the distance in his head. Maybe twenty steps. He'd managed to take twenty whole paces before somebody

38

decided to have a go. He wondered if it was a new record; thinking, *An all-time low.*

'It's Roddy,' Jenny said, half worried, half warning.

Sarah flinched.

Tim nodded. 'I guessed.'

'Ignore him,' his sister said.

Sarah walked quickly, wasn't even going to turn and look. But Tim knew ignoring Roddy Morgan was never quite as simple as it sounded. So he stood his ground.

'What d'you want, Roddy?'

Jenny and Sarah exchanged an anxious glance. Tim pretended not to notice.

Roddy Morgan shoved his way through the bustle of kids to catch up with them. 'I've been waiting for you all morning.'

Sarah was staring at her feet. Again Tim said, 'What do you want?'

He had scruffy blond hair, was skinny not scrawny, looking like he was made out of twisted wire. 'I've been looking for you all over the place.'

'And now you've found me. So what do you want?'

He took a folded sheet of paper out of his jacket. 'I want you to do me a favour.'

A *favour*? Tim nearly laughed out loud. Like that was ever going to happen. 'Can't, Roddy. Sorry. Bit busy at the minute.'

'It won't even take a minute.' He waved the sheet of paper.

'I'm in a rush. I've still got homework to do.'

'This isn't homework. This is important.' He chuckled to himself, because he thought he was funny.

Unconsciously they'd squared up to each other. Roddy had never been the worst; there had always been older lads more vicious and little kids more irritating when it came to ripping the piss out of Tim and the tradition and the Mourn. But Roddy had been the first to call him 'Monster Boy' and Tim was quite happy to hate him for the rest of his life just for that alone. Although he'd become noticeably more spiteful over the past year and Tim didn't think it was coincidence that he'd also started working for Vic Stones at WetFun round about the same time. Roddy had a talent for all things mechanical apparently, spent long hours at the weekend coaxing life from the most clapped-out jet-skis and outboard motors. According to Roddy's constant crowing, Vic Stones couldn't sing his praises loud enough. In return Roddy claimed Stones was a generous boss, a 'top bloke'. The two of them were a mutual fan club.

Tim had told Jenny that he'd probably learned everything he knew about engines from nicking cars – yet couldn't help feeling a prickling of envy towards him. His mechanical skill, the fact that he could *do* something. Tim had never been able to do anything. The typewriter and the guitar and the photography books in his bedroom were proof of that, weren't they?

But there was a more obvious jealousy on Roddy's side. Last Christmas he'd asked Sarah out, bought her a cuddly toy (a horrible, cute, sickly bear or something) with some of the money he'd earned from WetFun. She'd refused him, embarrassing him, and then in February she and Tim had started seeing each other. These days Roddy liked to pretend she didn't even exist.

He was refusing to acknowledge her now, had his back to her. 'Come on. Just one favour,' he said to Tim. He grinned in what he must have thought was a friendly way, but just looked like he had a bad taste in his mouth. He waved the folded sheet of paper under Tim's nose.

Tim looked down at the white sheet suspiciously. He saw the oil and dirt under Roddy's fingernails. 'Sorry, Roddy.' He put his arm around Sarah's shoulder, made to lead her away. 'Like I said, bit busy at the minute.' But Sarah wasn't about to be used in the argument and squirmed out from under him. Tim immediately regretted his action, felt stupid because of his own tactlessness, and tried to follow her.

'No. Hang on.' Roddy jumped in front of him to block the path. 'Don't you want to see . . . ?' He was unfolding the paper.

Jenny stepped in his way. 'We're not interested. We'd rather chew silver foil than do you a favour. Goodbye.'

Tim shouldered her to one side, glaring at her. Then, to Roddy: 'Read my lips: Piss off.'

'Make me.'

It was a well-practised antagonism. Tim held Roddy's stare for one, two, three seconds. Only then did he try to follow Sarah again.

But Roddy wasn't going to give up. He was back grinning

41

again. 'This is your duty. You can't turn your back on your *duty*.'

'Did you hear a mouse squeak?' Jenny asked her brother.

Which only helped wind him up more. He could fight his own battles.

Roddy said, 'What would your dad say if he knew you weren't doing your *duty*?'

It bit Tim deeper than he'd expected. He turned on Roddy. He saw, and ignored, the look on his sister's face. 'Come on then, what is it? What's made you come crawling to me begging for my help?'

Roddy ignored the dig. 'I've got my list of names for tomorrow's Feed.'

It was perhaps the last thing Tim would have expected. 'And?'

'I can't make it myself tomorrow. It's a pity, I know. But, busy busy busy, and all that. You could give it to your dad for me, though, right?'

Tim looked at the white sheet in Roddy's grubby fingers.

One of the most important aspects of the Feed was when the Mourner read aloud the list of names he'd been given by the gathered Fearful. Back in the olden days it was usually the names of the fishermen who earned their living out on the lake and had been given by their anxious wives or mothers. Reading it aloud was the Mourner's way of asking the creature to spare these people, in exchange for the sack of feed itself. These days, now that the town no longer relied on its fish market to survive, it had become a list of loved ones who their families believed were in need of special remembrance, or could do with saving from more general ills. Tim knew his father would never refuse a list of names – no matter who had written it.

Jenny got in between the two of them, but Tim elbowed her out of the way before she could say anything. He met Roddy's eyes and they sparkled sharply. There were alarm bells in his head but he took the list anyway.

'Cheers, Monster Boy. Thanks.' Roddy beamed.

Tim turned to go.

'Read it. Don't you need to check it?'

Tim realized that this was Roddy's punchline; he needed Tim to see the list for his spiteful joke to work. So the last thing he was going to do right now was read the names on that sheet of paper.

'Read it. Go on.'

'I'll give it to my dad to read.' He made a show of folding it again, to shove in his back pocket. But Roddy suddenly made to grab it. Tim tried to hold it out of his reach, but Roddy was taller – and stronger.

He swiped it away; flourished it. 'Vic Stones!' He waved it in front of Tim's face. 'I want Vic Stones saving!'

The name stung Tim – he saw Jenny flinch slightly too – but he didn't get the joke just yet.

Roddy said, 'He'll put you out of business. He's building a hotel of his own. No one's gonna want to stay in your *Monster House*.' He was eager to see the looks on Tim's and Jenny's faces, and was evidently disappointed.

'Old news,' Tim said, relieved that the punchline had fallen flat. Very relieved he'd already heard the worst. 'I thought you were going to tell us something exciting.' He was smarting just the same, but managed to hide it behind a careless smile far faker than Roddy's. 'We probably knew before you did,' he lied.

Roddy was clearly annoyed he hadn't managed to cause the amount of upset he'd been hoping to. But he recovered quickly. 'Who's gonna want to stay in your shit-heap when there's brand-new rooms at WetFun?'

Tim shrugged, pretending Roddy's darts were just bouncing off him, not sticking in deep. It was time to get going – he needed to get away. He looked at his sister, who played along. Together they turned their backs and walked the way Sarah had gone.

'You're going *down*, Monster Boy. You'll have to eat your own feed!'

'Old news, Roddy. Old news.' He hoped his words sounded like he couldn't care less. He kept his back turned through sheer force of will.

Roddy was behind him, shoving, aggravating, kicking at his ankles. He kept walking, desperate to get away, but knowing he couldn't be seen to be backing down any. He glanced at Jenny by his side: her forced smile had slipped and her face was tense, anxious. He guessed he must look the same. Other kids were watching now. Roddy was at his shoulder, shouting in his ear, his spittle spraying the back of Tim's neck.

'Why don't you piss off and leave Moutonby – *for ever*!'

He could feel Roddy's hate like heat. He tried not to walk too quickly, but he had to get away. He wanted to be far far away from all of this – for ever.

'Everybody hates you! Everybody thinks you're a *freak*!'

They reached Sarah, who was standing by the entrance to the main block. They'd attracted quite a crowd – Monster Boy-baiting could often be relied on for entertainment. He tried to ignore them; was wary of their stares. He made to follow his sister in through the door, but Roddy clutched at his arm.

'*Fucking* freak!'

Almost instinctively, without actually thinking about it, he jabbed his elbow back, sharp and hard. It was to get away; it was because he didn't want to be pulled back into the middle of all those stares. But it smashed into Roddy's face.

And Roddy yowled. He was sent back-pedalling. He stumbled over his own feet and went down.

There was a whoop from the crowd and they pushed closer, keen to see.

Part of Tim was shocked and bewildered by what he'd just done and he almost apologized – it was his first impulse. Roddy sat stunned on the ground with blood spurting from his nose and Tim almost helped him get up. It was the crush of the crowd that stopped him.

Roddy covered the lower half of his face with his hand but the bright blood flowed down onto his chin and neck and dripped onto his chest. The crowd of kids jostled around them, wanting to see more. Tim stood as if frozen with his own surprise at what he'd just done. His elbow throbbed and he cradled it in his hand, simply staring as Roddy staggered to his feet. He might have even let Roddy grab him and beat him to a pulp if Mr Cropper hadn't appeared. The teacher demanded to know what was going on.

Roddy's eyes glistened with watery pain. 'Nothing.'

'Doesn't look like nothing to me, Morgan.' Mr Cropper scanned the already vanishing crowd, looking for the likely other half of a fight, skipping Tim completely. His gaze didn't even pause as it swept by because Tim Milmullen would be the last person expected to smash Roddy Morgan's nose.

Roddy looked as though he was thinking exactly that thought too. 'I walked into the door.'

'Did you indeed?' Mr Cropper didn't believe it for a second. 'Not very bright of you, Morgan. Should we be teaching GCSE "How Doors Work" these days?' Then, when Roddy didn't reply and the crowd of suspects had all but vanished, he said, 'I suppose I'd better come with you to the medical room, then, hadn't I? There are at least three doors to navigate along the way and I'd hate you to bleed to death figuring out how to get through them.'

The fingers of the hand Roddy had covering his nose and mouth were slick with blood. He let Mr Cropper lead him away but his stare told Tim this wasn't the end – far from it. Tim watched them go, slowly rubbing at his tender elbow, and knew that his life had just taken a scary turn for the worse. Roddy had always been an annoyance, a pain in the arse; now he was an enemy.

'Are you okay?' Jenny asked. Then: 'You shouldn't have taken his list. You know what he's like.'

Tim could feel the adrenaline still coursing through him;

his legs felt shaky with it. 'Yeah? And what was I meant to do instead?' He was nervous about what had happened, about how Roddy was going to react. It made him angry, so he took it out on her. 'He wasn't calling you *Monster Girl*, was he? No one ever does, do they? No one says anything to you.'

'I used to get called it.'

Tim didn't reply. He just let the 'used to' hang in the chilly morning air between them.

They'd always been close – they were twins, it was impossible for them not to be. But when they were younger they'd found themselves isolated from a lot of the other children because of their father and what he did. If they hadn't been friends with each other then they might not have been friends with anyone.

Although Jenny was managing to grow up that bit more easily than Tim – or so it seemed from his point of view. While he was inheriting their father's life and duty, she'd made new friends, she was doing well at school, was making her way in the world. And Tim did his level best not to resent her.

'He was getting at me too. Vic Stones's hotel affects the whole family.'

'I know that, don't I? I'm not stupid.' He slung his bag over his shoulder.

'Where are you going?'

'As far away from Roddy Morgan as I can get.'

Sarah was hesitant. 'We'll come with you.' She looked pale with what she'd just witnessed.

But Tim shook his head. He strode away, trying to ignore the shaking in his legs.

Life was getting far too difficult. He had too much to think about and he couldn't focus on all of it at the same time. His head was stuffed full with things he had to give attention to, and remember, and concentrate on.

He had to keep his dad happy; he had to prepare for his birthday; he had to pretend with Sarah; he was going to get done for not finishing his homework; and now he was on the run from Roddy Morgan. It was like trying to juggle too many balls, and sooner or later one was going to fall. He just wasn't clever enough to keep them all in the air at the same time.

The morning dragged. His elbow ached surprisingly painfully and flowered into a dark bruise. There was a small part of him that was kind of proud of what he'd done and he naively wondered if people might see him in a slightly different light because of it. Maybe give him a hint of credibility. Perhaps make them think twice before having a go next time?

He avoided both Jenny and Sarah at break (Roddy Morgan too, obviously) by staying inside to make a half-hearted stab at his homework, but couldn't concentrate properly. It wasn't just because of those balls he was trying to juggle in his head, but also the feeling that something had changed today. He'd known his family were outsiders, but he'd never understood quite how despised they were by the likes of Roddy Morgan. And 'despised' was the only word he could come up with.

He remembered feeling that hot hatred on the back of his neck as Roddy had shouted at him. He tried to get his head around the fact that it was because of the Mourn – a legend; a story.

By lunch he was beginning to panic about still not having finished his homework. He ate quickly and alone in the dining hall, wanting to get to the library as soon as possible. English was the first lesson of the afternoon and he wanted to have something, anything, to hand in.

The shepherd's pie the dinner lady had slopped onto his plate wasn't particularly appetizing so he left most of it. He took his plate to scrape it into the waste bucket, but the large black bucket wasn't in its usual place next to the cutlery racks. So he left the dirty plate on an empty table on his way out. No one was allowed to take their bags into the dining hall; they were chucked down by hungry, rushing students, heaped in the cloakroom with a dinner lady supposedly standing guard. Tim dug his holdall out from underneath some others and headed off towards the library.

As soon as he set foot outside he spotted Roddy Morgan waiting for him. He pretended he hadn't noticed, but walked quickly.

Moutonby High was an uneven mix of the old girls' grammar school his mum used to attend when she was fifteen and a stuck-on boxy block built in the nineties. Tim had always found it irritating and ugly that the old and new bits didn't match. In his mind it didn't look like the modern architect had even bothered to take a glance at what was already here before shoving the most boring and unimaginative brick cube on the end. He had English in that cube and didn't want to have to walk past the windows if, by chance, Mr Wing was in his room, but it was the shortest route to the library. And he wanted to get to the library before Roddy could get to him.

He reckoned he was less worried about his English teacher than about Roddy, so cut straight across in front of the new block, face turned away from the windows just in case, and headed for the footpath that led towards the library. He was halfway there before he realized something was wrong.

The handle of his bag was slimy, sticky in his grip. He'd been too concerned with Roddy to properly notice until now. He had the holdall slung over his shoulder and it stank something horrible.

He dropped it quickly. His hand was covered in a brown gunge from where he'd held it. The bag's zip wasn't done up all the way; it too was covered in dark slime, and he immediately realized someone had been messing with his bag. He dropped it to the ground. Brown gunk was all over it.

He looked closer.

Gravy?

With a feeling like his belly was going cold and slowly deflating he crouched down and pinched the slimy, greasy zip between a tentative finger and thumb. He pulled his bag all the way open.

It was full of leftover food slops. Half-eaten burgers, beans, custard, chips, apple crumble, carrots, but mostly mince, mashed potatoes and gravy. And now he knew why the waste bucket in the dining hall had been missing. His schoolbooks and folders were swamped and filthy.

'Think of it as a donation,' Roddy Morgan said from over his shoulder. 'You know, for the Feed tomorrow.'

Tim was quick to turn and get to his feet.

Roddy's nose was purple and blue with a bruise that could have been the mirror image of Tim's elbow. But not just that: his top lip had a nasty cut and when he spoke Tim could see one of his front teeth was jaggedly broken.

'It's my offering,' he said. 'I have to give the Mourn some feed so it'll save Vic – that's the way it works, isn't it?' He leaned forward to look into the bag. 'Hmmm, yeah, nice. The Mourn'll love it. Nice bit of shepherd's pie. Bet it doesn't get that kind of thing very often.'

Tim didn't know how to react; his head was blank.

Roddy glared at him.

Tim had been expecting a fight, not this. 'I didn't mean to break your tooth,' he said.

'I walked into a door.'

'What?'

'As if *you* could break my tooth. I walked into a door.'

'I thought . . . This morning, when I – you know? I thought—'

'Shut up. I walked into a door.'

Tim backed up a step. 'If you say so.'

'I do. You couldn't have me in a fight. Are you saying you could have me?'

Tim didn't know what he was saying. 'Just leave it, then, okay? I got you, now you've got me back.'

'You didn't get me.' Roddy's eyes were slits.

Tim picked up his bag again. He wasn't even worrying about the mess inside just yet, reckoning the best thing he could do was get away as quickly as possible.

'I could have you any time, Monster Boy.'

Like an action replay of that morning, Tim started to walk away.

And Roddy was at his ear. 'Try it. Try it again and see what you get.'

Tim wasn't trying anything again; far from it. He turned to face Roddy with the idea of placating him. But Roddy went for him anyway.

He was knocked to the ground with the bigger kid's full weight on his back. He let his bag go to save his fall and the grit of the paving slabs bit into his palms. 'Get off!' He tried to twist round, tried to get up. Roddy jabbed him twice with a solid fist in his side, wrenched his arm up at his back. 'Get off me!'

'You're a freak of nature, Monster Boy. You and your family are all *freaks*!' But that wasn't enough; Roddy suddenly had a better idea.

Tim heard his black holdall being dragged across the ground and knew what was going to happen next. He struggled and squirmed, but Roddy was on him with his full weight.

He felt the thick, cold contents of his bag being poured over his head.

Roddy laughed like he might bust a kidney or something and jumped up off him. Tim was able to sit up, but that only let the mess run down his collar, drip down his brow and his cheeks. The crowd was quick to gather and Tim felt their laughter like blows to his head.

'Now *you're* feed,' Roddy told him, laughing the way an empty stomach rumbles. 'Get the Mourn to lick you clean. Now you know what the feed feels like!'

Tim slowly stood up. Roddy jumped back from the splatter of leftovers that hit the pavement. Kids were actually running the full length of the footpath to see what was happening, to join in the fun. There were faces at classroom windows.

He had to get to a toilet to try and clean himself up. He felt empty – no anger, no tears. Just empty. The absolute humiliation of it left him drained and cold. He would have preferred a beating. This was the worst kind of childish humiliation – it was something little kids would do and it made Tim seem like the littlest kid of all.

He wanted to go home but didn't know how he could let his parents see him looking like this.

He tried to wipe his face clean with his sleeve, much to the delight of everyone else. He reached for his bag. His schoolbooks were tipped on the ground and he gathered them up even though they were ruined. Everything was ruined.

The Feed

Another chill morning, with a thin wind carrying spits of icy rain. The dozen or so people standing in Mourn Home's garden all looked chubby with bulky layers to keep out the cold. They were waiting for Bill, for their Mourner's weekly words of reassurance. Some of them clutched plastic bags full of offerings. They stood with their backs to the tall house and shuffled their feet, pulled their collars up higher, pushed their hands deeper in their pockets and silently faced the dark water. Every one of them wondered if something in the water was silently staring back. Most of them believed it was. The steep, tree-lined sides of the valley and high hills enclosing them made the grey slice of sky overhead appear to be only as large as the lake at their feet – the lake reflected the sky, the sky reflected the lake.

When Bill appeared he was struggling with the heavy sack of feed. Everybody parted to let him through to the Mourn Stone, where he did his best to gently swing the awkwardly bulging sack off his shoulder and balance it on top.

The stone was a rectangular slab of granite, standing just over a metre tall and maybe half a metre wide. It was the main focus for the weekly Feed. Weather-pitted and coarse, it stood so close to the water's edge that after heavy rain – such as there'd been this past week – the lake lapped around its base. And Bill was wearing wellingtons this morning.

'Thank you all for coming,' he said, lifting his voice above the wind. 'It's an unpleasant morning and I know you probably had to dig deep to make the effort, so thank you for that. I'd like to begin by—'

He hadn't managed to balance the sack quite right; the awkward bulges inside tumbled over each other and it rolled, flopped over the edge of the narrow stone. It hit the wet ground with a hefty *splush*.

Tim, who was standing with Jenny to one side of the group, knew why the sack was so heavy this morning and what those bulges were. Inside was half of Mrs Kirkwooding's dog, Marshal. Not that he was sure which half; he just knew his father was feeding some of the dog this morning and saving the rest for next Saturday – for Tim's birthday and Carving celebrations.

Bill apologized to those standing close enough to the stone to have been splashed and fought with the sack to get it up on top again. Sarah's father stepped forward to help him.

Tim glanced across at Mrs Kirkwooding. Wrapped up in a heavy coat, with her scarf tight enough around her thin throat that it might throttle her, she stood as stiff and solid as ever. She parted the cold wind like a concrete pillar. Maybe as heartless as one too? No, she was just doing what she thought was right and dutiful. Just the same as everybody else who'd dragged themselves out of their cosy beds to stand here and shiver this morning. They were the Fearful.

55

'I think I'd better start over,' Bill said with a small, self-conscious tug on his beard.

Tim noticed Sarah was watching him – again. She was standing with her mother in the middle of the group and he was able to pretend he was looking beyond her to his father at the Stone. But she kept glancing over her shoulder at him every so often as if making sure he was still there.

He'd been avoiding her. She'd rung five times last night and once this morning before coming to the Feed. He was annoyed that she hadn't got the message, hadn't realized he'd been ignoring *everybody*. Jenny had; she was good like that – it was one of the decent things about being a twin. She knew him well enough to suss out something was going on inside his head and it was best to steer clear. He'd just needed, absolutely, to be alone. He'd been licking his wounds.

He'd gone straight to the boys' showers next to the sports hall and cleaned himself up as well as he could. He'd been laughed at, pointed at, goggled at. And after making everybody's day superbly entertaining and particularly memorable, he'd slunk off home. The only luck he'd had was that both Bill and Anne had been out and didn't know he was skipping school for the afternoon. Jack Spicer had seen him – he'd been down by the lake – but neither of them had acknowledged the other. And after washing his clothes as well as he could in the bath, he'd been able to barricade himself in his room.

Of course he'd run through the obvious emotions – self-pity to hatred to desperately needing, *craving* revenge. Again and again he'd gone over what he could have done, *should* have done. If he was able to smash Roddy's nose and teeth one minute, he should have been able to finish the job the next, surely? He could have fought harder. He should have fought back. Roddy had made him look so stupid and small.

Amongst all of this, like the snake hidden within a coil of rope, was the special bitterness reserved for his father – for all of these people here today in fact. He couldn't help thinking the legend was due its fair share of the blame, could he?

Bill was saying, 'The reading I've chosen for this morning is from July 1704, Old William's fifth year as Mourner. The creature had invaded his dreams while he slept, but he'd defeated it even in this shocking nightmare manifestation, and he awoke feeling anxious yet stronger for the new knowledge he'd gained.'

He was holding the pages he'd copied from Old William's diary. The diary itself was the most precious possession in the Milmullen household. So much more than a simple heirloom, it was kept locked in a glass cabinet in Bill's study. Each of the Mourners over the years had kept their own diary but it was obviously Old William's which held the most significance. It was all in there: the tragic day in 1699 when the 'dragon in the lake' had risen from the depths and devoured the five schoolboys, the building of Mourn Home, the laying down of the tradition of the Mourners . . . Everything.

'"Yet the more ways the Mourn found to besiege me, the greater it revealed itself,"' Bill read. '"Every layer of its malevolence that was peeled away, I took as victory, for the Beast was permitting me closer observance of its unnatural being. I was gladdened to know my children would inherit many of the ways to protect our lives."'

He paused long enough to allow everyone to turn to look at Tim. Who looked at his feet. Then Bill continued with the story of Old William's dream victory. "'My days as a schoolteacher seemed so very far from me now . . ."'

Tim only looked up again when he was sure all eyes were back on Bill. But he wasn't really listening any more. He let his gaze drift among the people gathered. He wondered if they knew all the crap he had to go through because of them. He didn't owe them anything, he didn't even *like* half of them, yet he was supposed to let Roddy Morgan do and say whatever he wanted just to keep them happy by being their Mourner.

He knew that if he could find a way out before his birthday, before his Carving, he'd take it.

Bill finished the reading. He folded the pages and put them back inside his cagoule. 'May I have the lists of names?'

Everything was running the same as it always did, step by step. Tim watched his father and couldn't help but feel a little impressed by him. His demeanour hid his true feelings of anxiety. No one would guess the amount of upset and worry the news of Vic Stones's hotel had caused yesterday. He looked tired around the eyes maybe, a little rumpled, but still every bit the strong, reassuring Mourner.

Earlier he'd asked Tim and Jenny not to mention any of

it to any of the Fearful; he wanted to deal with the implications himself first. Those implications being, of course, that if all their guests went to WetFun's hotel, Mourn Home would certainly go out of business – Roddy had been right about that. The Milmullens would no longer be able to afford to live in their house. And the idea of Mourn Home without a Mourner was unthinkable.

He'd checked on the builders' progress this morning as soon as he'd got up and was guiltily disappointed to see they took weekends off. There was a small, albeit completely naive hope that they'd build the hotel before next Saturday and scupper his chances of being the Mourner. But *Dream on*, he thought.

Bill nodded to Sarah's father. Mr Gregory had been standing at the front of the gathering, just to one side of the Stone; as the Underbearer he had to collect the lists. He was a plump man with wispy, curly blonde hair and a doughy face – he looked like a fifty-year-old baby. He owned the butcher's in the market square and was often helpful in filling the feed sack. He moved among the people gathered, thanking them for their lists, then handed them to Bill. Tim had a sickening feeling Roddy would somehow have got his single-name list in there as well, but Bill read aloud the usual names the Fearful cared for and fretted over. The only difference being that everybody had included Tim.

Everybody wanted their new Mourner safe. Bill had warned him to expect it, but Tim blushed all the same. Not out of modesty; more out of guilt.

Following the traditional structure as written down by

Old William in his diary – each step in turn – Bill said, 'Now we thank those who have gone before.'

Engraved into the flat, north-facing side of the Mourn Stone were twelve names that spanned more than three hundred years. The list of Mourners, Tim's ancestors, Milmullen fathers and their sixteen-year-old sons. The people gathered recited the names in chorus, out of respect, lifting their voices above the wind. There was room enough on the Stone for Tim's name (number thirteen – now that was a laugh). In a single, solitary week's time he'd see his father take a hammer and chisel and carve it into the granite – where it would be fixed, immutable, everlasting.

He read the list silently to himself after everybody else had finished, trying to remember a time when he'd wanted to see his name there too.

Again he let his eyes roam over everyone standing respectfully in front of the Mourn Stone, staring out at the lake. Nana Dalry, the Jessop family, Sarah and her mum. Was it really just him who wondered and questioned?

One by one those people who had brought an offering stepped up to the stone clutching their plastic bags and dropped their gift to the Mourn into the feed sack: Mr and Mrs Hinton, Clive Tucker the librarian. When ninety-three-year-old Eileen Such was helped forward by Sarah's father she looked so grey and feeble that Tim wondered why she didn't just climb into the sack herself and be done with it. But she'd brought a chicken carcass instead.

'Thank you. Thank you all,' Bill said.

Old William had slit a lamb's throat open and let it bleed

to death on the stone while he'd chanted at the lake with his arms held high. It was just polite thanks these days. The feed sack was more than likely filled with roadkill and helpful offerings from the friendly butcher or a sympathetic vet. Squashed hedgehog, a couple of pounds of tripe and poor old Hammy Hamster, weighted with a rock which would quickly drag it down deep.

Bill struggled to heave the sack up onto his shoulder again, then he and Sarah's father headed for the feeding pier and the little rowing boat tied up at the far end. The Underbearer would row the Mourner out into the centre of the lake, where the feed could be tipped over the side. Meaning, for one week more, the town of Moutonby would be safe from the creature these people believed lived somewhere in the cold, dark waters of Lake Mou.

Bill and Mr Gregory hadn't quite made it as far as the pier when someone shouted, 'Wait. Wait! We missed it!'

Everybody turned to see the American couple hurrying down the garden towards them. Sylvie was waving her arms, even though she hadn't quite managed to get all of her coat on just yet. Mike was trying to keep up with her while holding a digital camcorder at arm's length and not tripping or slipping over. He wasn't doing a particularly good job.

'Oh, we missed you. We *missed* you. Can you do it again?' Sylvie was distraught.

The gathered Fearful didn't look impressed.

Tim's mother was quick to intercept Sylvie because it

really looked like she might make a dive for Bill. 'I'm sorry,' she said. 'I'm sorry, Sylvie, but we've finished now.'

Sylvie shook her head in dismay. 'Can't you do it again for us? The folks back home just won't believe us unless we get a movie of you doing your, you know . . . your *thing*.'

'Come and join us inside.' Anne tried to lead her away by the flapping arm of her coat. 'We always have tea and scones afterwards. We like to have a bit of a feed ourselves.'

Sylvie wasn't paying her much attention; she was too busy directing her husband's camera-work. 'Make sure you get them out on the lake.' She waved at Bill and Mr Gregory. 'Go out with them. I want you to get him feeding the monster.'

'There won't be enough room for him in the boat,' Anne said as politely as she could. 'The *Bonnie Claire* only just manages Bill and Mr Gregory with the sack of feed between them.'

Sylvie frowned, frustrated. She wasn't happy. She lowered her voice. 'Why do you need the fat guy anyway, honey? I'm sure he could—'

There were indignant gasps from one or two people who overheard. Luckily Sarah and Mrs Gregory were well out of earshot.

'He's very important,' Anne assured Sylvie. 'Oh, we couldn't do without Mr Gregory. If anything had happened to my husband he would have been the one to look after Mourn Home until Tim turned sixteen.' She noticed Nana Dalry, one of the most ardent and vocal of the Fearful, stepping forward and getting ready to open her mouth, so quickly added: 'Everything is very traditional for the Feed. Shall I explain what the significance is?' She gestured for Sylvie to follow her.

Mike had continued his slip-sliding way down to the shoreline with the camcorder up to his face. He stood with the water soaking his slippers and the bottom of his pyjamas, which were poking out from underneath his trouser legs. Tim realized he must have pulled his clothes on over the top of what he wore to bed in his hurry. Or rather, in Sylvie's hurry.

She sighed heavily. 'We came all this way off our route and we missed everything. I wish you'd told us you were doing your thing.' She followed Anne towards the house only reluctantly.

Tim stayed where he was, watching his father. Next week, he thought, that'll be me. And that made him feel . . . ?

'That'll be you next week.' Jenny was standing next to him. She grinned widely, wanting him to join in.

'Hmm,' he said.

She seemed put out by his lack of enthusiasm, but ploughed on regardless. 'I know you're looking forward to it.'

He met her stare, wondering how well she could read him. 'I'd be mad not to be, right?'

Again her face said she was taken aback by his attitude, but: 'You'll be good, you know. I'd be nervous too, but I think you'll make a really great Mourner. Dad's always said so.'

He realized she simply thought he was nervous about taking over their father's role; she didn't know what his true feelings were. And that surprised him. He'd believed for most of his life that his twin could read his mind. It was a sad and disappointing realization.

'Hi.' Sarah had joined them but stayed a few tentative steps away.

Jenny grinned at her. 'I was just telling him how exciting it was going to be next week. My favourite brother's having his Carving!' She honestly sounded proud. She actually clapped him on the back.

Tim noticed Sarah was unsure of how to approach him after he'd ignored her calls and not spoken to her so far this morning. She smiled as brightly as she could. 'I'm really looking forward to it.'

'Let's just hope it's still out there, then,' he said.

The two girls looked confused.

He nodded at the water. 'The Mourn. Can you imagine how embarrassing it'd be if it had gone somewhere else? Or if it had died or something? There I am, dropping dead rabbits and stuff into the lake, and it's not even *there* any more.'

Jenny said, 'Tim . . .' but didn't seem to know where to go from there.

He shrugged. 'Nobody would need me then, would they?' He turned away, gave a quick snort of laughter. 'I'd have to go and work in McDonald's or something. Do you think collecting feed is good training for making burgers?'

Jenny was going to argue: she pulled a face which looked a bit too similar to Nana Dalry for comfort. But then Gully and Scott came strolling out through the main door towards them and she immediately became that demure young woman she always was around them. Part of Tim was impressed by the swiftness of the transformation, while another part was appalled.

'What's been happening here?' Gully asked, yawning. He was wrapped up in a thick jacket and scarf and obviously hadn't combed his hair this morning. It stuck up all over the place – not that he seemed to care. 'We missed a party or something?'

Scott looked much the same as he had yesterday morning. His denim jacket was too thin for the sharp weather and he shivered as he stood there, hunched up, his hands shoved in his pockets. Even so, he was watching the Fearful with a sly twinkle of amusement in his eye. 'Tourists?' he asked.

Tim waited for Jenny to reply. She fussed with her hair, brushed it back off her face and smiled. He tutted at her, but felt obliged to say something in reply. 'They're locals,' he said. 'They come every week.'

'Right. Mugs, then,' Scott said.

Tim didn't reply, not liking the way the two of them made him feel young and stupid. He stood up straighter, as if that would help.

'So, have you made it safe for us?' Gully asked Jenny with a smile.

Jenny gave a small shrug. 'Maybe.'

'You've done your monster stuff and now we can have some fun out there without getting eaten, right?'

She laughed – not that Tim had found anything particularly funny. He saw the look in Gully's eye, the way he was forcing Jenny to lock her gaze with his. He realized Gully knew exactly how his sister felt. He was obviously no slouch when it came to these things.

As if to prove it he asked, 'Why don't you come with us?'

'Where?'

'WetFun.' He nodded in the general direction of the club.

Jenny was doing her best to look casual, cool, to look as though this happened every day of her life, but she couldn't hide her pleasure at being asked. Even so: 'I can't. It's my mum and dad; they don't get on with the man who runs the place.'

Gully rolled his eyes. 'Yeah. Parents and all their shit. Why do we always have to put up with it?' He grinned at her.

Jenny was gazing up at him through her long lashes – and it was Tim's turn to roll his eyes. She was as good at this as Gully. Where on earth had she learned it all? 'I'm really not supposed to,' she said.

Gully glanced over his shoulder at the house, by way of pointing out that everybody had gone inside. And on the lake Bill and Mr Gregory were already too far out to be able to see what was happening. 'Who's gonna know?' He made a point of looking at Tim and Sarah in turn. 'Nobody'll say anything.'

Tim waited for Jenny to say no. He waited a good ten seconds or so while she prodded the ground with the toe of her trainers. Then she said, 'Okay. But I'm not going out on the lake. I'm only watching.'

'You can't!' Tim turned on her.

'Why not? I said I'm only watching, didn't I?'

'What if Mum and Dad find out?'

'They won't if you don't tell them.' There was the sly sliver of a threat in Gully's words.

Tim did his best to pretend he hadn't noticed. 'Jenny . . .'

But she was already letting Gully lead her away.

Scott winked at Sarah, took a step closer. 'What do you say? How d'you fancy—?'

'No!' She blushed furiously and snatched hold of Tim's hand.

Scott chuckled quietly and held up his own hands as if in submission. 'Sorry, mate,' he said to Tim. 'No offence. Didn't realize.'

Tim didn't know what to say. 'Jenny?'

She glanced at him over her shoulder.

He fought for a good-sense argument. 'What if . . . ?'

'Just cover for me. *And don't tell Dad.*'

He watched her hurry along the shore with the students on either side. He was amazed at the strength of her disobedience. And put out that she was going to the one place he'd always wished he could go himself.

The Fearful

Reluctantly Tim followed Sarah into the house, into the kitchen, where everybody was enjoying the warmth of tea and gossip. It crossed his mind to tell his mother about Jenny, but he knew he'd never stoop so low. He wondered if she'd bump into Roddy Morgan, but reckoned that was her own lookout. He'd only just managed to get his coat off when he was cornered by a conspiratorial Cagey Brown.

'Tim, Tim. Just the chap. Can I have a word, eh?' He moved even closer, pinning Tim against the wall. He was short, bald, with chunky metal glasses, and always wore saggy woolly jumpers that smelled of cat's pee. At least, Tim hoped it was the jumpers. He spoke in what he must have thought was a whisper. 'I know your dad's never been too keen on me helping him out, but, you know, if you're ever stuck or worried or anything . . . ? It'd be a pleasure. Absolutely. I'd be glad to help. So, I'm just saying, don't ever feel shy about calling on me, if you need me, if I can help. I'd be glad to.'

Tim thanked him uncertainly.

Cagey kept on smiling. 'You'd be surprised what I can get. I could fill that feed sack for you quick and easy. And

I know, I know, you've got ties to Gregory and his butcher's.' He cast a quick, anxious eye around the kitchen to make sure Sarah's dad hadn't returned from his duties out on the lake just yet. He nodded as he talked. 'I know that – what with him being your *dad's* Underbearer. And he's good at it; I'm not saying he's not, am I? I'm not saying that. But maybe it's time for a change. You know, in *your* eyes, when *you* become top man.' He was still nodding, as if pushing for Tim's affirmation.

'Thanks, Mr Brown. I appreciate it.'

'No, no, call me Brian. You're the Mourner now. Well, as good as. And I just want you to know that I can fill the sack as well as Gregory's butcher's. No worries, yes? Mine's only a small pet shop, I admit that, but as long as you know, I'm there if you need me.'

Tim didn't have a clue what to say. His forced smile was beginning to ache. He glanced around the room for help, looking for someone to escape to.

The regulars were all here. Brian Brown, of course – called 'Cagey' by Tim and Jenny since they'd first visited his tiny pet shop and seen the shelves of wooden cages filled with shrill birds, scratting mice and dopey rabbits. (Tim had always quite liked that pet shop, had thought it looked cared for and clean, but Cagey's words just now had certainly been the wrong side of weird for his tastes.) Nana Dalry and Mrs Kirkwooding were gossiping competitively with Nana's neighbours, Tom and Rhonda Bye. Timid Mr and Mrs Hinton were quietly hiding in the corner by the oven. Ancient Eileen Such was being propped upright by the librarian Clive Tucker, both talking, as always, about years long gone and over-fondly remembered. The Jessop family were at one end of the table; the two young children constantly being told to stop fidgeting, to sit up straight, to say thank you, to stop fidgeting . . . Sarah's mum was helping Anne by making more tea.

It didn't take a genius to work out that, apart from the Jessop kids, Tim, Jenny and Sarah were the youngest Saturday morning regulars by a good twenty-five years. Tom and Rhonda Bye's son used to come – until he'd got too old to be forced.

Jack Spicer appeared and was greeted like an old friend. He wasn't one of the Fearful himself, not officially, but he was well-liked and well-respected by everybody here. He had seen the Mourn after all. He moved around the room, clearly enjoying his particular status among them – like a more-famous actor turning up backstage at somebody else's play.

Tim managed to extricate himself – politely – from the conversation with Cagey Brown, but didn't get very far before Nana Dalry made a grab for him. Her grey hair was sticking up at clownish angles because of the wind and drizzle and she had sticky scone crumbs at the corners of her mouth.

'Here he is!' she said loud enough for *everybody* to hear. 'Here's my handsome grandson!'

He cringed, blushed uncontrollably.

She fussed around him. 'Oh, but I expect you're excited about next week.'

If I had a pound for everybody who'd said that . . .

She prodded him and stroked him and straightened his clothes. 'And I'm *so* proud, Timmy. We're all *so* proud. Aren't we *proud*, Grace?'

Mrs Kirkwooding smiled widely at him. 'Of course we are. Who wouldn't be?'

He tried to duck away, but the old ladies had him cornered, trapped. Tom and Rhonda Bye were quick to close in, making him feel surrounded. It was up to Anne to attempt a rescue.

'Please stop clucking, Mother,' she said, filling Nana Dalry's cup of tea for what could be the third time.

But Nana was having none of it. Her cheeks glowed with pride. 'Have you chosen your reading for next week yet? I thought your father's was *very* nice today. So *very* nice. Wasn't it *nice*, Grace?'

'Very,' Mrs Kirkwooding agreed. 'I enjoyed it immensely.'

'You'll have to choose a nice one for your Carving, Timmy. I remember your father's first Feed when—'

'Your father has a gift,' Rhonda Bye interrupted loudly, ignoring the scowl on Nana's face. 'Indeed he does. A real feel. He knows how to reassure us of all our worries and troubles.' She wasn't that much younger than Nana or Mrs Kirkwooding but shopped for clothes in the same places Jenny and Sarah did, and only unconvincingly squeezed herself into them. She was tanned like marmalade. 'I'm told your grandfather had the gift as well. You have a pair or two of large boots to fill, young man.'

'He'll fill them,' Nana Dalry stated almost aggressively. 'He's very much like both his grandfathers. The gift of the

Milmullens, but there's equal Dalry in him too.' She squinted at Mrs Bye mischievously. 'He's got a look of my Alan about him, don't you think? You were in the same class at school with my Alan – you must remember.'

Not for one second was Rhonda Bye going to admit she was the same age as Tim's grandfather. She turned to her husband. 'Tom might be a better judge.'

But Tom Bye looked pissed already. 'Hmm?' He seemed both surprised and frightened to be included.

'Maybe you could have a word with Sylvie,' Anne said to Nana, judiciously changing the subject.

'That dreadful American woman?' Nana Dalry wasn't impressed.

'She's upset about missing the Feed, having come all this way. Maybe you could explain to her what it is we do, and why. I think she'd appreciate learning more about the old traditions.'

Nana perked up immediately. 'What a good idea. Shall we, Grace?' Mrs Kirkwooding followed her.

Tim smiled gratefully at his mother and let her steer him away. He liked Nana Dalry – she was always generous at Christmas and birthdays – but she could be a bit full on when it came to the Mourn. And when she got together with Mrs Kirkwooding, they were formidable. Twice this past summer they'd torn a strip off some poor, confused tourist for not being respectful enough during the Feed. He was amazed she'd not said anything to Mike and Sylvie already. But looking at her, he guessed she was just building up to it.

'Where's Jenny disappeared to?' his mother asked. 'I could do with a hand.'

Tim pretended to look around the room for her. 'Is she upstairs?' He moved on before she could question him further.

He didn't get very far. These people had sticky fingers; sticking to his clothes, gluing themselves around his wrist, dragging him back towards them.

The librarian, Clive Tucker, was loud and effusive. 'Mark my words. Great day for Moutonby.' He beamed at Tim from under his silver 'tache, his thumbs tucked behind his shabby red braces, and rocked on his heels. 'First Mourner of the new millennium. Big responsibility. Reckon you're up to it? We'll see, won't we? See if you're made of the same stuff your dad is.' He nodded once, emphatically. 'Now, Henry's Carving in 1813 . . . ?' He sighed like a happy man sliding into a warm bath. 'What a day for the history books!' Tim hated history.

Mr and Mrs Hinton were hidden in the corner. They were the most timorous of the bunch, who usually left at the first polite opportunity (after eating only half a scone and drinking half a cup of tea, but full of mousy apologies). Yet today even they found the courage to tell him how eagerly they awaited his Carving.

'We're both looking forward to it,' Mr Hinton said, not making eye contact.

His tiny wife nodded quickly. 'Yes,' was all she dared say.

Tim smiled well, feigned gratitude like a professional,

even though in his head he was rattling at the bars of a cage. And he couldn't help thinking that these people were supposedly his army and his allies against the likes of Roddy Morgan. But just imagine if Roddy Morgan could see him now! He actually flinched away when the ninety-three-year-old, paper-thin, paper-dry Eileen Such tried to take his arm. He didn't want to be near these people. He wanted to be far, far away.

As soon as his father and Mr Gregory appeared, ruddy-faced and damp with spray after their row out to the middle of the lake, everyone's attention turned to them. The Fearful all wanted to praise and paw the two of them now. They all wanted to tell Bill how much they'd enjoyed the reading and how wonderful a Mourner he was. So Tim took full advantage and sneaked away. He heard Sylvie asking her husband if he was sure he'd got everything on film as he made a run for his stairs.

Sarah followed him. 'Tim . . . ?'

He knew he couldn't duck out of talking to her now, but he was halfway up the stairs and didn't want to stop in case he was spotted and dragged back down again. 'Come on,' he said, maybe looking a touch more furtive than he should. 'Come up to my room.' He kept taking the stairs two at a time.

'Don't worry. It doesn't matter. Not if you're in such a hurry.'

He caught the underlying tone of her voice and reluctantly stopped, wanting to avoid any arguments if he could.

'No, come on up. Please. I'm not being mardy; I just want to get as far away from that lot as I can.' She wasn't happy; she stared at her feet. 'We need to talk anyway,' he said, trying to reassure her. But he still had to say please a second time before she acquiesced.

His bedroom was in no better state. 'Erm, still a bit of a mess. I meant to tidy up last night, but . . .'

She shook her head – didn't matter. 'You seem funny,' she said. 'Is it because of yesterday?'

He didn't want to talk about yesterday. 'I just had to get away from everybody. They make me feel, you know . . . They're such hard work all the time – and so *clingy*.'

'Clingy?'

She didn't seem to understand, but when he met her eye she looked genuinely concerned. He held her gaze, wondering how much he could tell her. Keeping secrets could be a lonely thing to do. Maybe she was the right person to confide in; he needed someone to talk to, didn't he? He found himself really wanting her to understand.

'It's the way they talk to me and want me to be best friends with them and everything. And they all seem to think they *know* me. I reckon they must think I'm some-body I'm not. It's like they've already decided who I am, even though I still haven't figured it out for myself yet.'

Sarah looked disappointingly bemused. He saw the light half-smile on her lips, which could be twisted into a quick grimace of sympathy if needed – she just wasn't sure what to do with it. She was trying; she wanted to know why he was acting weird. But she just wasn't getting it.

'Wouldn't you rather be doing something else on a Saturday morning anyway?' he asked, changing tack.

'What like?'

'I don't know – drama club or something?'

'*Drama* club?' She was becoming more confused by the second.

'Well, yeah, anything like that, I suppose. There're kids at school who go to that drama club in town, aren't there? And there're lads who do footie practice or go swimming or something. Or go to the cinema; maybe just hang around the shops. But at least they're all together, having a laugh with their mates. We can't do any of that because every Saturday we have to have a Feed.'

'We have to have a Feed, or—'

'Yeah, I know. I know all that. It's just . . .' He wasn't all that sure he was making complete sense to himself now, but pushed on anyway. 'I'm just worried that those people downstairs are going to be my only friends.'

Sarah smiled coyly, tried to insinuate herself into a cuddle. 'I'm your friend.'

He stepped back, more interested in having her grasp what he was struggling to say. 'Yeah, of course. I know. But everybody downstairs—'

'They're not really *friends* friends,' she said. 'They look up to you. As the Mourner.'

Which only made Tim feel worse. 'Exactly. They're only my friends because of that. They might not even like me as a person.'

'Of course they do.'

'But what you've just said is that they only want to know me because I'm going to be the Mourner. If I decide I don't want to be the Mourner then they'll all hate me. It's not the Tim bit of me they want; it's the Milmullen part.'

Sarah shook her head in distaste. 'You're being funny again.' Her nose was crinkled as though his words smelled bad.

It was enough to convince him to shut up.

He stood at the window that looked towards WetFun in the hope of spotting Jenny and the two students. Only one small sailing boat was out on the water this morning; even so he could guarantee his sister wouldn't be sitting in it. A jet-ski buzzed back and forth and he reckoned it was probably Gully showing off. There was a large colour-coordinated group of people milling around on the shore, all wearing orange and yellow life vests. He saw a dark coat that he thought might be Jenny's, and if it was her she was keeping well away from the water's edge. Like Bill had always instructed.

'Can you see Jenny?' Sarah asked, stepping up to the window. 'Is that her?'

'Think so.'

'What will your dad say if he sees her?'

'He'll not be happy about it, that's for sure.'

'She'd never go out in a boat, though. She's too Fearful.'

'It's not just that, is it? It's because Dad can't stand Vic Stones, while Vic Stones purposely winds Dad up. Dad's always forbidden us from going anywhere near the place. And now with this hotel and everything it'd be worse, because it would feel like she was being a traitor.'

'That's silly. She'd never be a traitor; she's more Fearful than anyone. It's only because she fancies Gully.'

'Yeah. Suppose. But what's so special about Gully?' He looked at Sarah, who shrugged. 'Do you think he's good looking?'

'In a way.'

'But he's a nob-head.'

'It doesn't stop him from being good-looking.'

Tim pulled a face. Who was he more jealous of? Gully for his careless freedom and attitude, or Jenny for having the guts to break their parents' rules? And what was the point in taking the risk of going to WetFun if you weren't going to thrash about on a jet-ski or roar across the lake in a speedboat? It was true his sister was far too much of a believer to even think about going out on the water, but if Tim was over there, then just maybe *he* would.

'I tried phoning last night,' Sarah said.

Here we go. 'Yeah. I'm sorry. It wasn't that I was avoiding you on purpose. I just . . . You know.'

'I was worried about you.'

'I'm okay. I'm always okay.' He was using the same smile on her as he'd used with everyone downstairs. 'When am I ever not okay?' He forced the smile as wide as it would go.

She wasn't convinced. 'What about us? Is everything okay with us?'

And suddenly a split-second window of opportunity opened for him to admit he didn't want to see her any more.

But: 'Of course.' He lied because he couldn't tell her to

her face. Over the phone would be better, easier. Maybe even get Jenny to tell her instead.

He was still trying hard with that smile and hoped she couldn't see the awkwardness he felt with her. He wondered whether he should kiss her, but realized that might just make her stay longer. It wasn't her fault, he wanted to tell her. It was him. But that was crap and tacky and clichéd. And not wholly true either.

She was playing with the buttons of her cardigan. 'I can stay over. If you still want me to.'

It threw him for a second.

'You asked me to stay over, remember?'

'And you're allowed?'

'It's what we both want, isn't it?'

'Yeah, definitely. It's just that . . .' He saw her face change from irritated to annoyed; a subtle tilt of her eyebrows, a slight shift of her mouth. 'It's just great. *Really* great. When?'

'It has to be tomorrow night. I told my mum Jenny and I had a project to finish and that we were already late with it. She had a go at me for not doing my schoolwork properly, but it's worth it if I can stay the night with you, isn't it?'

He was concerned that he'd only asked her because he hadn't believed she'd go through with it. Never in a million years did he think . . . Then, at long last, his mind caught up – like a car changing gear, or an arrow hitting a bull's-eye. And he thought about what might happen. Alone for a whole night. With her.

'It's really great.' He nodded hard, grinning despite himself because he realized he actually meant it. Because spending a night meant sex, didn't it? He forgot about everybody and everything down in the kitchen for the time being. Because he was a boy. 'I'll find us a free room. There's plenty not booked.'

There was a worry. It was risky; could they get away with it without getting caught? Mr Gregory might well kill him. It was a big worry.

But he couldn't help letting his fantasies come first. He let his eagerness show through in his smile. A smile that was real for the first time all morning.

She giggled and came towards him, wanting a hug. He gave one willingly. 'But can we talk too?' she asked.

'Yeah.'

'About everything?'

'Promise,' he said, even though his mind was somewhere else entirely. Maybe life was good after all.

Although Sarah seemed determined to spoil things. 'Jenny said you've not told your mum and dad.'

'What about?'

'About yesterday. Roddy.'

He didn't like the sound of this. He stepped backwards out of the hug.

'About what happened at lunch time.'

He took another step away from her. 'I didn't see the point. I mean, there's not much they can do about it, is there? Not really.'

'I told mine.'

'What?' His good mood vanished as quickly as it had appeared. The world came crashing in. 'Why?'

'I thought it was important. He shouldn't be allowed to do things like that. Why didn't you—?'

He was shaking his head. 'Your dad will tell mine.' He swore: 'Shit. *Shit!*'

Sarah tried to come to him again, but he wouldn't let her this time.

'I never tell my mum and dad anything like that. Nothing about Roddy Morgan or any of the other arseholes at school.'

'Why not?'

'I just don't, okay? I just don't.'

'But maybe they could—'

'What could they do? Come on. What? They couldn't do anything. I can handle it myself. I always have.'

She shrugged, pulled her usual trick of looking down so she could hide her face behind the fall of her hair. And for some reason the gesture hit a nerve in him.

'If you've got something to say, just say it. I hate it when you do this. It's like you've got something really wise and wonderful to say, but don't want to tell me because I'm a whole month younger than you so couldn't possibly be expected to understand.'

She was shocked by the sharpness of his voice. 'I didn't mean . . .' But she couldn't say what she hadn't meant.

'It pisses me off.'

She wanted to leave. 'I'd better go. My mum will be wondering where I am.'

'I never tell my dad what happens at school,' Tim said again. 'Do you know how embarrassing it'd be? Do you know how bad it'd make him feel?'

81

Sarah didn't have an answer.

'My dad thinks I'm the most popular kid in school because of what he does. He doesn't get it that everybody else thinks it's just a big joke. He thinks I get red carpets and rose petals to walk on, trumpets played in the background—'

'No, Tim. I don't.'

Neither Tim nor Sarah had heard Bill coming up the stairs. He stood in the doorway, frowning, disappointed. He tugged on his beard. 'I may be a little hard of hearing now and again, but I'm not blind to what goes on just yet.'

Tim's face said it all. The surprise and guilt and embarrassment were easy to read. And he knew it, so he turned his back to stare out at the lake through his windows. There was a conversation coming that he didn't want to have.

The 12th Mourner

Bill was first to break the silence. 'Maybe you could help out downstairs,' he said to Sarah.

She dithered for a second or two, then said goodbye to Tim. He didn't answer.

Bill sat down on the edge of the bed. Tim watched him over his shoulder. His back was rounded, his chin close to his chest. He looked slightly deflated, as though he'd lost some air. 'People are asking for you downstairs,' he said.

'I'm not feeling very well.'

'Yes. Too ill to keep your room tidy by the look of things.' He tutted at the mess.

Tim didn't like his father being in his room, felt uncomfortable with him finding fault. This was *his* room, *his* retreat. Bill picked up a discarded jumper from the floor and folded it neatly before placing it on the bed next to him. Tim recoiled slightly at his father's intrusiveness.

'Are you going to start or am I?' Bill asked.

'What do you mean?'

'Are you going to explain what happened, or should I tell you what Colin Gregory told me?'

'It was just Roddy Morgan being Roddy Morgan. It's

what he does.' There was still part of him that didn't want to admit how bad it had been yesterday.

'Is he the lad Stones has got working at WetFun?'

Tim nodded. 'I'm not the only one he likes to have a go at. I'm not worried about it.'

'But more often than not, it's you who's on the receiving end when he does decide to have a go.' Bill sighed. He steepled his fingers and stared at them. 'There were a couple of Roddy Morgans when I was at school, a couple of people who knew how to make life tough for me. I can't count the number of times I got it in the neck from some mean-spirited bugger or other.'

Tim had never heard his father talk like this before. It surprised him, but intrigued him more. 'Was it bad?' he asked. He'd always imagined everybody in Moutonby to be Fearful in those days, and that the town's disregard for the legend was a particularly recent feeling.

'It was, when I was younger. Younger than you, I mean. The town still paid the Monster Tax back then, but no one was happy about it. The government taxed them enough; they didn't like giving up extra pounds and pence for something that, even then, they thought of as just an embarrassing folk story. I can remember the kids at school picking fights with me because *their* mum and dad had to pay for *my* mum and dad. At least, that was the reason they gave. I always thought most of the insults they threw in my face in the playground were the things they'd heard their parents complaining about over the dinner table. I had my fair share of black eyes and bloody lips. And the problem was, you see, that there were one or two of the teachers who agreed with them.'

'Didn't they try to stop the other kids from having a go at you?'

Bill raised his eyebrows. 'Maybe not as much as they could have done. But I was thirteen when the vote to abolish the tax went through, and over the next couple of years things slowly got better for me.' He tugged on his beard; a line in his brow creased and deepened. 'Didn't get much better for your granddad, that was the pity.'

Tim knew the story. Granddad Arthur had been so sick with worry when the Monster Tax was abolished that he'd eventually become bedridden. Granddad's Underbearer should have been the one to take on the responsibilities of the Feed, but Bill had stepped in to become the Mourner a year early, at the age of fifteen.

'It was your Uncle Doug who had the big idea of turning us into a guesthouse,' Bill continued with a small, private smile. 'And he was only twelve at the time. I wasn't having any of it at first; just another of his wild notions – he was full of them even back then. But your granddad said it could be the best solution to our problems. Well, it certainly didn't solve *all* of them, but it's kept us going ever since.' He chuckled to himself. 'Not that he's ever been seen as the hero, eh? If there's ever a black sheep in the Milmullen fold, Douglas certainly does his best to fit the bill.'

Tim smiled too, but he'd heard his uncle labelled as such before. He was, however, still intrigued by his father's confession. Maybe they had more in common than he'd thought. 'Did Uncle Doug get bullied too?'

Bill thought about it. 'Yes. Yes, he did. Though maybe not as much as me.'

'Because he wasn't going to be the Mourner?'

'Maybe. But your uncle gave as good as he got. He was bigger than me, more reckless than me, and he knew how to hit back.' He saw the thought that crossed Tim's face. 'But that was *Doug*. As you say, he wasn't going to be the Mourner. Even if I had been as big as him I couldn't have gone around fighting everyone. What's the point in having someone to protect the town from the Mourn only so he can harm or hurt them himself?' He caught Tim's eye. 'You see what I'm saying?'

Tim nodded. It was as direct an order as he'd ever really been given.

'I knew there'd be people who'd make life hard for you. But because you never talked about it I thought you were handling things well enough. I guess I was wrong – and I'm sorry for that. Sorry for you. I should have remembered a bit clearer what happened to me.'

Tim wasn't sure how obvious he was being, and he held onto the question for a good few seconds before asking, 'Did it ever make you not want to be the Mourner?'

His father wasn't stupid. Tim saw the look in his eyes and instantly regretted the question. He opened his mouth to say something else, to backtrack, but couldn't think of a single thing. It was a big clumsy boot stepping over the invisible line.

Bill wasn't angry, but there was an edge to his words. 'I was always very proud to be the Mourner.' He sat up straighter, squared his shoulders.

'Yeah, of course. I know. I just meant . . .' But he knew his father understood exactly what he'd meant.

'Even when I lost my hearing,' Bill continued, unconsciously raising his hand to his left ear, 'I knew how special a task it was to be the Mourner.'

This was something else Tim had never known his father talk about. He'd always thought he'd been born with his dodgy ear. 'Did someone—?'

'I was walloped around the head with an oar.' He snorted a half-laugh through his nose. It wasn't really funny – just a long time ago.

'Because you were going to be Mourner?'

Bill nodded.

'Who did it? Was it Vic Stones?' Tim knew they'd been at school together.

Bill ignored the question. 'Being the Mourner is a special task. It's a duty, but it's an honour too, passed down a long line of good, brave men. And I can understand how overwhelming it must seem, how big the responsibility is to you as a young man. Don't forget, I've been there myself.'

Tim could hear the conviction in his father's voice, but it didn't move him like perhaps it should have done. Because no, Bill never had been in his position. Because, as far as he knew, Bill had never questioned the legend. And wasn't this Tim's biggest problem? Weren't these the thoughts that really kept him awake at night?

He wanted to go out on the lake like Gully and Scott because he'd told himself he wasn't scared. He was embarrassed by the Feed because he thought it was pointless. He'd looked for the creature every day for as long as he could remember, but he'd never seen it. He didn't want to be the Mourner . . . *Because I don't believe the Mourn is real.*

His father knew nothing of these thoughts. He said, 'And I do know what people say about us. I don't have my head buried in the sand.' He pointed at the floor and down to the kitchen below. 'The people in this house are the only ones who still follow the tradition, but thank goodness for them. You know the legend better than anyone: if we don't feed the Mourn it will kill again, like it killed those poor schoolboys. Thank goodness for the people in this house who won't stand by and let that happen, don't you think?'

Tim didn't – couldn't – reply. He didn't think anything would happen to anyone if they never had another Feed again.

'You'll be a fine Mourner,' Bill said.

The words stung. He knew they hadn't been intended to hurt, but the fact that for his father this statement had never been in question was very obvious and painful. Tim was never going to be a pilot, or an architect, or a teacher, or a journalist. Not in his father's mind.

Yes, Bill had suffered too; he'd been bullied, picked on, even lost his hearing. But it had all been for a greater outcome in his eyes. An outcome Tim didn't want, so why should he have to suffer in the first place?

He spoke carefully. 'Hardly anyone believes in the Mourn any more.'

'They're fools to themselves.'

And now, suddenly, there was a huge precipice in front of Tim. Did he speak the truth and plunge headfirst into it? Or did he shuffle backwards and hold his tongue? His father was sitting on the end of his bed, right here, right this very second.

He took a small step closer to the edge. 'What if they're right?'

Bill's face showed genuine surprise.

'I've looked every day, Dad, honest I have. But I've never seen it.'

'Neither have I. I thank my lucky stars I've never had to look at it. I hope we *never* see it.'

Tim teetered on the edge. He knew that if he took too big a step he'd be beyond the point of no return. 'Maybe it's dead.'

Bill got to his feet; clearly uncomfortable with what was being said. He reached for his hearing aid, and Tim thought he might pull his old trick of pretending he couldn't hear. But he seemed to change his mind.

'Read the book,' he said, turning to face Tim. 'I'll give you the key to the cabinet in the study and you read for yourself Old William's exact words from his diary.' He managed to smile at his son. 'They can move you, those words. The Mourn is a frightening thing, but I've often found that what Old William writes can help me overcome the worst of it.'

Tim took a step back, physically and mentally. His father's belief in the Mourn, in the tradition, was like fog. It couldn't be dented or cut or punctured.

'And it's not just a book about a lake monster,' Bill

continued. 'It's about growing up; it's about becoming a man. At sixteen a Milmullen son has to be man enough to bear the weight of the responsibility. Old William talks a lot about how well his son took over the role from him, and about his grandson Henry. He talks about the Carving being a proud moment for both father *and* son.' He patted Tim's shoulder. 'And I know they are men whose lives seem daunting, no doubt about it, but you're just as much a Milmullen as they were. I've got faith in you, just so long as you accept that you're a man now, not a little boy any more.' He searched his son's eyes for his answer.

Tim held his father's gaze, but only because that was what Bill wanted him to do. The truth was he didn't have the courage to prove his real feelings by looking away.

'Good. I'm proud of you.' Bill's smile widened, strengthened. 'I'll get you that key. A week today and it'll be your study anyway, I suppose. I just hope you can find some odd jobs for your old man to do. I still reckon forty-six is far too young for retirement. But that's what it says in my contract.' He chuckled at his own joke.

He left Tim alone. And the second the door clicked shut, Tim grabbed that jumper his father had so neatly folded and flung it with all his strength against the wall across the other side of the room. Whenever he couldn't understand his feelings, whenever his head didn't seem to be coping, he got angry. Anger was straightforward. It was less complicated, easier to deal with than the scary tangle of emotions that wrapped up and constricted his real thoughts.

He couldn't believe he'd been told to *read the book* – not after yesterday, after the childishly vicious thing Roddy had done to him; after all that humiliation. He was furious at his father.

But not just him. At Sarah too, for not feeling the way he did. And at the Fearful for trapping him. And at Jenny for breaking the rules when he didn't dare.

Although the people he was angry at were nowhere near as important as the anger itself. He could fool himself into believing that it had a purpose, a momentum – feeling like this was almost as good as actually doing something about it. He punched his pillow, battered it flat; slammed his wardrobe door, savoured the bang. And, of course, blaming everyone else stopped him from blaming himself.

He'd missed his chance. He hadn't had the courage to tell his father what he really felt. Next Saturday was still next Saturday. He was still going to be the Mourner.

It hadn't just been an argument he'd been worried about; he could handle raised voices and a slanging match. The truth was, he didn't think his father would have started shouting anyway. It would have been a much worse reaction. Bill wouldn't have believed that Tim didn't believe – it was an impossible thought. There would have been a complete lack of understanding and an almost palpable disappointment.

He thought about his father sitting on the edge of his bed, about how he'd looked. Apart from one or two stray threads of grey in his beard he looked exactly the same as he had last year, and the year before. Bill didn't change.

When Tim was younger Bill used to tell him scary

adventure stories about being an explorer. Tim had believed them completely, because with his scruffy hair and beard his dad looked just like explorers should look, hadn't he? But the stories were all about exploring the lake shore, because Bill had never travelled far, never seen much of the rest of the country, and had certainly never been abroad. Not that Tim cared. The stories were too good to worry about that kind of thing back then. Now, however, they seemed like such small stories compared to the ones that could have been told.

Old William's diary was a small story about a small legend. *Read the book*, Bill said. *Read the book*. The diary was his answer to everything. But what hurt most was the way he'd told Tim to grow up. 'You're not a little boy any more. The book is about growing up. You've got to be a man now.'

Well, when Sarah stayed over tomorrow night, that would be being a man, wouldn't it? He wouldn't be a boy any more after that, would he? There were plenty of ways to be a man.

Read the book.

FUCK the book!

But throwing tantrums in his bedroom was no way to deal with all these feelings, all this anger. He needed to react. He needed to lash out, fight, hurt someone back.

Out of his window he could see a couple of windsurfers skimming across the lake, the people on the shore at WetFun. If Jenny could go there then so could he. If she could break the rules, he could too.

Mutiny seemed like an excellent choice. He grabbed his coat.

Jenny

The anger carried him as far as the water's edge before dumping him back on his own two feet. It had hurried him down the stairs and bustled him out into the garden through the main door, but now he felt it let go its grip. He stood for a moment, staring across the lake towards the water-sports club, confused that his temper had so suddenly cooled. Maybe it was the wind.

He panted heavily, as though he was trying to catch his breath. Did he really want to disobey his father? Was it so important to be so defiant? He looked back at Mourn Home. Then turned to face the lake again.

There were three bright sails out there this morning: one small boat cutting through the water east to west and two windsurfers who had the gusts at their backs as they skimmed and leaped over the chop. It had stopped raining. For the briefest of moments the sun broke through a tear in the clouds. Its thin rays sharpened the edges of the water. The white tips of the shallow waves glittered like myriad knives. And the Hundredwaters threatened, was boastful of its danger.

Don't fall in.

But that was ridiculous. That was his father talking. That was sixteen years of conditioning, sixteen years of having the legend pounded into him. All his life he'd been told how unsafe it was to go near the water. He shook his head as if to dislodge all that talk. It was just a lake. There were lots of lakes in the world, just like this one. It was no more dangerous than any other.

Because I don't believe in monsters.

He didn't have to dig too deep to stir up the anger and resentment again. Right now it was the most important thing in the world to do what *he* wanted to do. And he wanted to go to WetFun. So he turned his back on the house and pushed himself on around the shore.

It might have only been a fifteen-minute walk from Mourn Home but Tim had never set foot on WetFun property before. Yes, he'd wandered as close as he dared (as close as he thought he could get away with without being spotted and bollocked by his dad) but this was his first step across the invisible border and onto forbidden soil, as it were. And during the short walk he checked over his shoulder eight, ten, twelve times, cautiously looking back at the house.

The building site for the new hotel was cordoned off behind a temporary chain-link fence. The JCB was idle, but it had already ripped up a sizeable patch of land – large enough to prove the extent of Vic Stones's ambition. The doors to the three grey metal storage sheds where Roddy Morgan spent so much of his time with a screwdriver or whatever were padlocked up and Tim was happy to guess it probably meant Roddy wasn't around today.

But this was WetFun, this was enemy territory. Was he a different person now that he was here? He doubted it. Perhaps the lack of ringing alarms exposing his presence was an anticlimax. Or maybe it was for the best. He was certainly wary of the clubhouse. If there just happened, by chance, to be anyone who might recognize him sitting at the bar, gazing out at the lake through those huge plate-glass windows, he'd be hard to miss. It wasn't like there was a summer crowd of trippers he could lose himself amongst. The kiosk where ice creams were sold and fishing rods rented during high season was closed for winter. A speedboat, looking to Tim's eyes like a sleek, silver bullet of a machine, rested on its trailer high up the shore. He couldn't help thinking it seemed unnatural on dry land somehow, as it waited impatiently for a water-skier brave enough to hang on. It was a little disappointing that the one time he'd managed to pluck up the courage to come here was the time when so little was going on. The only activity this morning was happening around the two narrow jetties where the small sailboats were tied up.

At the near jetty was a group of about fifteen little kids who appeared to be part of a sailing club. They all wore matching orange and yellow life jackets and were gathered around a small dinghy that had been dragged onto the pebbly shore, high up out of the water. Two of the group sat inside the boat practising with the sail, following the shouted orders of one of the adult instructors. They seemed to pass the test because as Tim approached they were allowed to clamber out, and then the whole group trooped off along the jetty to the dinghies moored there. Everyone called enthusiastically to bagsy the boat they wanted – obviously excited to be having a go at the real thing. And Tim couldn't ignore the flicker of concern he felt at the thought of them out on the lake, but he managed to push it deep down. It was that sixteen years of brainwashing again.

He hurried past the end of the jetty, skirting round the practice dinghy, not looking at them.

Jenny and the two students were at the foot of the second, further jetty, where maybe as many as a dozen small motorboats were tied up. Tim wanted his sister to see him, wanted her to be as impressed with his defiance as he had been with hers. He waved at them.

They didn't see him at first. They seemed to be having too much fun to notice him. Gully was wearing a life jacket and his hair was already sticking up in wet spikes, as though he'd only just jumped off the jet-ski that was beached on the shore close by. He threw back his head as he laughed loudly at some great joke or other his friend had come out with, and Tim was eager to be involved. He reckoned they'd be trying every trick they knew to persuade Jenny into having a go on the back of the jet-ski. But she was shaking he head, holding up her hands in a warding-off gesture. No. She was probably telling them she'd never go out on the water.

Tim was thinking, *I'll have a go*. He glanced back yet again at Mourn Home to make sure there was no one watching. *Ask me. I don't care. I'll have a go*, he boasted to himself.

The squealing of one of the young kids caught his attention, although he couldn't see exactly which orange and yellow life jacket was making the fuss. An instructor shouted for everyone to concentrate, be sensible. It didn't look as though anybody had fallen in – just over-excitement. And Tim hoped the adults were as in control as they thought they were.

As he turned back to the second jetty he saw Gully suddenly reach out and grab his sister. Jenny tried to push him away. But then Scott also had a hand on her arm. Tim heard her shout and swear and knew she wasn't having fun any more. The students overpowered her, pinned her arms by her sides, dragged her onto the wooden jetty and out over the water.

'Hey!' he called, forgetting instantly about the young kids. 'Leave her alone.' He hurried towards them. He didn't run; he didn't think they'd actually throw her in. No way would they go that far.

Jenny was arguing and struggling. They jostled her along the jetty between the motorboats moored on either side. Tim still didn't quite run. He thought the students were just acting up, teasing her, and he didn't want to look like an over-protective brother – or worse, a foolish killjoy. He reached the foot of the jetty himself and saw that they had her teetering over the very end. He heard Scott say something about monsters and the Mourn, taunting her, holding her so her toes literally dangled in thin air.

Gully said, 'Come on the jet-ski with me or we'll chuck you in.'

Tim started out over the water himself, annoyed at their spitefulness, yet still not believing they were doing any more than winding her up. 'Leave her alone. You're not funny.'

Gully finally noticed him and said something to Scott that Tim couldn't quite catch. Scott glanced back over his shoulder, saw Tim jogging along the jetty towards them, grinned and winked. Quickly, roughly, he tipped Jenny backwards into his arms, holding her off-balance by the wrists. Gully went for her ankles. She struggled and one of her trainers popped off, but he still managed to sweep her up off her feet. Under different circumstance they could have been friends about to give her the 'bumps' on her birthday. But it had clearly long stopped being a game for Jenny.

She bucked and shrieked. Too late Tim heard her real fear. '*Don't!*' He raced towards them. '*No!*'

But on the count of three they threw her over the edge.

'Jenny!'

His immediate impulse was to catch her and he leaped forward, but it was a vain hope. She twisted in the air like a cat, as though she was going to land on all fours. And she fell out of sight below the end of the wooden jetty. She didn't stop screaming until she hit the water.

'*Jenny!*'

He barged between the guffawing students and teetered on the edge himself as he looked down. She'd gone all the way under. The water had swept back over to fill and cover the splash she'd made.

'She can't swim, you bastards!'

He was horrified. He couldn't see her. She'd gone all the way *under*. Everything his father had ever said and warned and threatened rushed through his head. He was frantic. He knew he should go in after her. He knew he should fetch Bill. He didn't dare do either.

'She can't *swim*!'

His brain seemed to slip out of synch somehow and he was aware of all sorts of different things at once – like the kids at the sailing school all watching, like the grey sky and sharp wind, like the students laughing – and time seemed to have slowed down, yet his thoughts were racing, trying to come up with some kind of reasonable explanation for what was going on that didn't end in catastrophe. Jenny was in the Hundredwaters. *Stay away from the water*, their father had always told them. But Jenny had gone all the way under.

And he didn't dare go in after her.

'JENNY!'

Suddenly she burst up to the surface, spluttering, floundering, gasping for breath. She flailed her arms for something solid to grab hold of and slipped under again. Tim kept shouting her name. He sprawled flat on his belly, reaching for her, but the jetty's wooden platform was too high above the water. He could see the churning, frothing waves she was making as she fought. But he still couldn't go in after her.

Again she broke the surface and this time managed to get her feet underneath her. She staggered, spitting and coughing. Thankfully the lake was nowhere near as deep here as it was around the feeding pier at Mourn Home; it only came to her shoulders, although whenever she moved it splashed up around her mouth. She held her arms out in front of her – Tim guessed she was on her tiptoes – her hair plastered across her white, frightened face. He tried reaching for her again and when she gripped his hand the icy cold of her skin shocked him.

He knew he'd never be strong enough to pull her back up onto the jetty. 'You'll have to go round. Jenny, listen. You'll have to walk round and up the shore.'

'Go in and get her,' Gully said from behind him. 'It's not deep.' He even nudged him with his foot as though he was considering kicking him in as well.

Tim savagely shoved the foot away. 'Get off me, you bastard!'

Scott just laughed. 'Go on. Dive in and save her. Quick before the monster comes!'

Gully started humming the *Jaws* theme tune.

Jenny was shivering and white; she wouldn't let go of Tim's hand – he was at full stretch just to be able to reach her. She was desperate to scrape her hair out of her eyes and she spluttered and coughed as the water splashed around her mouth and nose. She was turning this way and that, her eyes wide, searching the water frantically. Because she would also have their father's words running through her head. *Never go in the water*. She'd had sixteen years of listening to the legend exactly the same as Tim had.

'You've got to go round.' He tugged on her hand to try and get her moving. The kids from the sailing school were all staring; one of the instructors shouted to ask if everything was okay. 'Come on, Jenny. You've got to get out.'

'You go in and get her,' Scott said. 'Why don't you help her?'

Tim didn't understand how they could be so flippantly cruel, because one look at Jenny's face was surely enough proof for anybody to believe just how terrified she was. He found it impossible not to glance out at the deeper water.

'Come on, Jenny. Please.' He was begging her. He yanked on her freezing hand.

'Just get out of my way,' Gully said. He knocked Tim to one side as he took a two-step run-up and jumped off the jetty himself. He curled into a bomb before he hit the water, making the biggest splash he possibly could.

Jenny shrieked. Tim leaped back so he wouldn't get showered by cold, dirty lake water. Scott thought it was the funniest thing in the world.

Gully surged up to the surface. The wave he caused would have swamped Jenny again if he hadn't swept her up in his arms. Like all the best movie heroes he waded towards shore with her clinging to him.

Tim hurried down the jetty to the pebbly beach. 'Are you okay? Jenny?'

Once on dry land she squirmed and writhed in Gully's arms, so he had drop her onto her own feet straight away.

'Hey, you're a hero,' Scott told him.

He squirted a mouthful of water in a long jet. 'Yeah. I

101

know.' He grinned widely. It was all just one big game. He probably didn't even realize how frightened Jenny really was.

Tim took his coat off and put it over her shoulders. 'You're okay, yeah? You're all right?'

'. . . freezing . . .' she told him in a small voice. She was dripping, teeth chattering. Water ran in quick little rivulets down her forehead and face. She looked back yet again at the water, as if expecting the Mourn to swish by, just missing her, like monsters did in the movies. And she took a quick couple of steps further up the shore.

He tried to rub a bit of heat into her. 'We'd better get home; get you warm.'

She nodded, shuddering violently with the cold, wiping the water from her eyes again and again.

Gully had a stupid smirk all over his face. 'We had to do it,' he said. He swept his dripping hair back off his forehead. 'To prove to you there's nothing to worry about. And now you know that nothing's gonna get you, you can come out on the back of the jet-ski with me.'

'Just piss off,' Tim told him.

Scott stepped in front of them. 'Hey, is that all the thanks he gets for saving your sister when you were too chicken-shit to do it yourself?'

Tim tried to pull Jenny away, but she wouldn't let him.

'Why did you do it?' she asked, honestly wondering.

'We were messing about,' Gully said, defensive now. His grin slipped; he was shivering too. 'It was just meant to be a joke.'

'You knew I was frightened, and you still threw me in.'

102

'Didn't think you'd *really* freak out.' He rolled his eyes, tried to laugh. 'It was just a joke.' He wrapped his arms around himself as he shuddered with the cold.

'Yeah. Very funny.' She turned her back on him.

Tim held his arm around her shoulders. 'Come on.' He led her away, ignoring Gully's protestations.

'Don't you want this?' Scott held out Jenny's lost trainer.

Tim snatched it from him but pulled his sister away before she had a chance to put it back on.

'Don't tell Mum and Dad.'

Tim shook his head. They hurried past the stares of the kids in the sailing club and he kept his arm around her shoulders, trying to cuddle some warmth into her. She was shivering violently so he forced her to jog most of the way home. She was a mess. Her hair hung in ropes, she smelled of cold and dirty water and her trainers squelched with every step. He felt guiltier than he had ever done in his life before because he'd not even got the toe-tip of his own trainers damp.

The Feed was over for another week; there was no sign of the guests, the Fearful or their parents so they managed to slip inside through the main entrance and went immediately to Jenny's bedroom. Anne was probably driving Nana Dalry home while Bill would be around the far side of the lake.

Jenny's room was on the floor below Tim's and although it was smaller it was a heck of a lot tidier – he often wondered how she managed it. It must have been a couple of months since the last time he was in here and he noticed she'd recently taken most of her cheesy band posters down. They'd been replaced by more arty stuff: a New York skyline, a print of a famous painting he recognized but couldn't name. Her bookshelf was also full of books he'd never seen before. He was embarrassed by the childish mess of his own room all over again. How much proof did he really need that Jenny was growing up quicker than him?

He didn't know whether or not she actually wanted him hanging around right now but he wasn't about to leave. He wanted to talk to her even if she didn't want to talk to him. His head was spinning with all the things he wanted to say.

He stood at her single window as she changed. The view wasn't quite as impressive as from his room: her window faced south-west, onto the stretch of shoreline and lake which included the Mourn Stone, the feeding pier and the ragged curve of the water towards the woods. As he stood there he saw their father emerge from the trees, heading back this way.

'Looks like we only just made it in time,' he said. 'Another ten minutes and we would have walked right into Dad.'

Jenny pulled on a jumper and also looked out. 'Do you think he saw what happened?'

'Even if he did, we were all the way over on the other side and he wouldn't have been able to tell it was us.'

Jenny nodded, but still seemed worried.

'Are you okay?' It was maybe the tenth time he'd asked. And when she nodded again he said, 'You're sure, yeah?' It was guilt making him keep on asking.

She sat on her bed, pulled her knees up under chin and wrapped her arms around them as if she was still cold.

'Why did they do it? I didn't think they would. I can't believe they just threw you in like that.' Tim couldn't settle. He hovered at the window. Then, with a tut and sigh, he moved over to sit at her desk, where he swivelled back and forth on the thinly cushioned seat as though he was uncomfortable. 'I don't get why they did it.'

'Because they're wankers,' Jenny said.

He got up again, walked over to her new bookshelf, began prodding and poking at her books. He couldn't help but feel impressed with her. She'd been bullied, terrorized and freezing cold, and not once had she cried.

'Because they don't care about anybody else and think they can get away with doing anything they want,' she said.

'But why did you go with them in the first place?'

'You knew I fancied Gully. And he was paying me attention. How many boys do you know around here who bother paying me any attention?'

'Going to WetFun, though? Dad would—'

'I wanted to see what was happening at the building site. I wanted to see how big the hotel was going to be.'

'Massive. Bigger than this place.' He was back looking out of the window. Bill was halfway home along the shore already.

'So what made *you* come to WetFun? Did you fancy Gully as well?'

He almost laughed, but not quite. 'I'd had an argument with Dad. I wanted to be a rebel like you.'

'What were you arguing about?'

'Next Saturday.'

'Your Carving?'

He nodded slowly, not wanting to elaborate – he'd learned his lesson trying to talk to Sarah and his father. And just looking around Jenny's room proved how big the distance between the two of them had become, twins or not.

'You're nervous about becoming the Mourner?'

'It's a bit more complicated than that.'

'How do you mean?'

'Doesn't matter. It's all messed up anyway.' He saw the way she was looking at him and her sympathy embarrassed him. 'And anyway, shouldn't it be me comforting you?'

She managed a small smile at this. But it only made him feel guilty again because he was so completely *dry*.

'I'm sorry,' he said. 'I should have tried to save you. I should have jumped in to, you know . . . I should have been in the water to help you.'

She sat up straighter, sucked in a big breath. 'First off: the feminist in me would have something to say about the man always thinking he has to save the woman, and about male dominating behaviour.' She didn't give him the chance to ask if she was joking. 'And secondly: I don't blame you for not wanting to dive headfirst into the Hundredwaters. It's *the Hundredwaters*. It's where the Mourn is. Gully's just too stupid to care.'

Through the window Tim watched as their father stopped and shielded his eyes with one hand, scanning the lake, probably making sure there was no problem with the kids' sailing school. He had his back to her when he said, 'That's the problem. Up until Gully and Scott chucked you in I'd convinced myself the Mourn didn't exist.'

'What do you mean?'

He was at the bookshelf again, purposely looking at the books and not at her. 'It's why I don't want to be the Mourner. One of the reasons, anyway.'

The silence that greeted his admission felt horribly heavy. He fidgeted. *Said too much. Shitshitshit.* He hadn't meant to say anything. 'Don't tell Dad. You won't, will you?'

There was an audible clunk as Jenny managed to close her mouth. At last she said, 'He's going to find out sooner or later.'

'Later would be great,' Tim said with a failed chuckle. He shrugged a single shoulder. 'I tried to talk to him, but he didn't really want to listen.'

'I mean, I knew you were worried about becoming the Mourner, but I just thought you were nervous. I didn't realize . . .' She shook her head, obviously taken aback. 'You really don't believe in it?'

'I didn't think I did. I kept telling myself I didn't. But then I didn't dare jump into the lake to help you. Everything Dad had ever warned us about just kept running through my head.' He was miserable and ashamed when he admitted: 'I was too scared to help you.'

'So you *do* believe in it?'

'I don't know.' He slumped down onto the bed beside her, leaned back against the wall. 'I honestly don't know what to think any more.' He went on, 'When you were in the water, did you . . . ? Did you see it?'

'No.'

'But was it there? Did you feel it? You know, sort of *sense* it?'

107

'Maybe. I kept thinking it was behind me, getting closer. Although part of my head kept saying it wouldn't attack me because we'd just had a Feed.'

'But it could have just been your imagination, couldn't it?'

'Maybe.' She changed the subject. 'And you really don't want to be the Mourner?'

'If I don't think the Mourn's real, there doesn't seem much point, does there? But you've got to admit, it's probably the worst job in the world anyway, isn't it? Spending most days with a spade and sack collecting dead stuff, and having everyone laughing at you behind your back all the time.' He wanted to explain it to her as best as he could. 'I love Dad,' he said. 'I just don't want to *be* Dad.' He was worried by the look on her face. 'You promise you won't tell him?'

She shook her head.

But he didn't know what that meant. Did she mean no, she wouldn't tell him or no, she didn't promise?

She asked: 'Are you sure it's not just because of Roddy Morgan?'

'Well, stuff like yesterday kind of helped me make my mind up, obviously.'

'But it's such a special thing to do,' Jenny said. 'When I was little I always used to hide under the covers when I went to sleep, because I was scared that if the Mourn looked in through my window and saw me, it would come and get me. I knew it would never eat you, because you were going to be the Mourner, but what was to stop it eating me? I was just an extra. That was how I felt, being your twin. Then I remember there was a really loud storm outside and I was curled up under my sheets listening to it. I suddenly realized that Dad's job was to stop the Mourn from attacking the town, and I was part of the town, wasn't I? So I stuck my foot out – and nothing happened. And so I poked my head out. Dad would never let the Mourn get me because that was what Dad did. Other dads worked in shops or offices, but my dad kept me and everybody else safe. So I kicked back all my blankets and lay in the dark for ages, just listening to the wind and the rain. And nothing happened to me. I knew I'd always be safe because Dad did what he did.'

'Okay, that's all great, but—'

'No; listen. I worried at some point about him not always being around, but I soon realized that when Dad wasn't here, you would be. And I began to think what a fantastic thing it must be to be the one person who could make everybody else sleep safe at night. That's what the Mourner does, that's why it's such a special job. It must be great to read the list of names at the Feed and know it's you who's keeping those people safe. For me it feels good just to be one of the Fearful and know I'm doing my bit to help others too.'

Tim thought about it. After a while he asked: 'Is that all true?'

His sister nodded. 'Cross my heart.'

'Maybe it's you who should be the Mourner, then.'

'Don't be stupid! There's no girls' names on the Mourn Stone, is there? There's never been a woman Mourner – it's always first-born *sons*.' She pulled a face. 'But I'm sixteen next week too, don't forget. And I've got no idea what I'm meant to do, or where I should go, or anything. At least you've got something to do with your life – something that matters. You're lucky; there aren't many sixteen-year-olds who can say that.'

Tim was sceptical. 'But if the Mourn isn't real, then it's all just a massive waste of time, isn't it?'

'Why don't you think it's real?'

'Because I've never seen it.'

'So?'

'So everything. I want some proof. Where's the proof?' He was annoyed she couldn't see it from his point of view.

'This house is proof, isn't it? And the Fearful. And Old William's diary. Even Dad's proof, because of what he does.'

'But he's never seen it either!'

'Exactly. What more proof do you need? Why would all this be here if it was all just a story? There's over three hundred years of proof, isn't there?'

He jumped up off the bed, feeling twitchy all over again, and stalked over to the window. He saw that Bill was almost home. 'So you're saying you don't care what Gully and Scott, or Roddy Morgan, or whoever else are all saying behind your back.'

'No.'

He searched her face, looking for the lie he thought must be there. He couldn't find it, which agitated him further.

'I'm glad I'm different to them; I don't want to be anything like them,' she said.

'Yeah, well, like I said yesterday, nobody calls you *Monster Girl*, do they?' He didn't let her answer. He paced the room. 'It's just after what happened yesterday. It's just everything. I hate it. It's just so shit, isn't it? And look at today. It's getting worse, isn't it? I'm up to here with it – everybody always having a go. All because of the Mourn, and I didn't ask to be its keeper or anything; why get at me all the time?'

'It wasn't about you. They threw *me* in the lake, not you.'

'I know, but—'

'They didn't do it to get at *you*. Not everything that happens around here is about *you*.'

'But they're probably laughing right now, aren't they? Thinking they're funny. Having a laugh at all of us, but I'm the one who's got to be the Mourner, and I didn't ask to be.'

'And I never asked to be your sister either.'

That confused him. 'So?'

'So I'm fed up of hearing about you all the time. I said it's my birthday too next Saturday, didn't I? Have you bought my present yet? What have you got me?'

Tim hadn't got her anything – because he'd not even thought about it. He knew she could tell by the look on his face.

'How many people came up to me this morning to tell me they're looking forward to my birthday, do you think? How many people will remember, or even know it's my birthday too?'

111

'Well, maybe you really should be the Mourner, then. I'll go ask Dad now, shall I? You know, see if it's okay with him?'

She tutted. 'Grow up.'

That hurt. He remembered what Bill had said to him earlier. 'You grow up!' It was such a feeble retort but the anger had flared inside him again. 'You grow up! I'm not the one who believes in monsters, am I?'

'So why were you too scared to jump into the lake?'

He slammed the door on his way out.

Then instantly regretted it. Tentatively he poked his head back inside her room. 'You're not going to tell Dad, are you?'

'Get *out*!' She hurled a book at him, and only just missed.

His head fizzed. He felt hopeless with confusion. Had he been kidding himself when he'd said he didn't believe in the Mourn? Maybe he did believe.

Did he?

Maybe.

Would it help if he knew for certain? Would it be easier to be the Mourner if it was proved to him that the Mourn was real? His spinning mind fixed on this. He might be happy to do the worst job in the world if he truly believed in the Mourn. He could make himself happy to do it.

To his anxious, muddled mind this thought seemed to make perfect sense. He clung to it. Everything would be simpler, easier, *happier* if he knew for definite the Mourn was real.

It couldn't be so wrong to want some proof, could it? How could he be expected to dedicate his whole life to something he'd never seen? He was just a bit different from Jenny and their father. He needed proof.

He doubted he'd find it in Old William's diary and knew it was something Bill could never give him, because it came back to the same point over and over again: Bill had never seen the Mourn.

But as he stood there he realized there was somebody who claimed he had.

Jack Spicer's Story

Tim was suddenly in a hurry. He was getting his hopes up. He wanted something to happen *now*.

Suddenly, after years of not knowing exactly what was wrong with him, months of drifting helplessly not knowing which way to turn even when did understand his problem, he might have actually found an answer. Or if not an answer, at least some way of doing something about it. Because maybe Jack Spicer could offer him proof, could convince him in a way his father had never been able to.

And Tim had to talk to him *now*.

He hurried downstairs to find out which room Mr Spicer was staying in. He was going to check the guest book on the table by the main entrance but heard the side door open and close and voices in the kitchen. Both his mother and father had returned home. Tim waited at the bottom of the stairs to see where they were going – in case he needed to go the opposite way.

'Somebody's dumped a couple of filthy mattresses up in the trees,' Bill was saying. 'I'll need to use the van to get rid of them.' He saw keeping the lakeside rubbish-free as much a part of the job as keeping it safe.

The kitchen door was slightly ajar; through the slim gap Tim saw his mother heave three hefty plastic carrier bags up onto the kitchen table, letting them go with a relieved breath. 'I would have been a bit quicker if I'd known, but Mum wanted to talk about next Saturday. And the queues in the cash-and-carry were ridiculous.' She took her coat off, turned to hang it up.

Bill was behind her, still wearing his yellow waterproofs, helping carry another two stuffed-to-bursting bags. He put them on the table next to the others. 'We could maybe do with talking things through later as well. I'm worried about Tim. I had a chat with him earlier and he's been having a harder time of it than either of us have realized.'

Anne took one of the shopping bags out of Tim's line of vision. He heard her open the fridge door and bottles chinked together. 'It's understandable. Of course he's going to feel a little anxious with only a week to go.'

He wasn't usually the type to sneak or spy. He hesitated, in two minds what to do. The hurry to see Jack Spicer faded a little as his curiosity took hold of him. He wanted to know what his father thought about him after his near confession earlier. Jack Spicer's story could wait two or three minutes more. He crouched at the bottom of the stairs and held his breath to listen.

'I understand the nerves, Annie. But earlier I got the idea it's more than that.' Bill was helping unpack the shopping. 'He was talking like Tom and Rhonda's son. Tim should be the last person talking like that. I told him he had to read Old William's diary. I've left the key to the

115

study for him on the shelf.' There was a pause. 'Not that he's bothered to pick it up yet.'

Tim didn't know the full story behind why Tom and Rhonda Bye's son had stopped coming to the Feed. He'd always assumed Colin had simply decided the Mourn wasn't real, or that he couldn't take the constant mockery that Tim also suffered. So yes, maybe the two of them did talk alike.

'Do you think you should speak to him?' Anne asked.

'That's what I have been doing.'

'You said you told him to read the diary.'

'Old William's words are better than mine.'

'Maybe. But wouldn't he rather hear things from you? It's daunting the amount of responsibility he's got to take on next week, especially at his age.'

'I had to cope when I was only fifteen.'

'I know that, Bill,' Anne said, with a small edginess that implied she'd heard the story many times before. 'But you were lucky enough not to have the likes of Brian Brown or my mother pawing you every chance they got. Some of our friends are a lot to cope with at sixteen. And Tim has never been as bull-headed or stubborn as you.'

Bill sighed. 'That's just the way it is – I can't change more than three hundred years of history just because he's a little sensitive. His skin will thicken.'

'I know it will. I just wonder if that's such a good thing.'

Tim wasn't sure how that description made him feel. He'd never thought of himself as thin-skinned or sensitive. He found himself moving away from the stairs, sliding closer towards the gap in the door to hear more. He'd never really

116

considered that his parents might have a different view of him than he did of himself.

'I can't bend the tradition any more than I already am,' Bill said. 'My father would never have let me stay on at school. I would have been out the second I turned sixteen – if I hadn't already left.'

Anne was quiet.

'Clive Tucker was pulling me up about it earlier, saying the Mourner should *only* be the Mourner, not a student as well.'

'Well, that's all right for him to say.' Anne obviously wasn't impressed. She was back at the table, unpacking boxes of cornflakes and porridge, forcing Tim to slink back up one or two steps again. 'He already has his high and mighty university education.'

'He does have a point, though.'

'Times have changed. I don't see what the problem would be with letting Tim continue his studies as long as he wants to. You're fit and healthy; you keep saying you're far too young to retire. I can't see you taking up painting or gardening to keep your idle hands busy, can you? You'll be doing just as much as you are now. I always thought Tim could lead us in the Feed every Saturday, while you carried on the duties during the week. Just until he's decided if he wants to go to university or not.'

'And if he decides he does want to go to university?'

'He can come back at weekends. If he chooses Leeds or York, even Lancashire, he can catch a train on a Friday evening and be home by—'

117

'It's *not* a part-time job, Annie. The Mourner collects the feed; the Mourner keeps the lake and the town safe. How's he going to keep everyone safe when he's however many miles away getting pissed in the student bar?' Bill wasn't angry, but he was determined to make his point. 'Look at the two students who are staying here. Bloody waste of space, the pair of them. Do you want him turning out like them?' The rustling of his waterproofs sounded agitated. 'What are they doing here anyway? Shouldn't they be, you know, *studying*?'

'It's Reading Week,' Anne told him.

'Hmm. Then they should be reading, not playing silly buggers out on the lake, don't you think? Whichever way you look at it, Tim doesn't need university because he's the Mourner. Old William's diary can give him all the education he needs for that.'

'All I'm saying is that I hope you realize Tim won't suddenly turn into you next Saturday. It might take him a little longer to get used to his new responsibilities.'

'I'll be there for him every step of the way. Of course I will.'

'He's got more of my side of the family in him than yours. Jenny got his share of Milmullen.'

'She's inherited my stubborn bull-headedness, you mean?'

Anne laughed lightly. 'I didn't mean—'

'It makes me wonder why you ever married me.'

'Keep guessing.'

Bill laughed as well.

'Don't worry,' Anne said. 'Tim will make you proud. It's thirty years since your Carving, and as you always say yourself, so much has changed. Kids are different these days; the world expects different things from them. Just give him his own time and he'll make us all proud.'

'I know he will. I'm just concerned for the lad myself. Three hundred years is a lot to live up to and there are plenty of people in this town who would dearly love to see us fail.'

'I'm sure he knows that too.'

Bill pecked her on the cheek noisily and rustled his way to the back door in his waterproofs. 'I'm not sure what time I'll be back. Remind Tim about the key for me, would you?' Anne said she would and wished him goodbye. He headed out into the chilly day again.

Tim stayed where he was after the back door had closed again, listening to his mother unpack the rest of the shopping. He couldn't explain how all that his parents had said made him feel (and he'd never heard them talk so privately, so intimately before – which made him feel doubly weird). He *did* want to make his father proud, of course he did. But the only thing that would make Bill proud was the one thing Tim wasn't able to do. The whole situation left him feeling oddly claustrophobic. But maybe he could do it if he had proof it needed doing.

He waited a few moments more, then walked into the kitchen pretending he'd only just come downstairs.

'Is Dad out?' he asked, keeping up the pretence.

Anne turned from the sink where she was filling the kettle.

119

'Yes. But he's left the key to the study for you on the shelf by the fridge.'

'Okay, thanks.' He wanted to ask her what she meant by calling him sensitive, and whether it was a problem to be labelled as such. He managed to push the thought quickly aside. 'Which room is Mr Spicer in?' he asked instead. 'Is it number seven?'

'No, that's for your Uncle Doug when he comes tomorrow. *If* he comes tomorrow. Mr Spicer is in number six.'

'Thanks.' He turned to go. He was worried if he stayed too long he'd betray the fact that he'd been spying.

'But don't go bothering him if he doesn't want you hanging around.'

'I won't.' He was half out the door to the hallway.

'Don't forget the key.'

He hurried back to the shelf by the fridge. 'Got it.'

'And do you know where your sister's been hiding this morning? She promised to help me with the shopping.'

'Did she go to Sarah's?' he asked, because it was easier than an outright lie.

He took the main stairs two at a time. He was quietly amazed that his mother could talk about him behind his back and not even show the slightest signs of guilt. It made him wonder how often she and Bill did it.

He knocked twice at the door of room six, but Jack Spicer was out. Tim pulled a face, narked, impatient. He considered the key in his hand. Maybe he should do as he was told and read the book.

He checked his watch to see that it was gone twelve – the

pubs were open. He decided that if Mr Spicer wasn't in his room he'd probably be at his other favourite haunt: the Dows Bridges.

The pub stood on the lake (rather than the town) side of the twin, humpbacked bridges that were its namesake. Originally the tollhouse for anyone travelling into Moutonby, it wasn't that much younger than its more extravagant cousin, Mourn Home. And although the owners, Bert and Agna, had done their best to clean up its act in the last year or so, a paint job and new menu couldn't hide the overall impression that soon enough it was going to teeter over the edge and crumble into the river Hurry only a couple of metres below. One lane of the bridges had had to be rebuilt after the so-called earthquake of 1908, but the pub itself had always clung on tenaciously. It wasn't a place any of the Milmullens frequented and it took a swallow of courage for Tim to step inside.

The recently re-decorated family room at the front of the pub was bright and welcoming, and the vibrantly red-headed Agna flitted between the handful of tables that were taken up by young couples with toddlers. Tim was able to hurry through unnoticed. He knew not to look for Mr Spicer here.

The old-fashioned lounge bar at the back was dim, smoky, and if not exactly chock-a-block, busy enough with grumbling old men nursing their warm pints at rickety wooden tables. Tim hovered at the door. Bert guarded the bar, watching him. Bert knew him; of course he did, and knew he was under-age, but wouldn't say anything unless he tried to order a drink. Which he had no intention of doing. He just wanted to talk to Jack Spicer, who was sitting by himself at the window.

He weaved his way between the tables. 'Mr Spicer?'

The elderly man looked up, surprised to see him. He had to be seventy, easily, but still had a decent head of silver hair and walked tall and upright, if not particularly quickly.

'Sorry to disturb you, Mr Spicer.'

'There's not a problem back at Mourn Home, is there?'

Tim shook his head. 'No, no. Everything's fine.' He meant with the building itself, obviously. The people who lived there, however . . . 'I really don't want to disturb you if you're busy . . .'

'I don't reckon I can remember the last time I was busy.' Jack Spicer smiled sardonically. 'I'm not sure if you should be here, mind you. What do you reckon your mum might say if she catches you?'

Tim could only shrug.

Mr Spicer chuckled. 'Sit down, lad. Can I get you a drink?'

'No, it's okay, thanks. I'm not old enough anyway.'

'Of course you're not. Of course. But what about a pop?' He pointed at the dregs in his pint glass. 'Could do with a top-up myself anyway.' When Tim nodded he eased himself up from his chair like it was an effort to work his bones and headed for the bar.

Tim prickled with the stares of the other old men, but hoped it didn't show. Now he was here he wasn't sure how he was going to broach the subject with Mr Spicer. He had to be careful asking because the old man was easily irritated – as Tim and Jenny had now and again discovered to their cost. But when he turned to the window next to the table he realized the old man had a good view of the river Hurry and the lake – just the same as his table at breakfast, and his room in Mourn Home. Jack Spicer was still looking too.

'So what can I do you for?' The old man plonked a glass of Coke on the table, dribbling a splash of froth over the side. He tutted at the shaking of his hand as he sat down. He acknowledged Tim's thanks, sipped at his pint, then said: 'I don't know whether I'm willing to provide you with an alibi.'

Tim was confused.

'Twagging off school yesterday afternoon?'

Tim blushed, remembering being spotted when he'd tried to sneak home. 'Oh, no. No. That's not . . .' He tried to hide his face as he took a gulp of Coke. 'No.' He swallowed hard. 'It's about the Mourn.'

'Is it now?' Jack Spicer eyed him deliberately.

Tim wasn't sure where to go from here. 'You've seen it,' he said awkwardly.

The old man nodded.

'You were talking about it at breakfast yesterday.'

The old man nodded again.

'I was . . . Well, I wondered . . .'

At last Mr Spicer helped him. 'Surely you've heard the story many times before?' Perhaps it was meant as an admonishment, but Tim got the impression the old man was very willing to tell his tale again.

'Not really. Dad's mentioned it, told lots of people about you and everything' – Jack Spicer smiled at this – 'but I don't know *exactly* what happened.'

'"Exactly"?'

Tim shrugged. 'Well, yeah.'

The old man leaned back in his chair but never took his eyes off him. 'I'm not one of your Fearful lot,' he said.

'Oh, yeah, I know.' He took a breath, wanting to say the right thing. 'I suppose that's what . . .' He struggled for what he supposed. 'You're the only person who's seen it—'

'Recently.'

'Yeah, recently. So you believe in it, because you've seen it. My mum and dad never have, but . . . but they . . .'

'But they run the whole shebang.'

Tim was nodding furiously. 'Yes. Exactly. You come back all the time, and you never come to the Feed when you're here, you just always sit where you can see the lake.' He gestured at the table, the window. 'You've never seen it again, have you? And yet you still keep coming back . . .'

Jack Spicer took a deep breath. 'I'm only the most recent to see it, you know? Even your ancestor – Old William? – even he wasn't the first. He might have named it, but there'd been stories told by the fishermen of something in the water for a long, long time before that. There's always been stories about the lake.' He stopped and tutted at himself. 'Your dad tells that side of it better than me.' His eyes flicked to the window, the scene beyond. Tim waited impatiently.

Eventually Jack Spicer said, 'My story.' He turned his gaze on Tim again. 'My story is, I've been coming back every year for nigh on thirty years. Two big reasons – one not so big. I came here with my wife the first time, just for a short holiday. We wanted to walk in the hills. And we had a fine time. I certainly wasn't looking for the thing, but I saw it. I made two local papers, and one of the tabloids. I shared page three, but don't remember her name.' He smiled ruefully, took a drink. 'My wife, Mary, she died not long after we went home and got back to work. I come back over and over because I can think of her, and of one of the last good, happy times we spent together.'

Tim stayed quiet. Lots of questions already, but he managed to stay quiet for the time being.

'I also come back because of your family,' Jack Spicer continued. 'I like to keep myself to myself – I hope sometimes you don't even realize I'm around – but I've seen your father marry your mother, and you and your sister grow up. I held you as a baby, you know.' He cocked his eyebrow, took a drink. 'I like to think that you've adopted me a little. A lonely old man you've let into the fold, even if it's just in a small way.' He smiled at this.

'They're my two big reasons, Tim. They're the two things that drag me back three, maybe four times a year.' He returned to looking out of the window. 'Wanting to see the Mourn again is my not so big reason any more. But I can't deny that I like being around others who believe me. You could say I've had my fair share of leg-pulling and smart-aleck remarks where I come from. At least the people here believe me. I don't feel quite so mad or foolish around them.'

Tim remembered how Jack had been greeted by the Fearful earlier that morning. He asked: 'What did it look like?'

Jack Spicer took his time to answer. 'Nothing like Nessie,' he said. He heard Tim's frustrated sigh and shook his head. 'No, this is important. It's not a joke, lad. Everybody will tell you the Loch Ness Monster is a dinosaur – a freak of nature, but still an animal, if you like. Maybe it is. Who am I to argue? Or maybe we don't want to think about it being anything else. Maybe we *can't* think about it being anything else because modern times won't let us.'

Tim wasn't quite following this, but stayed quiet. For him Bert's smoky bar had virtually disappeared. He leaned forward, studying Jack Spicer's watery grey eyes, hearing nothing but his voice.

The words had an over-polished quality to them because he'd said them so many times before. 'It was a fair bit out, maybe about thirty or thirty-five foot from the shore; looked like it was going to swim up the river here, swim right under this pub. I saw its back, then its head – ugly, black thing. Maybe about twice as long as I am tall; unless it had a tail I couldn't see, then longer still. I thought it was an alligator, or crocodile, something like that. I went to shout for my Mary to come see. But I stopped myself because straight away I knew it wasn't anything like that. Not even if I had heard on the television that one had escaped from a zoo that very morning would I have believed they were the same thing. Because about the most I can tell you is that what I saw wasn't natural. The Mourn is not a creature Mother

Nature ever made. I've heard your father call it "the dragon in the lake", and that's about the best description I've got too. Because dragons aren't real, either.'

Tim waited for more, but Jack Spicer was only drinking now. The Dows Bridges seemed to fall into place around him again. 'It's not real?'

'It's not an animal. It's unearthly: not of this earth.'

Tim stared at the old man. It wasn't enough. 'Can you tell me any more?'

'What more do you want? I'd be lying if I said I'd seen it twice.'

'But could you tell me something . . . something else?'

Mr Spicer frowned at him. His voice sharpened the tiniest amount. 'I'm sure I haven't got the foggiest what you mean.'

Desperation made him bold. 'Could you tell me something more than just a *story*?'

'Are you calling me a liar, young man?'

Maybe Tim should have apologized but he was desperate to hear something he'd not heard before, desperate to have a hard, unarguable fact smack him between the eyes. Only that would have been good enough, proof enough. So instead of apologizing he found himself saying, 'I don't *think* you're lying . . .'

'What?' The old man's eyes immediately hardened.

At last Tim realized his mistake. Too late he began to apologize and say how grateful he was.

'I've had a few people call me a few things over the years, but I never believed I'd hear Bill Milmullen's son call me a *liar*.'

'No, Mr Spicer, I didn't mean it like that. Honestly I didn't.'

'I think I'm going to have to have a few words with your father about this. I've been a good friend to your family and I don't expect to be called a liar by you, young man.' He went on and on.

Tim managed to escape after his fifth or sixth apology, back through the family room and out into the car park in the wind. He stood for a few moments in the fresh air – a welcome relief after the smoky bar. He looked towards Mourn Home and Lake Mou, a little dazed by what had just happened. He realized that in the last hour he'd managed to drive a wedge between him and his sister as well as cause offence to his parents' most dependable customer. He wondered briefly how a day that had begun badly enough anyway could have got so much worse?

A small car crested the bridges and zoomed by, heading away from the town. It didn't turn off towards Mourn Home and the lake but kept going. He watched it as it followed the rise of the road towards the lip of the valley. For Tim that road was like an arrow pointing anywhere he wanted to go; places he was scared he might never get to see. Too late he stuck his thumb out for a lift, because the small car had already disappeared into the distance.

Part Two

Monster Boy II

Mourn Home was sleeping – except for Tim. He was sitting cross-legged on the floor of the study surrounded by his family's most precious possessions. The lamp on his father's desk spotlit him in the middle of the antique papers and bound manuscripts he'd taken from the glass cabinet. It was seventeen minutes past twelve – seventeen minutes into a new day, into another day closer to his sixteenth birthday, closer to his Carving. He didn't like the speed with which the days were passing. Less than a week now.

He'd been here since early evening. That crabby old bastard Jack Spicer had been as good as his word and told everyone who would listen what an ill-mannered and disrespectful brat Tim was. Fortunately the only person listening had been Anne because Bill had been at a meeting of townspeople opposed to Vic Stones's hotel all evening. Anne had given him the expected dressing down in front of Mr Spicer – the dressing down the cantankerous old git expected him to receive, that is. But when Mr Spicer had left them alone she'd told Tim that if he wanted to avoid upsetting his father any more, he should just do as he'd been asked.

He'd taken her advice. At first it felt like he'd been

banished to the study just to keep him out of everybody's hair, but he didn't mind too much – he'd always been someone who was happy enough to have time alone to think. He'd started reading only reluctantly to begin with, then had decided that he might as well try and find some of that elusive *proof*. So far, however, he'd been disappointed.

Old William's diary had pretty much defeated him, with its broken, jittery handwriting and archaic language. So he'd taken Richard's copy of the text. Richard had been Mourner from 1835 to 1866, and Tim reasoned that since he'd read and enjoyed *Frankenstein*, which was written round about the same time, he should be okay with it. And it was easier to follow, but twice the length of the original and deadly dull. Still, he waded through most of it, only to feel cheated when it didn't help his cause in the least.

Donald – who'd taken over as Mourner in 1900 when his older brother, Henry, died of TB without having any sons of his own – hadn't made a copy of the diary. Apparently he'd aspired to being the next Conan Doyle and had instead turned his account into an adventure yarn. Bill had tried to warn Tim off reading it, repeating again how important Old William's original words were. He said the reason successive Mourners had often made copies of the original diary was to gain greater knowledge and under-standing of those words. But Donald had been the last Mourner to claim he'd actually seen the Mourn.

According to his version of events the creature had risen from the dark depths of the lake 'with such violence and ferociousness' that it caused a terrifying earthquake which 'set every house and home in Moutonby trembling'. He wrote that he saw the beast 'rise from the maelstrom of black water with a roar like thunder'. Luckily Donald was safely on dry land at that precise moment, but he called for an immediate Feed which no Fearful declined to attend.

The history books did mention a 'minor earth tremor' in the area and the rebuilding of the Dows Bridges in 1908. Donald's sighting was only revealed in his diary and was as hotly disputed as Old William's. Even Bill admitted to being sceptical, but refused to believe any Mourner would need to lie, simply stating that Donald's diary was indeed sensational. Tim's view, however, was that it all read like a particularly bad *Hound of the Baskervilles* even with the earthquake.

Bill's notes on the original diary were of course the easiest to follow. But somehow they didn't help. The long-ago events they described, the supernatural occurrences and manifestations of the Mourn, sounded odd in his flat, modern tone of voice. Somehow Old William's archaic diatribe seemed to be the way it *should* be told.

But Tim's eyes were weary; he had pins and needles from sitting on the floor for so long. And he needed to clear his head. He was just too tired to think. But first he couldn't resist checking one more time; he had to read it again just in case.

He found the page in Old William's diary. He ran his finger under the lines.

. . . and the first-born of Mourn Home, my son William, will follow me at that time he turns sixteen. This will be precedent for all Mourners and their sons, for there must always be a Mourner for Moutonby's lost children . . .

It was one simple, short paragraph. But it was everything to his father and to him, although for each in a different way.

He gathered the manuscripts, putting them back in the glass cabinet carefully, exactly as he'd found them, and locking it all up with the key his father had left for him. He switched off the desk lamp, pitching the room into darkness. The study window looked onto his mother's flowerbeds and down to the lake. Habit made him turn his head and glance out that way as he headed for the door – he was as bad as Jack Spicer, he reckoned. He could see the shadowy lump of the Mourn Stone and the water behind it. What he wasn't expecting was to see a pale face appear on the other side of the glass.

He leaped back with the shock of it. Then wasn't sure what froze him to the spot: surprise or fear? Had he been seen? Did whoever it was know he was here? He could hear his heart and it sounded way too loud.

But as the face peered in, the shock slowly released its grip and he decided not, because he was several steps away from the window and the room was in total darkness. Then he recognized the face. Gully.

The student had his nose pressed up against the glass, squinting inside. Tim was more than just a little tempted to leap forward and thump on the window as hard as he could, and see who jumped *then*. Gully moved back of his own accord, however, and ran his hands around the frame. He pushed and prodded it, as if testing how secure it was.

Tim didn't have a clue what he was doing out there, but reckoned that wherever there was Gully there'd also be Scott. Cautiously he moved closer to the window. Gully was pacing backwards, craning his neck to see the upper floors. And there was Scott, off to one side, hunched up in his thin denim jacket and swigging from a can of lager. Tim guessed they'd been drinking late at WetFun's bar again, but had lost or forgotten their key and locked themselves out.

Good. Let them freeze.

Small revenge for what they'd done to Jenny perhaps, but not bad for starters. The problem was that it wouldn't take them long to get cold enough to ring the bell and wake the whole house. So maybe he should let them in. He moved closer still to the window and noticed a third person with them. He saw the burning tip of a cigarette first, then the tall, wiry silhouette standing behind Scott, over near the garage.

'Shit.'

Roddy Morgan.

It took only a moment to decide he wasn't going to wake anyone. Roddy was only here to provoke trouble, to cause as much grief as possible. But maybe by confronting him Tim could prove something.

Not exactly sure what that something was, he crept from the study to the kitchen. He didn't turn any lights on. From the kitchen window all three of them were in full view. Gully and Scott had joined Roddy by the garage. Silently

Tim pulled on his coat and trainers. He hovered with his hand on the back door's handle for a few seconds. He could recognize Scott's voice, but wasn't quite able to make out what he was saying.

Unsure whether he was more angry or more anxious he stepped out into the chilly night air. The gravel of the driveway crunched beneath his shoes and Roddy was the first to spot him.

'Hey! It's Monster Boy!' He sniffed the air. 'Is it just me, or can anyone else smell shepherd's pie?'

Tim ignored him, refusing to rise to the bait, because Scott was holding Gully's legs, steadying him as he climbed into the garage through its open window. But as soon as he realized Tim was there he let his friend go. And Gully tipped over the sill, plunging forward; there was the rattle and chink as his pockets emptied themselves of loose change, then his legs instantly disappeared as though the garage had sucked him inside. He gave a muffled grunt as he hit the floor.

'What's going on?' Tim's voice was a harsh whisper, conscious of the sleeping house. 'What do you think you're doing?'

Scott was drunk. 'Lost our key.' He wasn't particularly steady on his feet and it looked like his head was too heavy for his neck.

Tim checked the window. 'You didn't smash anything, did you?'

'It was already open,' Scott said. 'We didn't have to smash it.'

Tim double-checked it anyway, then stuck his head

inside. Gully was picking himself up off the concrete floor, feeling around for his scattered money. He couldn't see it in the dark.

'Get out, Gully.'

'We thought we'd sleep in here,' he said. It was obvious he was just as drunk. 'We didn't want to wake you up.'

'Why not? Worried my sister has grassed you up?'

He turned away. 'Lost my money.' He cast around in the dark again.

'Just get out, will you? My dad'll go mad when I tell him. I'm not joking.' He glanced at Mourn Home; the windows were still dark.

'Why've you got to tell him?' Scott asked. 'Just let us in quietly and nobody'll know anything.' He'd taken a couple of steps closer to Tim and although he was slurring slightly there was a sharper edge to his words. 'No one *needs* to know. Right?'

Tim had no real intention of telling anybody anything, but . . . 'Why should I do you any favours after what you did to my sister?'

'That was just us messing about.'

'She could have drowned.'

'She gave as good as she got. She kicked Gully in the balls.' He leaned in the garage window. 'Hey. She kicked you in the balls, didn't she?' He thought it was funny. 'We were just having a laugh,' Scott told him.

'Yeah, well, Jenny didn't find it very funny.'

'Did you really think she was going to get eaten?' Gully called from inside the garage. 'That's *wild* if you did.'

'Of course he did,' Scott said. 'That's why he didn't jump in after her. He may be *wild*, but he's not stupid.'

Tim stayed silent while they laughed.

'Are you going to let us in, then?' Scott eventually asked.

Roddy Morgan stepped up to them. 'Stop being a nob-head and let them in, Monster Boy.' He was standing behind Scott, but close up to his shoulder. He was with the big boys now and wanted Tim to know it.

'What's it got to do with you?' Tim said, hating the way he sounded like a kid. 'What're you doing here anyway?'

'We invited him,' Scott said. 'Told him he could come back to our room for a couple of beers. He wangled us some free drinks out of his boss and we wanted to pay him back.' Everything he said was a statement of intent, no question attached. Kind of, *This is what we're doing whether you like it or not.*

'Vic always gives me a few freebies at the end of the night,' Roddy said. 'I'm his right-hand man.'

'Yeah, I bet you are.'

Roddy didn't get it at first, not until Tim gave the international gesture for wanking. Then he went a deep, angry red and moved out from behind Scott. He was heated enough not to need the older lad now.

Scott laughed, but Roddy met Tim's eyes with real malice. He stepped up to the garage window and leaned inside, as if looking for something. 'Hey, Gully. Have a look in that freezer. You won't believe what they keep in their freezers at this place.'

Tim's heart went cold. Roddy smirked at him; it was

well known locally what was kept in their freezer. Tim pushed him away from the window. 'Get out of there, Gully. It's for the—' But too late.

'Bloody hell!' Gully was understandably amazed. 'Scott! Have you seen this? Look at all this stuff!' He dragged a frosty, lumpy plastic bag from inside and ripped it open.

Scott recoiled. 'Is that a cat?'

Gully held up the remains of the roadkill. 'Don't you know a fox when you see one?' Its back legs were crushed, twisted, its head the wrong shape, but it was definitely a fox. 'Gross!' He threw it at them – they all three ducked as one. It flew over their heads to land behind them in Anne's flowerbeds.

Tim immediately ran to grab it. Gingerly he picked it up by its rigid tail. The covering of cold, crispy frost on the fur felt like woolly gloves after a snowball fight. 'Just get out, Gully. I'll let you into the house, okay?'

Roddy thought it was hilarious. 'I always knew your family were freaks, Monster Boy. But this is *sick*.'

'What else is in there?' Scott was curious in an appalled kind of way.

'It's just feed,' Tim said, wanting to make it sound normal, thinking deep down he never could even in a million years.

'You eat dead foxes?' Gully called through the window. 'Wow! McDonald's are missing a trick there all right.'

'It's what they give their guests for breakfast.' Roddy was in stitches.

Tim turned on him. 'Yeah. Funny. It's for the Mourn, obviously.'

'*Obviously*,' he mimicked.

An icy hedgehog Frisbee flew out to land in the grass at his feet. Its spilled but frozen guts sparkled like jewels in the moonlight.

'Hey, watch where you're chucking that stuff!' Scott had to dodge a couple of stone-solid starlings with snapped wings and broken legs. 'Hey!'

'Come on, Gully,' Tim said. His anger had turned over to reveal the age-old embarrassment underneath. 'Leave it alone, will you? All this is needed for next week.' He was trying to pick up everything Gully was chucking out into the garden. 'Just pack it in.' He was watching for lights again, but none came on. Maybe he was lucky the old walls were so thick – maybe not. He knew all he had to do was fetch his dad, but somehow this had got well out of control and he felt he was to blame. He could have just let them into the house and none of this would have happened.

Gully was back at the window, another flat hedgehog in his hand. 'Would you like fries with that?'

Everybody laughed, except Tim.

Scott swallowed the last of his lager, crumpled the can and tossed it aside. He surprised Tim by grabbing the dead fox out of his hand before he could stop him. 'I'm going fishing,' he said. He swayed slightly on his unsteady feet then set off towards the feeding pier.

Gully was confused. 'Fishing?'

Scott held the frozen fox up above his head. 'Yeah, fishing. For *monsters*.'

Gully laughed loudly and virtually leaped out through

the garage window. He snatched up a dead bird or two to go with his hedgehog. 'Wait up! I want to see this!'

Tim hadn't believed the night could get any worse.

'Why didn't I ever think of that?' Roddy wanted to know. He picked up a starling of his own.

Too late now, Tim thought, but maybe he really should have woken his dad. He turned to look at the house. Maybe—

'You don't want to do that.' It was as if Roddy had read his mind. And then Gully was next to him too. 'Come on,' Roddy said. 'We're having a laugh, don't be your usual boring self and spoil it.'

If Roddy had been alone Tim would have stood up to him. But with Gully there as well all he could do was let them walk him out onto the feeding pier above the lake.

Their boots and trainers sounded loud on the planks, but Tim knew they were too far away from the house to be heard. The wind had died down during the day and now, although it was cold, there was not even a whisper of a breeze. The water beneath the pier could have been black ice. They went all the way out, right to the very end. The little rowing boat tied up to the side was motionless, looking like it had frozen into the blackness.

Gully was shivering. Scott got out a cigarette and Gully stole it from between his lips.

'Bet the water's freezing,' Scott said, lighting another. 'It's cold enough during the day.'

'Bloody perishing,' Gully agreed.

Tim was worried. With a heavy, sinking dread he knew that one of them would pretty soon come up with the idea of chucking him in. They'd done it to Jenny; they'd do it to him just as quick.

Again it was as if Roddy knew what he was thinking. 'Wouldn't want to fall in. You'd be an icicle in seconds. You'd never even reach the bottom.'

Tim shivered involuntarily.

'I didn't think it had a bottom. Or it's a hundred miles deep or something.' Gully said. 'Has anybody ever checked?' He stamped on the wooden planks. 'How come this doesn't sink then, if it is?'

Roddy tutted. 'Doesn't anyone know their local history except for me and Monster Boy?'

'We're not local,' Gully said.

Scott put his cigarette to the dead fox's fur and listened to it hiss. 'About which we're extremely pleased.'

Roddy waved his dead birds at Tim. 'I'll let you explain it if you want.'

But Tim only glared at him.

Roddy shrugged. 'It's only really deep once you get past here,' he said. 'They built this as far out as they could, before the bottom sort of falls away and suddenly goes down really steeply.' He stamped his foot like Gully had. 'But this is on solid rock.'

'You know a lot about something you reckon you hate,' Tim said.

'Why do you think I hate it so much?' There was real venom in Roddy's words. 'Don't you get it? I've had it rammed down my throat since the day I was born and it's all bollocks! It's impossible not to know about this stuff if you live around here.' Then to Gully again: 'No one really knows how deep it is the middle. Like everything else round here, you just have to believe what *his* family tells you to. And why should we give a shit what a family full of freaks says? They've never done anything except sponge off everyone else and make our town look stupid because people think we believe in monsters.'

Gully wasn't really interested in Roddy's ranting. He was staring at the water. 'It can't be a hundred miles deep. That'd be impossible.'

'I don't think anybody really believes it's that deep,' Tim said, as if to a child. 'It's just one of those really old names that stuck. It was called the Hundredwaters long before 1699.'

'You're admitting it's a lie!' Roddy cried.

Tim didn't want to argue about it. 'If you like.'

'You see, it's all bullshit! Everything his freaky family says, they expect you to believe. And we get it shoved down our throats all the time as little kids. It's like the three men who died building this feeding pier. It was a big storm and only one body was found afterwards. And the freaks round here expect you to believe that the big, bad monster ate the other two.'

'Believe what you want for all I care,' Tim said.

'I will, I will. Because *I* believe the Mourner killed them.'

'What?' Tim had to laugh.

Roddy was serious. 'It was your great-granddad, wasn't it?'

143

'Have you trapped your head in one of those outboard motors you were supposed to be mending or something?'

'If they were builders they probably just went down the pub and couldn't be arsed to come back,' Scott said. 'My old man's a builder. I should know.'

Gully was poking his dead starling suspiciously. One of its brittle legs broke and pinged off into the darkness. 'Is that who your boss was talking about at the bar?' he asked Roddy. 'He said it was the teacher that killed them or something?' He leaned over the edge and dropped the little speckled corpse over the side of the pier with a muted splash. The ripples spread quickly across the smooth blackness of water.

'No, that was the teacher who started it all: Old Willy the pervert. He killed the kids and made the whole legend up so no one would find out he'd been molesting them.' He eyed Tim carefully, and Tim met his stare without saying a word. Because he'd heard this story before – and from people far more intelligent than Roddy Morgan. He was just hoping the three of them would get bored and cold and want to go inside.

'Interesting theory,' Scott said. 'So you really don't believe in this monster?'

'I'll tell what I believe,' Roddy said. 'The whole family's a bunch of perverts and murderers, that's what.'

Scott turned to Tim. 'And what about you?'

Tim kept his face set, blank. 'Who knows what to believe?' he said.

Scott laughed. 'Excellent point – well made.'

Tim turned away. He was wondering if he could shove Roddy in. One hard push. Then run.

'Come on, let's see if we can catch us a legend.' Scott had the fox by its tail. 'Stiff as a broom,' he said.

'Brush,' Gully corrected him.

The three of them laughed. They were all just good mates together, united by Roddy's antagonism towards Tim. And Tim surprised himself by thinking how good it would be if the Mourn *was* real. Apart from wanting it to appear right here, right now, and bite a chunk out of Roddy (which would obviously be bloody marvellous for lots of reasons), he realized how great it would be to prove him wrong. He remembered what Jenny had said about wanting to be different to people like Roddy and Gully and Scott, and now he understood what she'd meant. He wanted people like them to be wrong. He wanted his father to be right. Because wouldn't that be the greatest revenge of all?

Gully was kneeling down dangling his crushed hedgehog over the edge. 'Come on then, you big bastard!' he shouted out at the lake. 'Come and eat me if you dare!' He hurled the hedgehog.

Tim watched him kneeling there. If he couldn't shove Roddy in, maybe Gully instead. Give the Mourn a helping hand. Do it for Jenny. It would be so easy to kick him over the side – he wasn't even looking.

It was now or never. He took a step forward. But Roddy saw him and grabbed his arm, twisting it up behind him, making him cry out. He put his face right up close to Tim's.

'You're too late,' a voice called from further down the pier.

Roddy instantly let go of him. Scott dropped the fox at his feet.

A tall man was striding towards them. 'It's already been fed. Won't be hungry till next Saturday at least.' He was wearing a tatty, black leather jacket, had his hands stuffed in the pockets. He was in his early forties, with a pale, oval face and a widow's peak of short black hair. He was grinning from ear to ear.

Tim couldn't help but let his relief show. He was always pleased to see his Uncle Doug, but this . . . This was *perfect* timing.

'How're you doing, Timmo?' He threw an arm around his nephew's shoulders, pulling him a couple of steps away from Roddy. 'Having fun?'

'*We* were,' Scott said.

Uncle Doug made a point of letting his grin slip. 'Was I talking to you?'

'I thought you weren't coming until tomorrow,' Tim said.

His uncle looked at his watch. 'It is tomorrow – if you know what I mean.' He turned to Roddy. 'So, let me introduce myself. I'm Tim's favourite uncle.' He held out his hand to Roddy. 'I'm Doug. You can call me Mr Milmullen.'

Roddy looked unsure, glanced over his shoulder at Gully and Scott. He didn't want to look intimidated in front of his new-found friends, so took Doug's hand with a sneery grin.

'Hello there.' Doug pumped Roddy's arm hard. Harder. 'Good to meet you.' He didn't let go and he was squeezing hard. He made to take a step forward, stumbled accidentally-on-purpose, and pushed Roddy right to the edge of the pier.

Roddy let out a yelp, and windmilled his free arm, his weight pulling him over. His foot slipped – he was going in.

But Uncle Doug yanked him back to safety. Dragged him so forcefully that his knees crunched as he fell forward onto the wooden planks.

'Whoa! Saved your life there, Big Guy.' Doug grinned down at him. 'You owe me one.'

Roddy slowly got to his feet, glaring at the man, undisguised loathing darkening his eyes.

Uncle Doug included the others in his smile. 'So, it's been a pleasure, but I've just driven all the way up from London and I'm gagging for a hot cup of tea. I'd invite you all to join me, but I've decided I don't like you. Pick your cans and fag ends up on your way off our property. Goodbye.'

Gully looked like he didn't have a clue what had just happened. 'We're staying here,' he said. 'In the guesthouse.'

'Are you? Oh well, guess our Bill can't pick and choose his customers these days. But that should change soon, with any luck.'

Scott said, 'Are you going to let us in, then?' And even now he still had that underlying edge to his voice.

'Guess I'll have to if you're paying for the privilege.'

Without a word, but somehow not seeming to back down, Scott slouched back along the pier towards the house. Gully flicked the last of his cigarette into the water and sloped after him.

Roddy didn't want to go. He was the type who needed to have the last word in a situation like this. 'See you at school, Monster Boy.' But he was quick to scuttle away once he'd said it.

Uncle Doug watched them go without losing his smile for an instant. 'Well, well, well,' he said to Tim. 'Want to talk about it?'

'Well . . . Not really.'

'No worries.'

Tim started to collect the frozen bits of feed that had been dropped.

'Just kick it in,' Doug told him, and booted the fox over the side.

As they walked back towards Mourn Home Tim said, 'Don't tell Dad, will you?'

'No need to worry about that, Tim, lad. We'll just tell him you woke up when you heard me clattering about letting myself in. He need never know, eh?'

'It's just that . . . I don't think I'm exactly, you know, flavour of the month at the minute.'

Uncle Doug once again put his arm around his nephew's shoulders. 'Timmo, believe me, I've kept darker secrets than this from my brother over the years.'

And Tim suddenly felt hopeful. Maybe he'd find an ally in Uncle Doug, someone to understand. He held onto that hope as they walked back along the pier.

Uncle Doug's Argument

'Personally, I think it's one of the best jobs I've ever had,' Uncle Doug proclaimed over Sunday dinner. They were eating in the family dining room, which was a rarity. It was bare and cold through lack of use; they were usually happier in the kitchen, and never used the guests' dining room. 'I'm good at it too,' he said with a wry smile.

He'd insisted that they eat in here today because of his 'surprise'. He said he wanted Old William to see it too, meaning the portrait hanging on the wall. It was a stately, morbid representation, which nobody in the family actually liked; it just hung there out of . . . tradition. The once ornate table was marked and the carpet was worn with years upon years of chair shuffling. The times when the Mourner of the day would use the room for entertaining local dignitaries were long gone. Only at Christmas had Tim ever seen the huge fireplace lit.

'Most of the big chains use mystery customers: Pizza Hut, Wetherspoon's, Little Chef – you name it. I have to check out the restaurants right under the staff's noses, without letting them know that's what I'm doing. And then when I send off my receipt, I get my meal for free.'

Jenny was impressed. 'Sounds cool.' Tim nodded his agreement.

'Thank you, Jenny. I think so too. It's the nearest I'll ever get to being a secret agent, eh?' He winked and laughed. 'But I'm one of the few people I know who lives off free lunches.'

There was an awkward silence from the other adults around the table. The chewing noises seemed especially loud.

At last Bill managed to say: 'As long as you're happy, Doug.'

'That I am, Bill. That I am.' He grinned at Tim, who beamed back at him.

'Doesn't sound like a job with many prospects to me,' Nana Dalry said.

'Mother,' Anne said in a strained voice, 'I'm sure Doug knows what he's doing.'

Nana Dalry didn't answer but her knife and fork rattled loudly against her plate as she finished her meal. She sat up stiffly, looking at no one in particular. She wasn't Doug's biggest fan, never had been since he'd gone to live in London, her belief being that he'd left her daughter and son-in-law in the lurch when they'd needed him most.

'No, no, you're right, Mrs Dalry,' Uncle Doug said. 'No prospects whatsoever!'

Jenny also rattled her knife and fork, then sat up just as straight as Nana. 'I still think it sounds cool.'

'Jenny . . .' her mother warned, not wanting any kind of bickering today.

'But I'll tell you what makes it such a good job,' Doug continued. 'It's given me lots of time to do other things, to do something that I've been wanting to do for years.'

'What's that?' Tim wanted to know.

'That's my surprise.'

The family sat waiting. Even Nana deigned to look at him.

'But I think we should have pudding first, don't you?'

Last night Tim had out and out decided that his uncle was a saviour and a hero. Not just because he'd kept secret what had happened out on the feeding pier (which had fortunately gone unnoticed by the rest of the family), but because he hoped Doug would understand what he was going through. He was the Milmullen who'd moved away, after all.

He was Bill's younger brother so he'd never had to worry about being the Mourner. He'd moved to London when Tim and Jenny were born, but drifted back occasionally for prolonged visits, seeing as he'd not been able to hold down a job for more than a couple of years at a time. Although he still wasn't married he'd introduced the family to Sophie, Claire and Isabelle separately over the years, each one proclaimed as the love of his life and the most important person in the world to him. But they'd only ever met each of these women once.

He almost always forgot birthdays, and Christmas presents could be a bit hit and miss. If he'd been working he was generous and seriously splashed out, but if his cash-flow situation was a problem the present was perhaps a little more *imaginative*. This explained why Tim and Jenny had each received a top-notch DVD player two Christmases ago, but only complimentary toiletries from some London hotel the following year.

He was well over six feet and ludicrously gangly. He picked up his glass of wine now and somehow reeled it in on his fishing-rod arm to take a drink. Despite his current job, despite all he ate, he was a stick insect – 'hollow legs' was Tim's mother's explanation – but he had enough good humour for someone three times his girth. And despite everything, the Milmullens were always pleased to have him around. It was difficult not to like the man.

Nana Dalry, however, wasn't a Milmullen. 'I won't be staying for pudding, dear,' she said. 'I have to be home.'

Anne rolled her eyes. 'Mother, you have never had to be home on a Sunday afternoon.'

'Well, perhaps today is different. Perhaps I've made arrangements with Grace Kirkwooding.'

'We both know very well that Grace goes to her grand-daughter's for Sunday dinner.'

Uncle Doug was shaking his head. 'No one is allowed to leave, I'm afraid. Not even you, Mrs Dalry. I'm not letting anyone set foot outside this dining room until I've shown you my surprise.'

Nana Dalry made a humphing sound but stayed seated. Anne said, 'I'd better hurry up with the pudding then, hadn't I? Or am I not allowed to leave the room to fetch it?'

'Pudding's an exception,' Doug assured her.

Bill stood up. 'I'll go. Jenny, will you collect the plates?' He moved through into the kitchen. Jenny followed.

Tim watched them both go, feeling a twinge of paranoia – worried they might talk about him. He'd felt nervy throughout the whole meal anyway, because this was the first time he'd had to face his sister since yesterday morning, and his father since Jack Spicer had caused trouble. In fact they'd all seemed to be treading on eggshells around each other, not wanting to be the one to start the seemingly unavoidable argument.

Tim had told Bill that he'd been reading the diaries, but all his father had offered in return was a nod and a gruff 'Good'. Nana Dalry's ears had pricked up at the mention of them, however, and she'd prodded at him with a couple of pointed questions. There had been no way he was going to elaborate for her why he was suddenly interested in the books, so he had become as uncommunicative as Bill. He certainly didn't want a lecture on the tradition from her today.

Right now she was grumbling about her next-door neighbour's cat using her flowerbeds as a toilet.

'Terrible, just terrible,' Uncle Doug sympathized. 'But remember, Mrs Dalry, today's nuisance moggy could easily be tomorrow's feed.' He seemed disappointed when nobody laughed.

Bill and Jenny served the apple crumble. Tim tried to catch his sister's eye to see if she'd said anything, but either she didn't notice or was purposely not looking at him. So Tim scrutinized his father. Unfortunately, same as always, Bill's feelings were well hidden behind his beard.

They ate quietly.

Tim decided he'd talk to his uncle as soon as he could. Because maybe Doug would know what it was he should do. He wished he'd mentioned something last night about how he felt, and explained exactly what the problem with Roddy and the students was. But he was sure Uncle Doug would be on his side. And he'd talk to him straight away, immediately after dinner if possible. Tonight at the latest.

But then he remembered he couldn't do anything tonight, because Sarah would be here. He shovelled down his dessert as fast as he could, suddenly nervous that if somebody looked at him right now, right this very second, they'd guess what he was planning. Every time he thought of tonight he forgot everything else – so he thought about it as often as possible.

'Fabulous, Annie,' Doug said, licking his spoon so clean he could see his face in it. 'You know, if you weren't married to my brother, I'd ask you to be my slave.'

Tim's mother smiled. 'Thank you, Douglas. You're very kind. But perhaps that's why you're not married.' She started to collect the dishes.

'Sit down, sit down,' Doug told her. 'Surprise time. Don't you *dare* move.'

He reached for the small haversack he'd stashed under his chair. 'Ready?' Eyebrows raised theatrically, he made everybody wait that little bit longer, milking the situation like a magician about to make a rabbit appear. Nana Dalry tutted at him, but it only widened his grin.

154

With a single smooth flourish he produced a huge hardback book from the bag and thumped it down onto the table. It was so large it made the glasses in the middle jump and chink together. Tim and Jenny leaned closer; their mother twisted her head to see. Even Nana Dalry was curious now.

Only Bill stayed where he was, but his smile was easily as wide as his younger brother's. 'This is it, then,' he said.

Uncle Doug puffed out his skinny chest. 'It certainly is, William. It certainly is. You didn't believe I'd do it, did you?'

Tim couldn't remember the last time he'd seen his father look quite so happy. 'But you've proved me wrong, Doug.' He even laughed.

Uncle Doug beamed.

Tim was amazed. On the glossy front cover of this tome was a photograph of their house, shrouded in an early morning mist, with Lake Mou looming just behind looking about ready to swallow the lot. The title *The Legend of the Hundredwaters* was written in embossed silver letters, and underneath: 'The Story of the Mourn'. Then, slightly smaller, but still in silver: 'Douglas Milmullen'.

'You've written a book,' Jenny said, eyes wide.

'About us?' Tim said in disbelief, not sure he liked the idea.

Uncle Doug nodded. 'About all of us. Your granddad, my granddad, his granddad; all the way back to the old guy on the wall and 1699.' He pointed at the portrait of Old William. 'That's why I wanted him to see it.' He even held

155

it up for the portrait to see. 'It's not a copy of the diary; it's more a history of the last three hundred years. But it's especially about you and your dad right now.'

'Wow,' Jenny said.

'Indeed,' Uncle Doug agreed.

Tim felt a quick pinch of anxiety in his stomach. No, he didn't like the idea of it being about him.

Nana Dalry, on the other hand, all of a sudden decided what an admirable and wonderful and clever man Uncle Doug was. 'You're making us all so proud of you,' she said.

Bill picked up the book. 'Dad'd be proud, Doug. This is some achievement.' He held it almost reverentially, feeling the weight then flipping slowly through the pages, even touching the print with the tips of his fingers. 'This is some achievement,' he repeated. He gave it to his wife. 'Look at this, hey? Look at it.'

'I can see it.' She smiled warmly at her brother-in-law. 'Well done, Douglas. It really is a wonderful achievement.'

'I told you I'd do it,' Uncle Doug said. 'I beavered away on it while I wasn't busy stuffing my face with cardboard pizzas and soggy burgers. I wasn't about to let the family down.' His smile was a touch sarcastic, but Nana Dalry didn't notice. 'You know, my publishers have agreed to throw a little launch party for me, and I realize it's short notice – very short in fact – but I wondered if we could have it this Saturday? At Tim's Carving?'

Tim wasn't sure what that meant, but he saw his father's brow wrinkle slightly. Not a good sign.

'I don't know about that, Doug,' Bill said, tugging on his beard. 'I was planning on it being a fairly quiet affair. Just for the Fearful – and the town.'

Uncle Doug took his book back. 'For the town? I think the town's shown time and again that it doesn't give two buggers for our family any more.' Bill made to speak, but his brother wouldn't let him. 'Wasn't last night's meeting of everyone who opposes Stones's hotel proof enough of that? Four people turned up, didn't you say?' He shook his head. 'No, Bill, you've got to think a little wider. We've got to remind the rest of the country about the Mourn and put Moutonby back on the map.' He was leaning across the table, waving his book like a preacher with a Bible. 'Bloody Nessie has had all the attention for far too long. And she didn't even eat anybody, did she, eh?'

Again Tim's father tried to speak, but—

'No, I'm sorry, Bill. Something has to be done and Tim's Carving will be the perfect opportunity to grab everybody's attention. He's going to be the first Mourner of the new millennium, don't forget.'

Father and son locked eyes. Tim hoped Bill couldn't see the mounting panic he was trying to hide in his.

Doug was busy sounding like a politician. 'We've got to focus the gaze of the world back on this little Yorkshire town and its lake. Bring back some dignity. That's why I've written the book. I think this family deserves a little bit more respect for what it has done – and is *still* doing.'

Bill was quiet.

Nana Dalry piped up, 'It's what I've been saying all

along,' she told him, suddenly Doug's new best friend and ally. 'I've been trying to tell you that for years.'

Tim's mouth had gone dry; there was a tightening fist of anxiety gripping his insides. The last thing he wanted, surely the worst thing that could happen, would be to have 'the gaze of the world' on his birthday. He knew the world was going to be full of people like Roddy Morgan.

'I've got to admit I've already had a word with the publishers,' Uncle Doug said, leaning back in his chair. 'And the wonderful women in the publicity department have already got the ball rolling. I've asked them to get local TV and radio here, a couple of the tabloids if possible. So with a bit of luck it's going to be big.'

Bill looked at his wife. Then turned to his brother again, shaking his head. 'Doug, I appreciate what you're doing, but—'

Uncle Doug was back over the table in an instant. 'Don't "but" me, Bill. Come on, don't you dare. You need this. Since the council abolished the Monster Tax what's this family been living on, eh? So we turned this old place into a guesthouse when Dad died. Fine. But where're the guests? The students and the Americans leave tomorrow; who've you got filling their rooms? You probably don't even charge old Jack Spicer full whack any more, do you? And when Stones opens his new place, what then?'

Tim's father didn't answer, knowing Doug didn't really need him to.

'Look, Bill, think of Dad, okay? He'd be so proud of the way you're fighting for this family and all we believe in. He always said it was the one thing that made the Milmullens different. Because we're Mourners it means we have a purpose and duty. So think how proud he'd be if we fought that little bit harder, if we brought recognition and pride back into this old house.'

Bill was looking at Tim. But Tim couldn't meet his dad's eyes any more.

Uncle Doug nodded at the portrait on the wall. 'Think of the old guy, and what he did way back when.'

Bill took the book from his brother again. 'I just don't think it's my way,' he said quietly.

'We've got the perfect opportunity this coming Saturday,' Uncle Doug told him. 'We celebrate a brand-new Mourner, and my marvellous book hits the shelves.'

Bill sighed heavily, his brow deeply creased.

Nana Dalry decided it was time for her two pennies worth. 'Well, you know what I think—'

'Yes, we probably do, Mother,' Anne said, and Nana Dalry harrumphed at being cut short.

'What do *you* think, Annie?' Bill asked her.

She considered the book herself for a few seconds. 'Maybe it's what this family needs: a kick-start.' She looked at Uncle Doug. 'But a tasteful one.'

He leaned back in his chair, spread his hands and smiled.

Bill was looking less than overjoyed. But was also looking as though he dearly wanted to be persuaded. 'If you think you can—'

'I *know* I can,' his brother said.

159

'Am I in your book, Uncle Doug?' Jenny asked. 'Am I going to be famous?'

Doug beamed at her. 'We're all going to be famous.' He swept his smile around the table. 'You want to be famous, don't you, Tim?'

Tim stared at the book. He remembered how he'd wanted the Mourn to show itself to Roddy Morgan and the students last night, and now more than ever he wanted that to happen. He was sure it was the only thing that would stop the whole world from laughing at him on his birthday.

The Hundredwaters

Sarah was crying. Small hitching sobs that caught in her throat.

'What?' Tim asked. 'What?' But he knew.

She pulled the sheets over to cover her, turned away from him.

'Sarah. Talk to me.' He stopped at the sound of footsteps in the hallway outside: Sylvie and Mike returning to their room. He waited for them to close their door. He lowered his voice to a whisper. 'Tell me what's wrong.'

She shook her head and he took the meaning to be, *I can't.*

'I thought . . .' he began. But what he'd been about to say was going to be a lie so he stopped himself. He knew this wasn't what she'd wanted. It was all him. Just him. Because it was going to make him a man. And the problem was, even though she was crying, he could still feel the heat of his want inside him.

'Sarah . . .' He tried to hold her, brushed his fingers across her belly. 'Come on, Sarah. Please . . .'

She used the flat of her hand to push him away. 'No.'

He got out of bed, pulled his boxers and jeans on and

sat in the chair on the other side of the room to her – needing the distance.

Sarah had spent the early evening with Jenny, then at about ten had made a point of saying goodbye to everyone, even Uncle Doug. Tim had declared he'd walk her home, but had brought her to room two. They'd giggled and acted up at their daring deception, exaggeratedly hushing each other with lots of kisses. The worries of the last few days had slid way down in the back of his mind. The deceit and the delicious nerves it caused seemed to be the best way to forget, as well as a wonderful aphrodisiac.

They lay on the bed together. 'Where do you want to be?' he'd asked her. The room was bright and spotlessly clean, but it was anonymous – plain and dull. Yet the ordinariness helped Tim's imagination. 'We could be anywhere.'

'I like it right here,' Sarah said, her head on his shoulder.

'But we're in a hotel room, and it could be any hotel room in any place anywhere in the world.'

'You choose. Wherever you want to go is where I want to go.'

He laughed. He tickled her, plucked at her bra strap through her T-shirt, tried to make her laugh with him. 'There's loads of places I want to go.'

She pulled his arms around her. 'I like it right here,' she repeated.

Which kind of annoyed him, but he didn't want to spoil things.

After three-quarters of an hour or so he went to tell everyone he was back and going up to his bedroom. Nobody minded – all too busy talking about Uncle Doug's book. When he returned to room two he found Sarah already under the sheets, nothing on except her black underwear. There'd been a lot more giggling going on; kissing, touching. But then . . .

And now . . .

He was getting cold sitting there half naked. The room was dark and Sarah was just a shape under the blankets.

'Sarah, I'm sorry. I . . . Are you okay?'

He heard her sniff at her tears, and saw her silhouette move as she rubbed her wet cheeks on the pillow. 'Why were you like that?'

'I thought that's what we were going to do.'

'We said we were going to spend the night together. We were going to hold each other all night, you said, because it was something we'd never been able to do before.'

He stayed quiet. All he'd really wanted was sex. And part of him was surprised she hadn't realized.

'Do you love me?'

He'd known this was going to be one of her first questions.

She answered for him. 'You don't love me. You just want to have sex.'

'Sarah, you wouldn't believe how much I wanted tonight to be special. It's been the only thing that's kept me happy all weekend.'

'That's a bit shallow, don't you think?'

He recoiled from the spite in her voice. He didn't know

what to think. She was crying again but he didn't have a clue how to comfort her.

'What have I done wrong?' she wanted to know. 'Have I done something to make you . . . ?' But the words got caught up in her tears and she had to bury her face in the pillow to quieten them.

'It's not you.' It was half the truth. 'It's me.' The whole truth would be that it was both of them.

He knew that loving her, loving her with all his heart, would be another tie that bound him to Mourn Home. Was it such a terrible thing for him to admit that he wanted to see the world? Was he a bad person for wanting to love other girls and women too?

He stared at her silhouette. He finally made the decision that had been nagging at the back of his mind for such a long time.

'I'm going away.'

Sarah sniffed loudly. 'What do you mean?'

He didn't want to say 'running away' because it sounded childish somehow. 'I just need to go somewhere else. I don't want to be here any more.'

He heard the catch in her voice. 'Is it me? Is it because I won't—?'

He shook his head quickly. 'No, no. Don't think that. No. Please.'

'What is it, then? Why do you—?'

'I don't want to be the Mourner.'

He'd expected her to be shocked, outraged, to jump up and down shouting, 'You're crazy! What are you *talking* about?' But she was silent. He tried to see the expression on her face, but she was still turned away from him and the room was too dark.

He said, 'I don't want all this stuff that my Uncle Doug's planning to happen and have the whole world laughing at me for believing in monsters. Because that's the problem: I don't believe in the Mourn.'

Silence.

He was shivering. He reached for his jumper on the floor and pulled it on.

'You must have believed in it once,' Sarah said at last.

'I did. At least I think I did. Kind of like the way I believed in Father Christmas when I was a little kid. And I've been wishing I still did believe, but—'

'So am I a little kid because I still believe in it?'

'That's not what I said.'

She rolled over so she could look at him, and he wondered how much of him she could see, because she was still just a silhouette to his eyes.

'Why *do* you believe?' he asked, knowing that this was the question he should have asked his father.

'I just do. I always have.'

'But why?'

'Because my parents always have, I suppose. It's just never been a question.'

'Don't you have a mind of your own?' He'd meant it to be a joke, but had forgotten she wouldn't see the slight smile on his face. 'That came out wrong,' he said quickly. But couldn't help wondering if it had.

'Of course I've got a mind of my own. I believe in it because it's true. You've got to believe in it if it's true.'

'But I've never known if it is true.'

'Why would people go on believing in it for all this time if it was all just a big lie?' She sat up in the bed, with her knees up under her chin and the sheets pulled over them. 'So what are you going to do instead of being the Mourner?'

'Don't know,' he said. 'That's part of the problem, I guess. As long as I don't have to be the Mourner I can be anything I want, can't I?' He just had to figure out what that was. Unlike most kids he hadn't spent his life dreaming about being this, that or the other because he'd only ever been going to be one thing. Now the choice seemed overwhelming and complicated. But having that choice was what mattered, wasn't it? The freedom of that choice. *Anything* I *choose.*

'What about everybody else?' Sarah asked.

'I'm worried about my dad,' he said. 'I'm scared of hurting him. I'm scared he'll never want to talk to me again.'

'I don't just mean your dad. I mean Moutonby – *everybody*. What will happen to us if you're wrong?'

'I don't—'

'*You* don't believe in the Mourn, but *you* could be wrong, couldn't you? What happens if the legend is true? What if the Mourn attacks us?'

Tim didn't like this train of thought. 'But it won't.'

'How do you know?'

'Because it's not true.'

'How do you know? You're just guessing, aren't you?

Same as us, I suppose. But if you were wrong, it'd be like you're a murderer.'

This, Tim suddenly understood, was much how his father felt. And he sensed those ties that bound him to Mourn Home tighten. He couldn't leave, could he? He couldn't try to be anything else. If the Mourn was real, and it did kill, it would all be his fault for running away. Was this the responsibility his father had talked about?

'I can't do anything,' he said. He stood up and paced the room. 'I don't know what to do, but I can't do anything anyway.'

Sarah tried to shush him, still concerned with the night's main deceit.

With a great effort he forced himself to sit down again. He tried to make a joke. 'Maybe I could train it to only eat people like Roddy Morgan, or Gully and Scott.'

Sarah didn't laugh.

He said, 'I've been thinking how much it would piss those kinds of people off if the legend was true. At one point last night it made me wish it *was* true. I didn't tell you what happened, did I?' He told her about the previous night's events out on the feeding pier and couldn't stop himself from getting even more worked up and frustrated as he told her, as he remembered everything Roddy and the students had said. 'Even I've got to admit that it would've been great to see the Mourn rise up out of the water and chomp a lump out of Gully.'

Sarah was thoughtful. 'Why haven't you ever tried to do something like that?' She seemed embarrassed by Tim's derisive snort. 'What I mean is, you haven't looked for it properly. In Loch Ness they have actual scientific studies; they use radar and sonar and things. But nobody's ever tried to look for the Mourn. Not properly.'

He was going to tell her to forget it, but the words never came out. Because he suddenly realized she might be right. He was quiet, still, and Sarah had to ask if he was okay. But his mind was turning it over. Maybe this was exactly what he was meant to do. He wanted proof, didn't he?

'Okay,' he said, standing up again. 'Okay. Let's do it.'

Sarah was confused. 'What?'

'Let's go looking for it. We'll get the boat and row out to the middle of the lake with some feed and try to make it come to us.'

Sarah sounded horrified by the idea. 'That's not what I meant.'

'But that's all we've got.' The more he thought about it, the more it sounded like the only thing to do. It might be the only way he'd ever know for sure.

'Tim, I—'

'Come on, it's your idea.' He checked his watch. 'It's gone midnight now; everybody else will be in bed. And you're right, I never have tried to look for it. I stand staring out my bedroom window expecting to see it pop up and wave at me, but I've never actually been out on the lake by myself, trying to make it come to me.'

'You're being silly.'

'It's your idea.'

'It's the middle of the night.'

'So? The middle of the night's when most monsters come out to play, isn't it?'

Five minutes later Sarah was wet and shivering in Mourn Home's garden. She poked her head in through the garage door, squinting in the dark for Tim. 'It's a really bad idea. The water looks really rough. And the rain's getting really heavy.'

'Really?' He pulled a random carrier bag out of the freezer and looked inside. A couple of starlings and a blackbird. That'd do.

'What if your dad comes?' Sarah wanted to know.

Tim pushed past her, swung the garage door closed and fastened the padlock. 'Let's hope he doesn't.' He pocketed the key.

'But . . .'

For the second cold night in a row Tim walked along the feeding pier out above the waters of Lake Mou. The wind tugged at him, threw waves at the thick wooden legs to splash and soak his trainers. He strode quickly all the way to the end. Maybe it was because his head felt so stuffed and confused, maybe because he needed to relieve the pressure, but he had a tightening knot of devil-may-care attitude inside. He was going to row out into the middle of the lake and try to summon the Mourn, not caring what happened if by some miracle or other it came. He really was. Because his head was too stuffed and confused to care how it could all turn out. Not tonight. Not now.

'What do you want me to do?' Sarah asked.

'You can hold this.' Tim gave her the carrier bag. He knelt down and untied the *Bonnie Claire* as it bobbed on the restless water.

Sarah held the bag outstretched from her body at the very end of her arm, wrist, hand, fingers. 'I don't want to go out on the lake,' she said.

'I might need you to help me row.'

'I can't row.'

'So what about as a witness? If the Mourn comes I'll need someone to pinch me and tell me I'm not dreaming.' He couldn't help it, he knew he was being particularly callous, but he felt like he needed someone to share in his frustration. 'Scared?' he asked.

Sarah looked away, then nodded. 'Yes.'

The lake was trying to pull the *Bonnie Claire* out of his grip and he held tight to the painter; the rope was almost solid with icy water. He refused to say as much, but the strength of the wind and the waves was scaring him a little too, because he'd never rowed at night before, and certainly not in this kind of weather.

'No one knows we're here,' Sarah said.

'No way would my dad let me do this, so I'm not about to tell him.'

Sarah nodded. 'That's what I mean.'

Tim looked at her, nonplussed. He had to keep a pretty good grip on the painter to stop the waves from dragging the rowing boat away into the dark. 'Just get in, will you?'

'What do we do if anything happens? What if we fall in? No one will know.'

Now Tim understood. He looked out at the lake, and couldn't see the hills or the woods on the other side. He couldn't see a single colourful mast of a sailing dinghy docked at WetFun. He couldn't even see the stars or the moon overhead because the cloud was so thick. For a brief moment his couldn't-care-less attitude slipped, because this close to the water, in the dark, it was easy to believe the cold, black lake went on for ever. Not across, but down. Fall in, go under, and you go down a long, long way.

Sarah was quick to pick up on his second or two of second thought. 'It's a silly idea, Tim.'

He nodded. 'I know.' But it wasn't going to stop him. He stared at the water chopping around the pier's thick stilts. He yanked on the painter sharply and the boat's wooden prow struck the edge of the pier. 'It's *my* lake. If you believe in the legend then the Mourner and the Hundredwaters are linked, so it would never do anything to harm me.' He pulled hard on the rope again, as if the rowing boat was a disobedient dog.

Sarah was quiet.

'I have to go.' She still didn't speak. 'I'm going,' he said.

He pulled the *Bonnie Claire* as close as he could. He stepped off the sturdy, solid pier into the little rocking boat, immediately sitting down on the middle thwart to try to calm its sway. He reached up for the carrier bag with the dead birds.

Sarah passed it to him reluctantly. 'I can't fetch your dad if anything happens. I'm not meant to be here.'

He pushed away from the pier and took up the oars. He rowed away.

He pulled hard on the oars, the waves seeming to fight against him. He heaved at them, digging them deep into the water. He was soon out of breath. He rowed without looking where he was going. The rain found a gap in his anorak collar and ran down the back of his neck, chilling the sweat that already slicked the length of his spine. He rowed far enough so that he lost sight of Sarah and the feeding pier in the darkness.

It was easy out here in the middle of the lake, in the cold, the dark, the rain, to feel slightly ridiculous. It would be easy to turn back and go to his warm bed, he knew that. But he wanted something to happen; he wanted to see the Mourn. *Proof.* He didn't know how far out he was when he finally stopped rowing and pulled the oars back in, leaving himself to drift. He had the carrier bag with the dead birds, but that only made him feel more ridiculous. Like feeding bread to ducks; like feeding dead things to a monster. He simply emptied the bag over the side.

'Come on,' he whispered under his breath. 'I want to see you.'

The wind was rough with him. He shivered through all his layers. The silence of the lake would have been complete if it hadn't been for the slapping of the waves or the rattle of the rain on the surface of the water.

'Come on.' If he could only see it. 'I can't believe in you unless I see you.'

He wondered who else had been out here looking for it. Surely he couldn't be the only Milmullen son ever to ask questions and go searching for some answers.

He let his mind drift back through the history he'd had drummed into him since he was small, back along the long line of Mourners. His father and his grandfather; Great-Grandfather Thomas, who'd built the feeding pier; Donald, the writer, and his older brother Henry, who'd died of TB before he could have any children of his own. Then John; Richard before him. James who'd insisted on swimming in the lake every day of his life, until he'd died at the ripe old age of seventy-four – on dry land. The first Thomas; Henry before him. Young William, and finally, at the very top of the tree, Old William back in 1699. Some of them might have very probably felt just like Tim did now, yet they'd all ended up as believers, they'd all continued the tradition. So why couldn't he?

Had they all been brave men, sensible men? Or had they all been crazy?

How many of them had seen it? Did it matter if they hadn't? Tim supposed possibly not – not back then anyway. In those days people seemed to live most of their lives by blind faith. But Tim knew he was a modern person, someone who lived in a world that relied on scientific evidence.

He peered into the darkness. But it was hard to see anything right now. The *Bonnie Claire* rode the lake uneasily.

It could be below him now, he thought. Emerging from

its watery depths, rising up from its bottomless pit. Old William wrote in his diary that its eyes were 'cold and ancient'; he said that it moved 'as swiftly through the water as a hunting bird can fly'. Maybe it was sliding through the black water now, coming closer, wanting to appraise its new keeper.

Imagine the creature down there. Imagine it circling beneath the little boat. Would he be able to see it coming in the dark? Would he be able to see it rise out of the water? Imagine it swimming closer.

An unusually large wave buffeted the boat and it shuddered beneath him. He froze, held his breath.

Had the creature really come to him? He didn't dare move. Was it there?

The rain was relentless; the wind threw it in his face, but he couldn't move. He waited, tense, everything strained to listen, peering into the darkness.

Is it really out there?

He couldn't see anything. All he could hear was the rain. He forced himself to keep still, breathing as shallowly as he could.

Another swelling wave.

The rowing boat lurched awkwardly to one side. His backside slipped on the damp thwart. His feet went from under him as he fell backwards, arms windmilling as he tried to grab hold of the sides. He smacked his back painfully against the wood and couldn't stop himself from crying out. And for the first time that night he was scared.

He was suddenly very aware of his noisy heart; he could

feel his blood pounding in his ears. He gripped the sides of the little boat as it shivered beneath him.

If he fell in . . . Would he be able to climb back into the boat if he fell in the lake? Or would the Mourn . . . ? Would it attack him?

He couldn't see anything in the dark. He didn't move, stayed crouched low as the *Bonnie Claire* rocked. The waves buffeted him this way, then that.

The rain fell heavier, soaking him. The wind was getting stronger. That was all. Just the wind. Nothing else. A sudden wave threatened to spill him. He yelped, clung on.

No. It's here, he insisted. The Mourn was below him, wanting to see him. Wanting him to see it.

He was on his feet, not caring about the way the boat pitched and swayed. He had to see it. He was searching the dark water for something just below the surface.

'Where are you?' he shouted into the rain. 'I want to see you. Where are you? Make me believe in you!' He couldn't see well enough; the wind and rain fought against him. '*Where are you?*'

He turned round, twisting back and forth, peering, searching the darkness; no longer frightened of upsetting the boat, just desperate. He had to see it. The boat rocked treacherously beneath him, his trainers felt greasy on the damp wood, but he didn't care. If it was there then why didn't it show itself?

'*Come on!*'

He snatched up an oar and beat at the water, smacking the wooden blade down harder and harder.

'*Where are you? Where are you?*'

He tried to hurt the water with the oar – smacking it down, smacking it down. The wind tugged at his anorak, whipped his hair. He beat at the waves.

'*Where are you?*'

Just the wind and the rain. Just the waves.

'You're dead!' he shouted. '*You're a lie!*'

There was no reply.

He slumped down, tipping the rowing boat dangerously. He no longer cared if he fell out.

'You're just a shitty *lie!*'

He felt hollow and exhausted. He was breathing hard, as if he'd just run a race – and lost.

'*Tim . . .*'

He tried to ignore the voice calling him at first, wanting to pretend it was just a sound carried by the wind. He closed his eyes to block it out. There was a slice of stars above the horizon as a gap in the cloud moved slowly across the sky.

'*Tim,*' his father called. '*Timothy.*'

Reluctantly he picked up the oars, and using the dim starlight was able to point himself in the direction of the feeding pier. Sarah had obviously run to fetch Bill. Her nerves must have been too much for her. But Tim didn't feel betrayed – at least, not by her. He rowed slowly, not feeling anything. He was empty inside. His arms ached with the effort of rowing and that took up all the concentration he had. The waves struggled against him all the way back.

The Dragon in the Lake

As soon as he opened his eyes he remembered, so closed them again. Tight. He didn't want to wake up – not this morning. He tried to cling to his sleep like he was clinging to his duvet.

But now his mind was awake and spinning through last night's events. The more he tried to ignore the morning light sneaking around the edges of his curtains the more impossible it was to pretend he was still fast asleep. Maybe it was all just a dream. Hah! No such luck.

Maybe today will be different, he thought. *Maybe today will be the day when everything changes.*

The first thing he realized was how much the muscles in his arms ached because of all that rowing. And he had blisters on his hands from where he'd gripped and tugged at the oars. Then, when he finally submitted to the idea that he was going to have to face the day, he saw that he was late. Very late.

His alarm clock told him it was 9:15. He should have been helping out with breakfast two hours ago, but he'd slept right through. Right now he should be sitting in his

Monday morning history lesson with Miss Webb. Nobody let anybody sleep late in this house. Bill, Anne or Jenny (sometimes all three) were usually extremely vocal about getting him up on time.

Now he didn't want to get up because he was worried about what might have happened. His imagination threw up several possibilities. They could have forgotten about him – but that was highly unlikely. They were pissed off with what had gone on last night and couldn't be bothered to worry about him any more – which definitely sounded more feasible. Or something had happened to them . . .

He opened his curtains to look out at the lake. It was a bright day, but there was a slowly melting frost on his mother's flowerbeds. He checked to make sure the *Bonnie Claire* was still there, then looked for his father's bright yellow figure somewhere close by. He couldn't see him, although the garage door was open so he guessed that must be where he'd be found. Over at WetFun he saw the builders were back; several busy bodies moving around the site. There were already some sailors out on the lake, scratching silver wakes across the dark surface. The speedboat that he'd seen on the trailer on Saturday was back in the water where it belonged. One of the students was zooming across the water's chop on the jet-ski. Probably Gully – he was the jet-ski fanatic. They were going home later today apparently, and good riddance to them. Looking around the lake he saw there were also a couple of anglers on the far shore in the lee of the trees. Everything *seemed* okay.

Even so he dressed quickly if apprehensively, and headed

downstairs. He'd told Sarah last night that he wanted to leave. He determined that if nothing else, today was going to be the day he laid plans.

Anne was in the kitchen, sitting at the table with a mug of tea and one of her chunky novels. The breakfast pots had all been washed and cleared away but the kitchen still smelled of fry-ups. Anne put the book down when he came in.

'You're up,' she said needlessly.

'Hmm,' he agreed. He hovered, waiting to see what she was going to say.

'Do you want breakfast?'

'Has something happened?'

'Happened?'

'It's half-past nine.'

She stood up and moved over to the fridge. 'Your father and I thought you might want an extra hour or so in bed after last night.'

'Oh.' It was unlike his dad to be so thoughtfully lax. 'Thank you.'

Anne took some bacon and eggs out the fridge and went to the stove.

'I'm not hungry,' Tim said.

'Are you sure?'

'I'll just have a glass of milk and then I'd better get to school.'

'You don't have to go in today. I called to let them know a few minutes ago.' She returned the food to the fridge and poured him some milk. 'Your father and I wanted to have a talk with you. About last night.'

He took the glass of milk but didn't sit down at the table. It appeared his parents had been having another one of their private chats about him. He wondered whether he'd rather be in Miss Webb's class, even though Roddy Morgan was in that class too.

'Has Jenny gone in?'

'Your Uncle Doug had to go into town, so he drove her and Sarah in on his way.'

'Is . . . Is Sarah okay?' What he was really asking was, *Do you know the truth about what she was doing here last night?*

Unfortunately his mother's answer was as ambiguous as his question. 'You gave her a bit of a fright, I think. She was the one who woke us. She thought you'd fallen in. She said you'd been shouting but she couldn't see you in the dark, and then all of a sudden you went quiet. Your father was ready to ask Vic Stones for one of his boats when we saw you rowing back in again.' Anne sat back at the table. 'I think you gave us all a bit of a fright.'

When he'd returned last night it wasn't just Bill standing on the feeding pier, but Anne, Uncle Doug and Jenny. They'd all had questions for him and he'd told them he was showing off to Sarah, trying to impress her, because he didn't think it sounded quite as stupid as the truth.

Anne had still wanted to know what on earth Sarah was doing at Mourn Home. Jenny had guessed what had been going on immediately and lied for them, saying she'd called Sarah really late last night to get her to sneak back round. Neither Anne nor Bill had been impressed, but had had to accept the answer because it was the only one they were going to be given. Tim couldn't have been more grateful to his sister and knew he owed her a favour or two in return now. He wondered whether it ought to involve some sort of revenge against Gully.

Anne sipped her tea slowly. He noticed the grey shadows under her eyes and realized she must have been up all night.

He took a gulp of his milk and went to put the glass down on the table. But the table moved.

The whole house moved.

The noise, the rumble, was like the loudest rolling thunder Tim had ever heard. But it was a low, crunching bass note that came from deep underground.

His glass smashed on the floor as if it had jumped out of his hand, splashing the white milk across the grey stone slabs. His head cried, *Earthquake!* But he wasn't sure if he believed it. His legs almost went from under him as the floor shifted suddenly one way then the other. The solidity of the world felt brittle.

Anne had dropped her mug of tea. She was gripping the table for dear life. Her chair had juddered right out from underneath her and toppled over backwards on the uneven floor. Everything shook. Everything juddered, shuddered, jerked, jolted, *shook*. Cupboard doors swung open. The crockery inside seemed to leap suicidally from the shelves, smashing itself to smithereens.

Tim staggered again and this time lost his legs; he fell flat on his backside. His mind spun at an incredible rate, a thousand thoughts per second. One thought caught hold and he remembered Donald's diary writing – his description of the terrifying earthquake back in 1908. He didn't think the man's words had been such an exaggeration after all.

He wasn't sure whether he should try to stand again. The shards of crockery danced and chattered on the floor around him. There was a sound like a whip – a loud *shh-nap* – and although the kitchen window stayed in its frame a crack instantly appeared diagonally from top to bottom in the glass. The door to the guest's dining room opened all by itself as if a ghost had just walked in.

'Outside!' Anne shouted, lurching to her feet.

Tim moved on drunken legs, scrambling up, reeling for the back door. The ceiling light shade swung like a pendulum. The doorknob vibrated in his hand. He half fell onto the gravel driveway with Anne treading on his heels in her haste. Bill was hurrying towards them from out of the garage.

The deafening rumble was fading, its echo ebbing away.

'Are you all right?' Bill was breathing hard. 'Annie? Tim? Are you hurt?'

Anne was shaking her head. 'We're fine, but—'

Tim was staring out at the lake. 'Dad! Look!'

A wave bigger than anything Tim had seen before rolled along the feeding pier. It tossed the *Bonnie Claire* up out of the water and onto the planks and kept coming. It surged up the shore, past the Mourn Stone, splashing and foaming around its rough edges, and reached almost as far as Anne's flowerbeds before at last slouching back. But Tim was pointing farther out to where the whole surface of the lake was churning. Two of the small sailing boats were lying on their sides; maybe as many as half a dozen people were struggling in the cold water.

'Call Vic Stones,' Bill said to Anne. Then he was running for the feeding pier, for the *Bonnie Claire*. 'Tell him to get one of his speedboats out to them.'

Anne didn't need telling twice, but Tim was following his father.

Bill suddenly turned on him. 'Feed!' he shouted. 'Get some feed!'

Tim ran into the garage, ignored the tools that lay scattered across the floor, the stepladder that had fallen off its wall-hooks, and pulled one of the plastic bags out of the freezer.

He raced along the pier as another wave rushed towards them. It was smaller than the first, yet it still managed to rock the rowing boat now sitting on the pier and swamp their feet and ankles. He caught up with his father and together they heaved the little boat back into the water. Tim thought he was going to be ordered to wait here, and although Bill hesitated for a fraction of a second, what he said was: 'I'll row.'

They pushed off from the side of the pier and Bill pulled hard on the oars. The lake was already beginning to settle but it was still as choppy as if they were in the middle of a storm. Bill had his back to the drama; Tim was looking beyond him to the people in the water. Two of them had managed to climb onto the exposed hulls of one boat; a third was clinging to the mast. He couldn't see the second boat clearly because it was too far away, but the figures did seem to be close to it rather than far adrift.

'I think they're okay,' he said.

But Bill didn't slow. Sweat stood out on his brow. He worked his jaw as if that would help his arms.

'Was it an earthquake?' Tim wanted to know. Bill didn't answer and out of habit, thinking of his hearing aid, he shouted, 'It was an earthquake, wasn't it?'

'Keep that feed handy,' Bill told him.

They edged closer. And suddenly the water rose up around them, a heavy wave thumped against the rowing boat. Aftershock. Tim gripped the sides; icy spray drenched him. He heard a faint yell. The sailors on the closest boat were washed into the water again after almost managing to scramble up onto the tipped hull.

Bill glanced over his shoulder but kept rowing as strongly as ever. 'Throw some of the feed over the side. Not the whole lot. Draw it to us if it's close.'

The *Bonnie Claire* pitched and rolled. Tim tore open the plastic bag and dropped into the water something that looked like it had come from Mr Gregory's shop. *Draw it to us*, he thought. Bill believed the Mourn was close.

Groups of frightened onlookers gathered on WetFun's shore. All they could do was watch. The anxious voices carried to Tim and his father. But they were lost in an instant as a roaring engine burst into life. A speedboat shot out across the lake as if fired from a catapult.

'It's Vic Stones.' Tim watched the way the sleek silver boat smashed through the waves rather than skimmed over them. It was quick to reach the sailing dinghy nearest the shore and Stones's passenger plucked the struggling sailors out of the cold lake. 'He's got them. They're okay. He's got them.'

'Throw in more feed,' Bill said. He was watching over his shoulder as the speedboat noisily leaped across the lake to the second capsized crew. Tim couldn't help wondering if his father wished he had a speedboat too, because it was meant to be his job to do the rescuing round here, wasn't it? To be honest, even over the thumping of his heart, Tim couldn't help feeling a little ridiculous in the back of the rowing boat.

The water seemed to settle once more. They bobbed in the *Bonnie Claire* and watched as Vic Stones circled the dinghy once, twice, assessing any damage, then started back towards the WetFun shore. But there was somebody running out along a jetty waving at the speedboat. It was one of the students. Tim recognized Scott and followed with his eyes to where he was waving, pointing.

Both Bill and Tim saw it at the same time. Tim felt his whole body go cold. Bill immediately started rowing hard again. Vic Stones on the other hand didn't seem to understand what Scott was trying to say. The speedboat sped towards him, too quick to see what Tim and Bill had seen.

'Throw in the rest of the feed.' Bill dug the oars into

the water with all his strength as he tried to power the little boat along. 'Throw it in, Tim!'

Tim did as he was told. Icy dread filled his belly, but he couldn't tear his eyes away from the shocking sight. There was a jet-ski bobbing in the waves. Riderless. Gully was nowhere to be seen.

Part Three

A Small Legend

Be careful what you wish for. Tim couldn't remember where he'd heard that before.

He was watching TV in his room; watching Uncle Doug being interviewed by the breakfast television news reporter, trying to explain about the legend and the Mourn and why what had happened had happened. And if Tim turned round to look through the window he'd see the two police boats out on the lake searching for Gully's body.

But he hadn't wished for this, had he? Not this much, this bad.

But the Mourn *had* answered him. And wasn't everything that was happening now his much sought-after proof? He felt forced into believing. He'd summoned the Mourn, he'd called for it to prove itself to him, and it had taken Gully just like it had taken those schoolboys back in 1699. Wasn't this what he had to believe now?

There was a gentle knock at his door. His mother came into the room. 'Can you switch that off and come downstairs, love? I want to have a quick word with you and Jenny before you go to school.'

As he reached forward to push the OFF button he heard

the reporter say: '. . . and what has been only a small legend for over three hundred years yesterday suddenly exploded into the national consciousness . . .'

He followed his mother down to the kitchen. The lights were all on because the cracked window had been boarded up. Jenny was already sitting at the table, a new mug of tea held in both hands. There were two cardboard boxes of fresh crockery on the floor waiting to be fully unpacked; so far they'd only taken out what had been needed for breakfast. Tim sat opposite his sister at the table. It was obvious she hadn't slept much last night; her complexion was sickly and she had deep grey shadows under her eyes. She looked like she'd been crying until only a few moments ago.

She hadn't said anything to anyone yesterday when she'd been brought home from school early. Anne had explained what had happened (she'd already known about the earthquake because the tremors had been felt at the school) and she'd disappeared up to her room without speaking to anyone – then stayed there. He wondered if she knew what he'd done, that it could be his fault. The only thing he couldn't work out was whether the creature had attacked Gully by chance, or whether it *knew* he hated him?

'You okay?' he asked.

She gave a small nod but didn't look up.

Yesterday had been difficult for the whole family. To Tim it had felt a bit like living in an underwater world. The proper, outside world of loud noises had been muted and it had taken a real effort to wade through the hours and minutes and seconds. But now that time had dried, there didn't seem to be a single drop of it left – he couldn't tell where the day had gone. He'd watched the TV vans with their satellite dishes and masses of cables take over the lakeside, churn up the mud, spill dozens of people and cameras onto the shore. But if anybody asked him now what time they'd arrived, he wouldn't have a clue.

Last night had been worse – lying in the dark, thinking in circles, feeling scared and guilty. He hadn't been the only one. He'd been to the toilet once at midnight, again just after three, and he'd seen Jenny's light was still on and had heard his parents talking with Uncle Doug in the study both times.

'Dad's going to run you to school in a few minutes,' Anne told them. 'We don't want you walking and having to fight off the reporters on the way. We'd rather you didn't talk to any reporters at all – Dad and Uncle Doug can do that, yes?'

They both nodded.

'It will be best if you try and treat school like as normal a day as possible.'

They nodded again, albeit reluctantly this time. Tim certainly wasn't looking forward to having to go at all; doubted Jenny was either. It didn't take a genius to work out that school was going to be kind of tough today.

Anne put a mug of tea on the table in front of him before turning her attention to the sink. The guests' breakfasts had already been dealt with but there was still the washing-up to be done. Tim got up to help just as Uncle Doug came in through the back door.

Anne was quickest to ask: 'Is everything all right?'

'Bedlam,' Doug said, kicking off his shoes. Then: 'They all want to interview Bill. I reckon they're getting a bit fed up of me.'

'He's patrolling the shore. It's even more important he keeps up his duties now.'

'I know, Annie, love. You know that, I know that. But these journalists are looking for an angle – as if a man-eating lake monster isn't enough!' He helped himself to tea from the pot. 'I can only repeat everything I already told them yesterday, and the police haven't found the poor bugger's body, which means they've got nothing new to say either. So to keep the story interesting they've started calling us a "cult".'

Anne shook her head. 'But that's ridiculous.'

'Again, Annie: we both know it.' He slumped down at the table beside Jenny. 'At first it was all questions about why I was sure the Mourn had attacked the lad rather than him simply losing control of the jet-ski during the earth-quake, falling in and drowning. And I think the point that the police haven't found sight nor sign of him yet answers that. But then this smart-arse from the BBC who seemed to have done a little more of his research started talking about how Bill had failed in his duty because he didn't protect the lad in the first place.'

Anne sucked in her breath through gritted teeth. Tim and Jenny exchanged edgy glances.

'Bill's going to have to talk to these people if he wants to defend himself,' Doug said.

'He won't.' Anne looked grim. 'He said he won't talk to *any* reporters. He says it's none of their business.'

'A young lad's been killed by the Mourn, Bill is the Mourner – the whole country sees it as their business. I don't think he understands how the media works these days. You can't ignore it. You may be able to avoid many things in life, but the media – same as the police or the government – has a tendency to seek you out whenever it feels like it. You know, if he doesn't stand up to these people and defend himself, he's going to end up with the blame.'

Tim had heard enough. 'But it's not his fault! He didn't—'

His mother shushed him. 'Please, Tim. It's—'

'Dad's not to blame!'

'Hey, of course he's not.' Uncle Doug held up his hand for calm. 'But he has to fight his own battles. Neither you nor I can do it for him.'

'That's not what I mean.'

Anne was sharp. 'Tim! Please! I don't want our guests hearing about all our problems.'

'But—'

'You go get ready for school. Don't cause your father any more worries by making him late as well this morning.'

He felt like a small child being banned from 'grown-up' conversation. It hurt him and provoked his anger in equal measure because they didn't know all the facts, and weren't even willing to listen. He still hadn't admitted what he was really doing out on the lake the other night. But when Jenny stood up to leave the room he followed, feeling it was important to talk to her as well.

They went to Jenny's bedroom, switched on her TV. It was the first time they'd been alone together since their argument on Saturday morning.

'I wanted to say thanks for not saying anything to Dad – about what I said.'

'I still might.'

He took the hint and shut up.

ITV were repeating an interview with Uncle Doug from last night.

'. . . we're not doubting the fact that there was an earthquake. There are records of other tremors in this area dating back centuries. But this morning's was perhaps the strongest one for many years, and we believe it was probably the reason for the Mourn's attack. The tremor caused a great disturbance deep down in the lake that must have roused the creature, bringing it closer to the surface than it's been in a long, long while . . .'

Tim shook his head. 'I don't think that's true.'

'You don't think *any*thing's true.'

Tim flinched. 'No, listen – I was wrong. What I said to you on Saturday, I'm admitting I was wrong, okay?'

'Why? Because it's all on telly now?'

'No. Of course not.'

'What then?'

'I know I said I didn't believe. I said I needed proof, didn't I? Well that's why I was out on the lake on Sunday night. I was trying—'

But he didn't get the chance to finish what he was saying

because their father was at the door. 'Turn that off,' he said. 'I'm taking you to school.'

Again Tim had to bite back his confession. It was harder to do second time around: the guilt was swelling inside him. He felt like it might burst him wide open.

It might have been exciting if it wasn't so nerve-racking. Tim sat in the back of the van, Jenny up front next to Bill. They had to drive through a rowdy scrum of journalists and photographers; a flash popped brightly, there were shouted questions and somebody thumped on the passenger-side window, making Jenny yelp. She looked pale. Tim just couldn't believe it; he'd never seen anything like it. Bill blared his horn and drove slowly but steadily, refusing to stop.

Tim didn't know if Uncle Doug had told him what the reporter had said – about him failing in his duty. If he did know, he was hiding it well. But then he'd always been good at hiding his feelings. Maybe he'd just turned his hearing aid off. Although Tim reckoned even that prop wouldn't have been able to block out this kind of noise.

They managed to get to the main road and over the Dows Bridges in one piece.

'Either your Uncle Doug or I will be there to pick you up tonight. I don't want you talking to anybody you don't know today. No sneaking out to the chippy for lunch, please. Just stay on the school grounds. I've already rung your Head – Mrs Collins, isn't it? – and she's promised to do everything she can to make it as normal a day as possible for everybody. Yes?'

Tim and his sister nodded silently.

'If anything does happen — and I'm not saying it will, but just in case — report it to her straight away. I know she's not Fearful, but she has a job to do. Luckily for us she knows that.'

Again they nodded.

Tim sat quietly in the back of the van as they drove along Goode Street, Couth Lane, getting closer to school. He was desperate to say something to Bill, but was scared he might not listen. Not that he knew what to say, or how to say it. He forced himself to speak before it was too late.

'Dad!' It was as if the word had leaped out with some force behind it. He rushed on. 'It's not your fault, Dad.'

Bill stayed facing forward as he drove. He made no sign of even hearing.

Jenny turned and frowned at him, wanting him to shut up, but he said, 'It's not your fault about Gully. You couldn't have done anything about it.'

'Thank you, Tim.' Bill said it so quietly Tim had to strain to hear him above the noise of the engine. He slowed and pulled up at a zebra crossing, letting two elderly women cross. One peered into the van and pointed them out to her companion. They both stared. He put his foot down again, perhaps a touch too hard. 'At least this has happened now. It's best it's happened at the end of my time instead of at the beginning of yours.'

Tim struggled with what to say. He still hadn't said what he wanted to. The van climbed the hill towards the school. 'I . . . I think *I* might have done it. I think I summoned the Mourn on Sunday night.' He ignored Jenny's glare. 'I wanted to see it, I challenged it to prove itself to me. I think I made it get Gully because . . .' He looked away from his sister. 'Because we'd had an argument. I hated him. I think it's my fault, not yours.'

Jenny's face had softened; she looked confused, not angry.

Bill stopped the van at the side of the road. He turned round fully in the driver's seat to look at his son. 'Some Mourners have claimed to have had the power to summon the Mourn – Old William, of course, but James and Donald too. I never have; I've never wanted to. Maybe you do – only time will tell. I'll warn you, though: don't ever think you can control it.'

He waited for Tim to nod his understanding.

'I don't like to hear you saying you hate anyone,' he said, turning round to stare up the road. 'But the Mourn took that lad as a show of its power, that's what I believe. We're coming up to an important time of change for all of us. This weekend we see the new Mourner initiated; the creature can no doubt sense this, and wants us to remember why we call ourselves "Fearful". That's what I believe. Perhaps I should have realized. Mr Spicer saw the creature not long after my Carving; these things happen for a reason.' He twisted his head to look at Tim again. 'I need you to read the diary, okay?'

'I am. I was—'

'Read what Old William has to say. That way you can help me make sure this never, *never*, happens again.'

Tim hid his dismay at again being told to read the book. But maybe this time he understood why. For Bill it was what made sense of the world when everything seemed to be going wrong. He watched his father's eyes in the rear-view mirror as he drove them the rest of the way to school. And if the diary worked so well for him then why couldn't it work like that for Tim too? He just hadn't tried hard enough to understand it on Saturday night, that was the problem. He had to make a proper effort.

'Wait for your uncle or me at the end of the day,' Bill reminded them as they climbed out of the van at the school gates. He waved once as he drove away.

Tim braced himself for the stares and the gossip that was bound to greet them inside, but Jenny had a hand on his arm.

'Did you mean what you said just then?'

'Yes. It's my fault. It has to be. Because of what I was doing on the lake.'

'I thought it was me,' Jenny said. 'I walked down to the lake and begged the Mourn to show itself, so Gully and Scott would feel shitty for what they did to me – and to make you see some sense.'

'Like Dad said, only Mourners can summon it. But maybe we both wanted it hard enough. We're both Milmullens.' He shrugged. 'Whatever, I guess I've been forced into believing in it now, haven't I?'

'So you are going to be Mourner?'

It might not be what he deep down wanted. He might hate having to do it. But he began to wonder if his father had ever actually *enjoyed* his duties. Being the Mourner wasn't about enjoyment, he realized; it was about stopping what happened to Gully happening to anyone else.

'It's my duty, isn't it?' he said. 'It's what I'm meant to do.'

The New Fearful

Tim might have decided he was going to be the Mourner, but it didn't make walking into school any easier that day. Even Jenny had her head down, wary of catching anybody's eye. Most of the kids were watching them – and those who weren't were soon told why everybody else was. They walked a gauntlet of gossip and stares along the footpath from the gates to the main block. It prickled Tim's skin worse than goose pimples.

Someone called his name.

He flinched. But the girl was smiling at him, even if it was in a nervy kind of way.

'What d'you want?' he said, a bit too sharply, making *her* flinch.

She was in his year, but he didn't share any classes with her and couldn't remember her name. She hovered, looking awkward, and with one hand pushed her long fringe out of her eyes. In her other hand she was holding a supermarket carrier bag. 'My mum's sent this for you.' She held the carrier bag out to him – Tesco's.

He stared down at it, then looked for Roddy Morgan. Where was he? He had to have something to do with this, right? But although there were plenty of other kids hanging around, curious about what was going on, Roddy was nowhere to be seen. And Roddy never did like doing anything if he couldn't accept the applause afterwards.

He turned to his sister. All she could do was shrug.

The girl squirmed now, looking horribly uncomfortable. Her nervous smile flickered.

He said, 'Thanks . . .'

She thrust the bag at him. 'For Saturday.' He had to grab it quick before she let it go. And she was obviously very happy to have got rid of it. She hurried back to her friends, who were waiting for her at the side of the footpath.

He was surprised by the bag's weight.

'Just see what's inside.' Jenny tried to peer in herself. 'What is it?'

'An oh-so-funny present from Roddy Morgan, probably.' But it wasn't. It was a massive lump of beef. He opened the carrier bag wide for his sister to see.

'Do you think it's feed?'

'Must be. She said it was for Saturday, didn't she?' He was searching the loose gangs of kids wandering by, but the girl's group of friends had moved on along the footpath towards the main block. 'What am I meant to do with it?' he asked.

'Put it in your locker until tonight, I suppose.' She looked as bemused as he felt.

They parted at the main block. Jenny headed for her form room, Tim for his locker so he could get rid of the meat. But hanging from his padlock was yet another plastic bag. Old habits die hard and he peered around. The corridor was busy but there was no sign of Roddy. Tentatively, without actually taking it down from where it hung, he looked inside. Chopped liver – with a note.

He threw both carrier bags into his locker and took the folded sheet of paper to his form room. Only when he was sitting at his desk, making sure no one else in the room was spying on him, did he open the note.

Dear Timothy Milmullen,

We apologize for never having contributed to the Feed before now, but we would like you to know how Fearful our family has always been. We are usually very busy on a Saturday morning (due to dance classes, swimming lessons etc.) but now feel sure we can play a more prominent role in the future.

Please pass on our gratitude and best wishes to your father for all of his selfless duty. We look forward to supporting you as our future Mourner.

Yours respectfully,

Mrs D. Custance and family

Under his breath Tim whispered, 'Bloody hell!' He glanced around the classroom as it slowly filled with students. Two more of his classmates were bearing carrier bags before them. '*Bloody hell!*' he repeated.

Miss Kelly, Tim's form tutor and German teacher, arrived five minutes after the bell for registration had rung. There'd already been hopeful comments from some of the kids that she might be ill and then a general disappointment when she hurried in. She looked as though she'd been rushing all morning, but swept her gaze around the room until she spotted Tim, and only then took out the register.

'Settle down, settle down. Quiet, everyone, please.'

Everybody took a seat. The chatter and fidgeting gradually subsided.

Miss Kelly bent over the open register. 'Answer your names clearly, please.'

She only managed to get as far as the Gs, however.

'Will someone please tell me what on earth that awful smell is?'

Tim, who had a pile of raw meat warming nicely inside the plastic carrier bags by his feet, slowly raised his hand in the air. 'I think it's my fault, miss,' he said, blushing.

Miss Kelly rolled her eyes. 'Someone help Tim take that to the kitchens. Ask the canteen staff if they would be kind enough to put it in the refrigerator until the end of the day.'

As Tim was leaving the room she touched his elbow and spoke to him in a hushed voice. 'Can you see me after today's German lesson? I went past the supermarket myself this morning.'

'It's because of what's happened,' Jenny said. 'Everybody's seen the telly and now they're scared because it proves the legend's all true. It's because of Gully. Everybody's scared.'

It was lunch time and Tim was sitting with Jenny and Sarah on the long wooden bench in the cloakroom outside the library. The morning had been one of the weirdest of his life – he'd been given another two bags of feed at break – and it didn't seem as though things were going to get any more normal before the end of the day. Looking at Jenny he could tell she felt the same too.

He kicked at a couple of sweet wrappers on the floor by his feet. 'I know what Dad said, but I can't help thinking it was me who summoned it.' He looked up at his sister, then at Sarah. 'Do you think I did?'

'We both wanted it to come,' Jenny said. 'After what Gully did to me I was desperate for something to happen.'

'I don't think I cared who it happened to. Gully, Scott or Roddy Morgan – I wasn't fussy.' He realized the words sounded harsh as soon as they were out of his mouth. 'I didn't mean . . .' But he couldn't swallow them back. 'I just needed to prove them wrong and the legend right. Like you said on Saturday, about wanting to be different to them.'

Jenny nodded. They were quiet, thoughtful. They could hear the racket from the other kids outside.

'It couldn't have known what we wanted, could it?'

'But we didn't mean *this*, did we? No way did we mean this. I didn't want anyone dead.'

'It's not definite he's dead,' Sarah said, then blushed when Tim and Jenny stared at her. 'He could have just drowned – by accident.'

Tim shrugged. 'Could have, but . . .'

Their silence was heavy above them.

'Do you think they'll find his body?' Sarah asked. She was talking about the police divers.

'If he drowned, yes. If it was the Mourn, no.'

On the wall opposite was artwork from their year group: a misshapen bowl of fruit, an insulting portrait, but a rather good landscape of the valley and Lake Mou. It was the landscape which caught Tim's eye. He stared at it. *Is that . . . ?* He got up and walked over to get a closer look.

'You definitely think it *was* the Mourn?' Sarah asked.

Tim squinted at the pencil marks. Was that meant to be a wave? Or had somebody drawn . . . ?

'I think it had to be,' Jenny said. 'Like Dad said about it sensing it's close to Tim's Carving, and if he was trying to get it to show itself, it seems logical that it answered its new keeper.' She was watching her brother. 'That's what you think, isn't it?' He ran his finger over the picture. 'Tim?' He had his nose virtually pressed up against it. 'What're you doing?'

He squinted hard. *Only a wave.* He blinked.

'Nothing,' he said too quickly, embarrassed. 'Just . . . Nothing.' He sat back down without meeting his sister's eye.

'*Do* you think it was the Mourn?' Sarah asked.

It took Tim a second or two to realize she wasn't talking about the picture. 'I don't know what else it could be.' This was the truth as he saw it. There was still that niggle at the back of his mind; obviously there was still doubt, but . . . 'It's kind of a lot of fuss if it isn't. I mean, with the newspapers and TV and everything.'

'That man from the paper is still at the gates,' Sarah said. 'He's been stopping people who go home for lunch and asking them questions.'

'About me?'

She nodded. 'I think so.'

It had been Mrs Collins, the Head, who'd told him to stay in the building. The weather was fine and dry; usually no one was allowed inside during break or lunch time unless it was raining. But a photographer from one of the tabloid newspapers had sneaked onto the school grounds in an attempt to take pictures of him in his lessons. The photographer had been firmly kicked out by both the Head and the caretaker, but Tim guessed they couldn't do anything more about him if he was outside the gates, off school property. He shuddered at the thought of what might be being said about him by the other kids. 'Oh yeah, we know Monster Boy. He's a right *freak*!'

Sarah was watching him closely. She'd been keeping her distance from him today; she hadn't given him the usual kiss or hug upon meeting. They hadn't seen each other to talk about what had happened on Sunday night yet; he'd just left her hanging, not sure where she stood exactly. But he was thinking that maybe yesterday had changed things. If he was going to be the Mourner after all, maybe they should stay together too?

He reached over and took hold of her hand, surprising her, making her jump. He smiled at her. Slowly, she smiled back; squeezed his hand.

There were footsteps coming towards them along the corridor and for some reason Tim wasn't in the least bit surprised to see Roddy Morgan. 'Hey! Monster Boy! I heard you were hiding yourself away.' He grinned and the tooth Tim had chipped seemed very obvious in amongst the rest.

'Leave it out, Roddy. I really don't care what you've got to say to me, not today.' He felt exhausted at the thought of having to argue with him.

'I just wanted to let you know that I'm going out to talk to that journalist bloke at the gates. I thought you might want to know what I was going to tell him.'

'Piss off.'

Roddy took no notice. 'I'm going to say you're a freak, your dad's a freak . . . in fact your whole family are freaks.'

'I've heard it all before,' Tim said, sounding bored, but getting aggravated.

'I'm also going to tell him my theory about all the Mourners being murderers and perverts.'

Jenny was shocked. 'What?'

Tim just sneered at Roddy. 'Yeah, yeah. If you like.' But he was angry at himself for letting this nob-head wind him up.

'And I'm also going to give him the front-page scoop,' Roddy continued, 'on my theory of how I reckon Gully really died. I'll tell him that your dad probably—'

Tim snapped. He was on his feet in an instant, glaring eye to eye. 'Maybe he was on a dodgy jet-ski. Ever thought of that? Faulty repairs.'

Roddy shook his head, still grinning. It was mission accomplished for him – all he'd wanted was to get under Tim's skin.

'Yeah, maybe I'll have a word with the reporter about *that* theory. Tell the police too.'

Roddy was laughing, shaking his head as if in pity. He backed away towards the outside door. 'I'm not the one who comes from a family of freaks and weirdos . . .' He swung the door open, then called over his shoulder as he stepped through: 'And *murderers*.'

Jenny was livid. 'He can't say that. How can he say that? What if he really does talk to that reporter?'

Tim ground his teeth. 'He probably already has.' He turned to her.

She shook her head. 'Don't say it.'

He pulled a face but Sarah asked: 'Don't say what?'

'That the Mourn ate the wrong arsehole.'

Bill had to help load the van with the offerings at the end of school. 'It's been like this all day,' he told them. 'We're not going to get it all in the freezer, but I can't turn anyone away. Not now.'

'It's been weird,' Tim said.

The afternoon had been almost unbelievable, with more and more people bringing feed after seeing the others doing it in the morning. He'd been invited round for tea to one girl's house. Two lads had squabbled over who was going to sit next to him in English. Even now a group of half a dozen boys walked by and three of them said, 'See you tomorrow.' A girl he didn't recognize waved.

Jenny summed it up. '*Everybody's* Fearful now.'

Bill didn't comment. Instead: 'Mrs Collins said something about a journalist hanging around.'

'We didn't speak to him,' Jenny said. 'He was asking the

other kids loads of questions. But it's okay, because they're all on our side now.'

'It's not about sides,' Bill said as he put the van into gear.

As they drove both Tim and Jenny listed all the names of the teachers and students who'd made donations, and the promises they'd given to come to the Feed more often. Then they sat in silence, all a little bemused, maybe even suspicious. Tim knew the long list had plenty of names on it that Bill had never even heard before, even in a small town like Moutonby.

They crossed the Dows Bridges, past Bert and Agna's pub. Jenny jabbed Tim's shoulder and pointed out the notice that had been stuck in the big front window: FEED YOUR-SELF AFTER FEEDING THE MOURN. MONSTER LUNCHTIME SPECIALS EVERY SATURDAY.

'Things are getting out of hand,' was Bill's response.

They turned off the main road onto the dirt track across the waste ground. At first Tim couldn't believe his eyes. There were maybe a dozen tents and caravans spread out along the lakeside. More TV vehicles had arrived. Everybody had binoculars or cameras.

'What's happening?' Jenny said, wide-eyed.

'Rubbernecks,' Bill growled. 'The kind of people who stop at traffic accidents to look for the blood.'

'Is this good?' Tim asked, wondering if this was what Uncle Doug had had in mind.

'If you like *ghouls*,' Bill said.

There were traffic cones across the front of the driveway to stop other people from parking there and Bill had to get out of the van to move them before he could drive through himself. A PRIVATE PROPERTY notice had also been put up. This was all very new and bizarre. Tim and Jenny exchanged glances.

There was a van already parked in the driveway, with ROSS FRASER GLAZIER written on the back doors – here for the kitchen window. Bill pulled up behind it and switched the engine off. He turned round to face the two of them. 'Just go inside. Take no notice of what anybody says, all right? Straight in.'

'Is everything okay?' Jenny asked.

Bill sighed; was perhaps considering not telling them. 'There's been another sighting,' he said.

Tim was amazed. 'What? Where?'

'Over on the western shore. Close to where it first appeared to Old William, as far as I can make out. I'm getting told as little as you at the minute.' He wasn't happy about it, and the strain of events was showing in his face.

Jenny asked quietly, 'Was anybody hurt?'

'No, fortunately. But nobody thought it was worth bothering to tell me until a couple of hours afterwards, so I've called for an extra Feed tomorrow – everybody knows.'

'There wasn't another earthquake, was there?'

Bill shook his head angrily. 'The Mourn doesn't need special effects. You should *know* that by now. For goodness' sake, this isn't the *movies*.' He near enough bit her head off.

Tim wondered what he was so angry about. Surely this could be seen as good news too, couldn't it? Then he wondered if it was because Bill hadn't seen the creature himself. He was the Mourner after all, and yet he'd still never set eyes on it.

'Who saw it?' he asked.

'It was some young woman from out of town. She says she tried to get a picture of it. We don't know if the picture's come out yet; we'll just have to wait and see.' He pushed open his door with a creak of metal. 'I've got to go out on the water again in case some idiot falls in. You two get yourselves inside.'

Tim took his time climbing out of the van and looking around the lake. Never in a million years had he believed he'd see something like this. It confused him. Was this good news or bad? He followed Jenny into the house, wanting to ask her opinion. For a second he almost forgot why it was all happening.

'Jenny . . . ?' But the question turned to dust in his mouth.

Anne was sitting at the kitchen table with a middle-aged couple he'd never seen before. The woman's eyes were red and obviously sore from a long day and night of tears. The man had a hand on her shoulder. He was still weeping. Next to them was Scott, stony-faced.

Tim instantly knew who these people were. Gully's parents. They were people who'd just lost their son. There was an almost physical thump in his chest as the facts of the matter hit home. Whatever was happening around the lake would never be good news for them.

Behind them, through the brand-new kitchen window, he could see the police boats trawling the deep water.

Sightings

It was headline news. Splashed across the front page in bold, black letters.

Caroline Bow: a nurse from Manchester, by chance visiting friends here in Moutonby. She'd heard about the 'kerfuffle' down at the lake and had gone along 'just to be nosy, really'. But she'd been the one to see what everybody else was talking about.

Jenny held the newspaper so that Tim was able to read it over her shoulder. 'What d'you think?'

He didn't answer, but took the paper from her so that he could read it again. He wanted to concentrate on each and every word to be absolutely certain of not missing anything. Yes, he'd read about her in another paper. Yes, he'd seen her interviewed on TV. But this particular story might have something different, something extra.

They were in room six, Jack Spicer's room, and had found the paper on the dressing table. They weren't snooping; they'd been asked by Anne to help clean the rooms. No school for either of them today. They had originally meant to go in late because of the emergency Feed Bill had called. He'd wanted them to go as soon as it was

211

over but the Head had phoned with the request that they take the day off altogether. Apparently there was not just one but a whole horde of reporters hanging around outside the school gates. Mrs Collins thought it would be far too disruptive for the other students if Jenny and Tim were to attend classes. All Bill and Anne could do was reluctantly consent. But not before putting brother and sister under strict house arrest.

They had plenty to keep them occupied, however, because Mourn Home was full. Every room was taken; it was so busy you'd be forgiven for thinking it was the height of summer. This was why Anne and Nana Dalry were doing an emergency shop at the wholesalers. The Feed earlier had been attended by what Tim reckoned was about a hundred people – a fair few of whom hadn't even been locals.

Tim looked at the photo of Caroline Bow in the newspaper. He couldn't say he remembered her being there, but then there had been so many new faces in the crowd.

Jenny was doing all the work. 'Tim?'

He shushed her. 'Just a minute.'

The nurse's description was a little different to what Jack Spicer claimed to have seen, but it was weird that she'd been at almost exactly the same spot where Old William and the schoolboys had been attacked. There was a photo of that spot – the trees crowding down to the shingle at the water's edge. There was a photo of Caroline Bow too. He studied the slightly fuzzy black and white image of her. She was youngish looking, not as old as Anne or Uncle Doug, with long, light hair. She'd obviously been posed pointing out at the lake. The expression on her face was hard to read – perhaps she looked a little embarrassed. What she didn't look was barmy.

'Do you believe her?' he asked Jenny.

She was bundling up the sheets she'd just stripped from the bed. 'Why bother to make it up?'

Good question – why? To get her picture in the paper? He reckoned there were better ways to do it, ways which didn't automatically get people calling you a *nutter*, anyway. There was a particular tone to the interview that he recognized all too well. It was insinuating, sniggering. It was the way he'd often heard people talk to his father. Why would a nurse from Manchester come all this way to make up a story?

'I think—' Tim started, but didn't get chance to say exactly what it was he thought because Jack Spicer appeared through the door. He jumped, realizing he was holding the old man's paper and immediately started apologizing. This was their first meeting since Saturday in the Dows Bridges, but Mr Spicer seemed to have other things on his mind.

'Don't bother yourselves, I'm not checking up on you. I've just come for my hat and scarf. It's too sharp for this old man out there.' He bent over the chest of drawers and had his back to them when he asked, 'What do you make of her, then? This nurse.'

Tim and Jenny exchanged glances. 'What do you mean?' Tim asked.

The old man was rummaging. 'I reckon she needs

glasses. She should know that, her being a nurse, don't you think?'

The twins remained quiet.

'Didn't you notice? She makes it sound more like a big wet wolf or something. Bit different to what *I* saw, wouldn't you say?'

Tim wasn't sure how to answer. Jenny was no help. She ducked out of the conversation by unfolding the clean sheets across the bed, busying herself.

Jack Spicer was insistent. 'I think what I saw tallies more with what we all know the Mourn to look like, don't you?' He pulled his scarf from the drawer like a magician pulling a silk handkerchief from his sleeve.

'She says she saw it at the same place Old William did.' Tim held up the paper in an attempt to show the photo. 'It's just here where the marker stone is and—'

Mr Spicer rode right over him. 'Fur on its head, she says. And a *muzzle*. It's the "dragon in the lake", not the big soggy *mutt*.' He was particularly scornful and threw his woolly scarf around his neck, yanked it tight. 'What do you think she saw?'

Tim squirmed. 'Erm . . .'

'I'm betting it *was* a dog. What're you betting, young Tim?' Then, when Tim remained stuck for an answer, the old man smiled thinly. 'Sensible lad. I would've had the shirt off your back. It was a dog, I say, and that's why her supposed photo has never been shown. The sooner she stops kidding herself the sooner she can stop kidding the rest of us. All she's doing is muddying the water. Look at it out there – bloody circus is what it is.'

He pointed out through his first-floor window at the view of the lake. Both Tim and Jenny followed his finger. Lake Mou had probably never seen anything like it. A loose necklace of people, tents, cars, TV vans and camera crews was strung from WetFun on the eastern shore all the way round the water's edge and into the woods to the west. Mourn Home was the pendant that hung in the middle of the chain. People were wrapped up against the cold but sitting on bright and stripy deckchairs, or in their parked cars pointed out at the water, or on picnic blankets, with mugs of hot tea steaming in their hands. Were they watching for the Mourn, or waiting in the hope of seeing Gully's body dredged up by the police divers? It was a circus all right. Even so, Tim thought he should be out there too.

'She should keep her mouth shut if she doesn't know what she's saying.' A vein, like a streak of lightning, appeared on the old man's forehead. 'It's just making your job harder, young Tim.' He wagged his spindly finger. 'I don't envy you and your dad.'

Tim just nodded. It seemed the safest thing to do. But he knew he should be out on the lake with his father, or patrolling the shore, or just keeping everybody out of the water. He was the Mourner in three days' time, wasn't he? And here he was making beds and emptying wastepaper baskets.

Mr Spicer nodded too, at his own supposed wisdom. Then he turned to Jenny. 'Make certain you tuck that bottom sheet in well, my dear. I can't sleep when it pulls itself out in the night.'

'I'll be sure it's done properly.'

'That's a girl.'

Tim caught the flash of resentment in Jenny's eye and guessed she believed she should also be out in the thick of it.

The old man was about to leave but he took the paper from Tim and stared at the photo. With a shake of his head he said, 'Some people, eh? Nothing better to do with their lives.' He folded the paper under his arm and disappeared out into the hallway.

Tim waited until the footsteps had receded. 'What was all that about?'

'Can't you guess?'

'Do you reckon he's jealous someone else has seen it too?'

'Well, you know how much he loved the attention he got last Saturday morning. And he is the only one who's been getting it for the last thirty years.'

'I would've thought he'd be pleased. You know, someone to prove him right.'

Jenny just shrugged. 'Who knows? But if you give me a hand we can get out of here quick in case he comes back.'

They moved along the hallway to what had been Uncle Doug's room. There were suitcases on the floor with clothes spilling out of them. The American couple, Mike and Sylvie, had moved in in a hurry, obviously just dumping their stuff before scurrying out with their camcorder's battery charged up and ready to roll.

Originally they'd planned on leaving today but everything

216

that had happened had persuaded them to stay on longer. Which would have been fine under normal circumstances, but Uncle Doug had booked all the rooms out to people from the British Geological Survey, who were here to investigate the earthquake. He was particularly keen on having them stay because he'd been able to charge them twice the normal room rate.

'Big organizations can afford more,' had been his reasoning. 'Mike and Sylvie are a lovely couple, but—'

'But they're *my* guests, Doug,' Bill had argued at breakfast. 'And I don't throw *my* guests out into the street.'

'Are you in any position to turn that kind of money down?' Doug had asked.

The thing was, Bill had been wary of allowing the BGS people rooms anyway – he'd already insisted that all journalists and TV people be refused accommodation. It wasn't until the scientists had assured him personally that they weren't here because of the Mourn, they were solely interested in the earthquake, that he'd acquiesced. Everybody agreed there *had* been an earthquake and they were here to collect data on it, not to join in the discussion of the Mourn, or give evidence for or against.

But he'd still not allowed Doug to turf Mike and Sylvie out, and in the end the only solution had been for Uncle Doug to give up his own room. He now had a sleeping bag on Tim's floor.

A room had been offered to Gully's parents but they'd decided to stay in the Travel Inn on the road out of town, away from what was now the folly of the lakeside, but still close. Scott had gone with them. When they'd told Bill last night that they would be staying in the area until Gully's body was recovered, he'd stayed quiet. Tim knew his father didn't believe the body would ever be found.

Jenny tugged the sheets Uncle Doug had slept in from the bed and set to with clean ones. 'At least we're not at school,' she said. 'I guess we should be grateful for small mercies.'

Tim bobbed his head in agreement. Life certainly seemed to be a case of spotting and extracting the good bits when you could.

'I hope Sarah's been okay. The resident arseholes all know she's the next best target after us.'

'Give her a ring later,' Tim said. 'See if she's been getting any hassle.'

'*You* ring her. She's your girlfriend.'

He nodded absently, because he was thinking whether or not he would ever get back to school himself; whether he needed to; whether or not Bill would let him.

'She still *is* your girlfriend, isn't she?' Jenny asked.

He was surprised by the tone of her voice. 'I suppose so, yeah.'

'You suppose so?'

'Well, okay then. *Of course* she's still my girlfriend.'

'It's just that I can't work the two of you out sometimes. She's idiot enough to adore you – why, I don't know – but sometimes you . . .'

'Sometimes I what?'

Jenny shook her head. 'Doesn't matter.'

'No, come on. Sometimes I what?'

'I don't know. Blow a bit hot and cold, I suppose.'

'Do I?' He raised his eyebrows at her. 'And what would you know about it?'

'She *is* my best friend. We *do* talk.'

He was paranoid now. 'Has she said something?'

'Just that things have changed. She said you seem such a different person from who she started going out with in February.'

'Well, things have been a bit weird recently, haven't they?'

Jenny shrugged. 'She says you don't laugh any more.'

He didn't know how to answer that.

'I've noticed it too. We used to always have a laugh together, but I hardly ever see you any more – even though we live in the same house. You just lock yourself away in your room all the time. You've got to admit, we don't act much like twins any more.'

Tim stared at her, a little thrown by what she was saying. He'd spent so long recently blaming Jenny for changing, but maybe he'd been doing quite a bit of his own changing too. He said: 'It's because of the Mourn and everything, isn't it? And Sarah's part of it all because of her dad.' It sounded lame and Jenny didn't look particularly impressed by the answer. But it was the only answer he had. 'I was going to leave home,' he told her. 'When I didn't think the Mourn was real I just wanted to get as far away from here as I could.'

'But you've changed your mind now?'

His first instinct was to say, *I think so*. But instead: 'Well, everything's changed now, hasn't it?'

'For you, maybe. Not necessarily for the rest of us.'

The utility room had originally been a privy years ago; now it held the industrial-size washing machine and dryer. They were kept in here because the walls were thick enough to deaden the incredible noise they made.

Jenny and Tim were stuffing the washing machine with probably far too big a load when Uncle Doug appeared at the door. 'Tim, lad; Timmo – found you. Need you for a sec – is that all right?'

Happy to get out of any more chores, he jumped at the chance. 'Yeah. Fine.'

Uncle Doug clapped him on the back. 'I knew you wouldn't let me down.'

'What's happening outside?' Jenny asked. 'Is it as bad as it looks from in here?' What she was really asking was, could she come too?

But Uncle Doug didn't seem to realize. 'You could say that. About five minutes ago we had somebody else shouting that they'd seen the Mourn.'

Jenny and Tim exchanged an almost comical look of surprise. 'Who? Where?' they said in unison.

'Just some little lad who should rightly be at school. He's only about ten or twelve so nobody's taking him seriously. Even I'm finding it tough to believe that after all this time the Mourn's decided to lose its stage fright.'

'Did it attack him?' Tim asked.

Doug shook his head. 'No, no. But it's caused a bit of fuss, if you know what I mean. So come on, Tim, lad. Got to stay ahead of the game.' He virtually dragged him away by his arm.

They left Jenny and went through to the kitchen, where Doug told him to shove his coat and shoes on – quick. 'Is everything okay? Is it Dad?'

'Your dad's fine. We're not going to disturb him.'

'Nothing's wrong?' His uncle's urgency was making him edgy.

'No, nothing to worry about. Just need you to talk to someone for me.' He had his hand in the middle of Tim's back to gee him along, but when his mobile phone trilled in his jacket pocket he dug it out to answer it. 'Yes, we're on our way . . . No, no problem . . . No, away from the house. That pub I told you about . . . Dows Bridges, that's right . . . Okay, see you in ten.'

'I'm not allowed to talk to anyone.' Tim couldn't help but feel suspicious.

Doug dropped the tiny phone back into his pocket. 'Why not?'

'Dad said so.'

'He'll be okay with this. He'll understand when I explain it to him.'

Tim wasn't being given a chance to argue as his uncle steered him out through the back door.

His eyes went straight to the water, to the two police boats. So what if the lake wasn't really a hundred miles deep? It certainly seemed vast enough to make their job impossible.

He asked, 'Dad does know, doesn't he?'

'I'm sure he'll be fine.' Doug wanted to go in the opposite direction. 'Don't you get yourself all worked up about it, but if we don't give the papers something they're not going to keep—' He shut up when he saw Bill striding towards them across the back garden. 'Ah,' he said. Or perhaps groaned. Tim wasn't sure.

'I thought I asked you to stay inside.' Bill glared at Tim. He'd only just rowed ashore; he was panting slightly, his face red and sweaty.

'I know, but Uncle Doug—'

Uncle Doug stepped between them. 'Bill, listen—'

Bill ignored him. 'Come on, Tim. You can't leave all the chores to Jenny.'

Doug said, 'I need him to talk to someone, Bill.'

And Tim realized he was in fact trapped.

'No reporters,' his father said. 'I've told you as much I don't know how many times.'

'We have to give them something,' Doug insisted. 'They're wondering why we're not talking to them, and if they get fed up they might decide to get nasty—'

'Let them get fed up. Let them get so fed up they bugger off and leave us alone.'

'We need them, Bill.'

'I don't.'

'They think you're being *aloof*. And they'll pay good money for an interview with the new Mourner. I'm talking *five figures*.'

'Funny, that. I thought you were talking *shite*.'

Tim couldn't help letting a quick, nervous laugh escape.

His dad turned on him. 'Go back inside and help your sister.'

Tim wasn't sure if this was the right time to start sticking up for himself or not. Still, he asked, 'What if I wanted to talk to them?' But he spoke so quietly the breeze almost carried his words away.

Uncle Doug heard him loud and clear, however. 'The lad's right, Bill. It's his decision, really.'

Bill's hearing aid was playing up. 'There's plenty needs doing around the house.'

'What are you going to do come Saturday?' Doug asked. 'He's the Mourner then.'

'He'll still be my *son*,' Bill growled.

'No, Bill. He'll be your *Mourner*.'

There was a stand-off between them. Tim didn't like it at all, not one bit. He didn't want to be the piggy in the middle of their argument. He agreed with what Uncle Doug was saying: he would be Mourner; in terms of the tradition he would be head of the Milmullen household and Mourn Home would be his. Yet he was appalled at the way his uncle was using that fact as a weapon against his father. Bill was angry, but there was an uncertainty in his eyes as well.

He turned his glare on Tim. 'Is this what you think too?'

'I . . . I suppose so.'

Bill turned to walk away.

Tim grabbed his arm. 'I mean, yes, I'm going to be Mourner. Like the tradition says. And if I am then I should be allowed to make some decisions, shouldn't I? I feel as though I'm being treated like a little kid today. But on Saturday I'm meant to be one hundred per cent grown up and responsible.'

Bill was watching him carefully, was listening too.

'It doesn't happen like that, does it?' Tim continued. 'Growing up? It doesn't happen overnight, just because it's my birthday. Did it for you? Did you snap your fingers and become an adult?'

'He's talking sense,' Uncle Doug said.

Both Bill and Tim ignored him. 'I want to help,' Tim said. 'I feel I *should* help.'

'You think talking to reporters and getting your face on the television is going to help?' Bill asked.

'No,' Tim admitted. 'But I could help you, out on the lake, couldn't I? You can't watch everywhere at once.'

Bill's eyes softened the tiniest amount. He breathed a long sigh through his nose.

'It's like the Mourn keeps popping its head out and you'd never know unless somebody told you. I can help you now; I don't have to wait until Saturday.'

'Yes,' Bill said quietly. He nodded, once, making the moment of thought definite in head. 'Yes, I suppose you're right, son. The bloody thing would have to be doing tricks and balancing a ball on its nose before I'd even notice.' He looked at Tim with an honest admiration and smiled.

Doug shook his head. 'For what it's worth, I think you're both making a mistake. If you talk to them they'll print what you say, but if you don't, they'll just print whatever they want. They'll have a go at you, Bill, that's for sure.'

Bill wasn't even acknowledging him any more. 'If I stay with the police divers out on the water, can you look after the shoreline?'

Tim nodded quickly. 'Yeah. Of course. No problem.' He'd never believed he could feel so good about being his father's son.

Marshal's Head

Along the western side of the lake the shoreline had at least a dozen small but oddly uniform coves or inlets – geographical quirks which, when viewed from above, gave the water's edge the toothed appearance of a cogwheel. It was a rock formation peculiar to Lake Mou. The trees spilling over the top of the surrounding hills into the valley bustled all the way down to the water, making snug, shady bays between the rocks that were the preferred haunts of the local anglers.

They each had their favourite spot (or 'swim') and were always mortified if some out-of-towner beat them to it during the high season. They'd steal a fellow's swim if they had to, if their hand was forced, and they would only ever share as a last resort. But there was one narrow cove they never used. This was the place where Old William had brought his pupils on that fateful day over three hundred years ago. It was marked by a simple stone, similar in height to the Mourn Stone, pale grey and crumbling as it stood amongst the shadows of the tall trees.

It was a pretty enough spot – easily as pretty as any of the other swims. But maybe the wood seemed denser here, the snug inlet that little bit gloomier under the trees. Maybe the lack of sunshine made the air of this particular spot feel a touch cooler. Maybe for the same reason the shaded water seemed darker somehow. Even the out-of-towners who set up for the day only stayed a few hours. Maybe they noticed there was no birdsong here. Maybe they became frustrated when the fish refused to bite. But the local anglers would all tell you that no one liked sitting all day with their back to that damn gravestone. It was a feeling that for many would be made concrete after this day's discovery.

A dog's head had washed up on the pebbly shore. It rocked back and forth gently with the lapping of the water, the wavelets turned it gently. One side of its face was missing. The flesh was torn, the muzzle broken, the eye popped like an over-ripe grape – looking for all the world like it had been bitten, chewed and spat back out.

It was mid morning as Tim made his way through the woods along the western shore. There was a thread of a footpath that sewed its way in between the trees and he followed it as long as he had a decent view of the water. Now and again it fell back too far from the shoreline, got lost in all that green and brown, and when it did he had to scramble across the rocks until he could pick it up again. His father had told him never to lose sight of the water.

It was a bright day, but cold. He could see his breath. The evergreen smell wasn't as heavy as it would be in the summer but there was little wind to stir whatever fragrance there might be. This far from Mourn Home the world seemed particularly silent.

Looking back that way he could see the sightseers, the rubbernecks, the gawpers and the *ghouls*, all still chasing shadows with their cameras along the stretch of shore from the building site for the new hotel to the edge of the woods; but he couldn't hear their constant buzz. On the Hundredwaters itself, over towards WetFun, were the boats being used by the police divers, with the speck that was the *Bonnie Claire* bobbing watchfully close by. Bill had insisted that if people were in the water he needed to be there with them and the police had eventually acquiesced. Anyone else was forbidden from taking to the lake because it would only make the divers' task all the more problematic. Which hadn't pleased Vic Stones – he knew he could fill his yachts, dinghies and pedaloes twice over right now, no matter what price he charged.

Tim stood for a minute or so watching the restless surface of the water. He was carrying a rucksack filled with feed and it was surprisingly heavy, making the back of his neck and shoulders ache. He would walk as far as the marker stone then head home again. He wouldn't say he was enjoying himself exactly, but it did feel as though he was doing something rather than nothing now. And doing something his father approved of.

Last night had been a good night. Bill and he had talked. They'd made plans for Saturday together. He hadn't realized just how lonely he'd been these past months when that barrier had been growing between them. But now he felt like his father's son again – the greatest feeling in the world.

Because it was going to happen: he was going to be

Mourner. Because he couldn't deny the Mourn's existence now, could he? He might not have seen it with his own eyes, but . . . But all this *was* proof. He couldn't abandon Moutonby to the creature. Gully had to be the last.

He watched the police boats. How long would they keep searching? he wondered. And what would he feel if they did find the body? What if the opposite proof was given: that the earthquake killed Gully?

'They won't find him,' he said aloud. And hearing it out loud made it convincing somehow.

He'd found it was important to keep convincing himself. There was still that irritating niggle at the back of his mind, reminding him how he'd felt this time last week. There was still a rational part of his mind telling him that the Mourn was impossible, but he knew the Mourn would never be a *rational* thing either. He buried the questions he had. He told himself his doubts would fade; they were leftover thoughts from how he used to think, and of course it was going to take him time to get used to his new beliefs.

He stared out at the water. The rucksack full of feed dragged his shoulders down.

It would be so good to see it, though. Because he knew doing this for the rest of his life was going to be so hard. If only he could see it with his own eyes.

He shook himself. It was no good to think like that any more. He had to be more like his father.

He climbed down off the rocks and continued through the trees. The marker stone wasn't far. He checked his watch.

He'd pay his respects to Moutonby's lost children, maybe tell them who he was, then head back.

The sound of somebody else up ahead surprised him. There was the snapping of branches and the rustle of waterproofs. He thought it might be a journalist – a reporter could have followed him. But it had been unexpectedly simple to keep out of their way. When he'd set off on his patrol earlier he'd happily strolled through the straggly crowd around Mourn Home without actually drawing a second glance. Mainly because they'd all been too busy staring at the lake, but also because hardly anyone really knew what he looked like. It was always Uncle Doug or Bill who got snapped by the photographers. Only one photo of him had appeared in the papers, a blurry image that had been blown up from a picture taken when he'd been an extra in the school production of *Bugsy Malone*. The caption underneath had read 'Can this teenager keep a whole town safe from the supernatural predator?' Jenny had agreed it was an odd thing to print underneath the picture of an eleven-year-old gangster.

He saw the fishing rod first, the slender tip bobbing among the trees; then the pale, bespectacled middle-aged man in a baseball cap and wellingtons carrying it came hurrying along the path. Tim didn't recognize him, didn't think he was local. And this assumption appeared correct because the angler didn't know who he was either.

The man was carrying a large wicker fishing basket on a thick strap over his shoulder. It banged and bumped against his back. His haste was a stumbling run in his knee-high wellies. 'No, no,' he said. 'I wouldn't go down there if I were you, sonny.' He used his rod to bar Tim's way. He spread his arms wide to usher Tim back along the footpath.

'Is everything okay?'

'It's not safe.' He took his cap off to mop his brow, and his salt-and-pepper hair was a sweaty mess underneath. 'That thing must be close by. Don't go anywhere near the water.' He looked around with wild eyes, flinched when he saw the water was only a few metres away through the trees.

Tim realized this man was genuinely frightened. 'Have you seen the Mourn?'

'As good as, I'd say. Nigh on had myself a bloody heart attack! It must be close by.'

His father had insisted Tim take his mobile with him, in case of emergencies. He surprised himself by not immediately grabbing for it. He wasn't nervous – it was more important to see the Mourn. But the man wouldn't let him pass.

'No, sonny, I can't let you go that way. It's too dangerous. Come on back this way and we'll get that Mourn man, or whatever he's called.'

'I'm his son,' Tim said. And for the first time in recent years felt proud to say it. 'I'm the new Mourner.'

The angler wasn't sure how to react to this and just stared as Tim squeezed past him on the footpath.

'What did you see?' Tim asked. 'Where were you?'

'It's near that gravestone,' the man replied. He was still looking slightly bewildered. 'You shouldn't go there. I'm not going back; I'll tell you that for nothing. Are you sure you'll be all right?'

Tim didn't answer as he hurried through the trees.

He started thinking the worst. It's one of the schoolboys, his mind told him – it's one of Old William's pupils finally washed up after three long centuries. It's Gully, his head insisted. Dead and bloated Gully. He followed the path at an awkward sprint, trying to both watch where he was going and fumble a lump of meat out of his backpack. It's the Mourn itself.

Maybe as much as two hundred metres further on he ducked through the trees to a spot he knew all too well. He'd been here many times with his father, many times alone too. The slowly crumbling, grey marker stone had so much foliage wrapped around its base it looked like it was rooted as solidly as any tree, no matter how worn its weathered surface.

He stopped by the stone, panting quickly, looking around cautiously. If it really was the Mourn he didn't want it to see him. He tried to steady his adrenaline as he crept the final few steps through the tangled undergrowth down to the water's edge.

And that was when he saw the mutilated dog's head bobbing gently against the shingle. He recognized Mrs Kirkwooding's golden retriever, Marshal, even though its fur was a matted, dirty brown.

He used his phone to contact Bill, made sure he was moving away from where the police divers were still searching and rowing in the right direction, then stepped back from the water's edge himself. He stayed a few paces away from the water but swept his eyes across the waves. The angler could be right: the Mourn could still be close by after all. He watched for any kind of suspicious movement on the surface – dark patches, ripples.

Was it a coincidence that the head had washed up here, by the marker, at the exact same spot all this had begun in 1699? Tim didn't know. Did the Mourn know? Perhaps that was the real question. Was the creature sentient enough to do something like this by design? And was it coincidental that this had happened just when Tim was having doubts again?

It was probably just his imagination getting the better of him, but he felt a cold shiver run up his spine, as though he was being watched. He scanned the water. But there was nothing to be seen.

He couldn't help feeling sorry for Marshal, even though the dog had already been dead. He remembered how he'd looked in Mrs Kirkwooding's kitchen, and then remembered standing among the Fearful on Saturday morning wondering which half of the golden retriever was in the feed sack. He supposed he knew now. It was the Mourner's job to prepare the feed sack and he wondered how long it would take him to become as immune to squeamishness as his father obviously was.

Looking out at the lake again he saw it was going to take Bill a good few minutes to reach the shore. The wind was against him. He also realized he wasn't the only one watching the *Bonnie Claire*. The journalists were good at spotting stories; it was what they were trained to do, after

233

all. So it wasn't too difficult to get the idea that only the juiciest titbit would make Bill leave his tireless vigil. The angler might easily have told his story to whoever he'd run into as well. Both observant journalists and over-excited spectators came running.

Bill barely managed to make it to shore before the circus arrived. He leaped out of the *Bonnie Claire* and waded through knee-high water. 'Couldn't you have covered it up?' was the first thing he said. 'Put it in your rucksack.'

'It's still full of feed,' Tim said, showing him the bulk of it on his back. And part of him was glad he couldn't fit that gory, stinking mess in there. The punctured eyeball stared blindly up at him, the ripped flesh around the mouth seemed to grin.

Bill tutted as though he was to blame. Then swore under his breath at the sound of snapping branches as two burly photographers pushed their way off the footpath and through the undergrowth.

Tim stood, startled, as the flashes lit up the dimness underneath the trees.

'Have you caught the monster, Mr Milmullen?'

'Don't be bloody ridiculous!' Bill spat.

The photographer didn't even flinch at his anger. 'Can we get you next to the gravestone, Mr Milmullen?' Bill chose to ignore him but the cameras flashed anyway, shattering the quiet with their brilliant white. Then one of them spotted Marshal's head. 'Is that a dog? Has your monster killed a dog, Mr Milmullen?'

'Tim,' Bill ordered. 'Get in the boat.'

'This your son, is it, Mr Milmullen? Can we get a shot of the two of you together? Old Mourner and new together.' Flash, flash. 'Maybe holding the dog's head?'

Tim's eyes flared with sparkled white and silver. He had time to realize that he wasn't going to see pictures of himself dressed as a gangster in the papers any more.

There were more people arriving, crashing along the narrow path between the trees; the tiny inlet was suddenly crowded.

Tim stepped forward. 'Please, keep back,' he said. 'Please.' He didn't know whether he was trying to help for his father's sake or for Marshal's. The cameras went off inches from his face. He couldn't understand what everybody wanted. Why they were all there.

'Is it the Mourn?' someone shouted. 'Can you see it? Where is it?'

'Is it the student? Have they found his body?'

'Can you see it?'

'It's the monster! It's the monster!'

Bill was physically pushing people away. 'There's nothing to see. What's wrong with you people?'

An elderly man with a tousle of white hair only just clinging to his scalp shoved Bill back. 'I demand to see the body. I have every right. This is history happening here.'

For a second Bill was too stunned to speak. When he managed to get his mouth working again he bellowed, 'What on earth do you want, man? His ripped and bloody T-shirt, or the stump of his leg? Get out of here, you *vulture*!'

But he couldn't hold everybody at bay. He took Tim's

arm and dragged him back to the water. He took off his cagoule and threw it over the poor dog's battered head, then picked it up and waded out to the little rowing boat with it under his arm. They clambered in, not caring about the sloshing of cold water, and Bill gave the head to Tim as he took up the oars. Tim could feel it even through the cagoule's thick, waterproof material and quickly placed it at his feet. The cameras still flashed and popped.

'Ghouls,' Bill snarled, digging in the oars, pulling hard. 'Bloody ghouls and vultures!'

Tim turned to look for the old marker stone but it was completely surrounded, lost in the fray.

Stones

Tim was upstairs when his father called for him. He'd been trying to tidy his room but it wasn't easy with Uncle Doug's gradually exploding suitcases. He found Bill sitting at the kitchen table with the phone held a little too hard against his good ear. His voice was calm but he spoke through gritted teeth, as though he'd much rather be bellowing.

'Can you spare half an hour or so this evening?' he asked.

'Yeah. If you need me.'

Bill spoke into the receiver. 'Yes. We can come now.' He kept his eyes on Tim while he listened to the reply. 'Well, you think about it. You need to speak to my son more than you do me, because it's him who's going to be running the show from Saturday.' Another pause, still watching Tim. 'Yes. We're on our way.'

He cut the call. Tim hovered, waiting.

'Get your coat on,' Bill told him, getting up.

They were about to leave when Anne came in from the driveway.

Bill was even gruff with her. 'Have you seen Doug?'

She pulled her gloves off one at a time. 'Not since breakfast.'

'If you do, tell him I want a word, will you?'

'Is everything okay?'

'Can you just tell him to stop avoiding me?' He opened the door for Tim to go first. 'We won't be long; we've been summoned to WetFun.'

'Oh.' Anne was obviously surprised. 'Are you sure everything's okay?'

'Your guess is as good as mine,' Bill said as he slammed the door behind him.

Dusk was sliding into twilight; another cold night was on its way. They walked quickly, following the shoreline. They might have been quicker rowing across, especially with the lake being so placid, but Bill never went out on the water unless it was necessary. The police had halted their search for another day because of the fading light and Tim wondered how many more days they'd keep looking. Soon some chief constable somewhere would have to make the judgement call that enough was enough. Tim couldn't help but feel thankful that it wasn't his call to make.

Most of the ghouls had also gone home, the encroaching dark and promised chill having driven them away. There were still a few persevering enough to want to keep night vigil and they stared openly as Tim and his father skirted around their little camps. They could see their breath as they walked. The fading light seemed to start at the top of the valley and lazily roll down the hills towards them, covering the trees and the far side of the lake first. The night was drawing in. It started to rain.

'What exactly does Mr Stones want?' Tim asked.

'Probably worried about losing business, at a guess. I don't know how much his hotel is costing him, but it's going to be far too expensive if he hasn't got anyone coming to fill it.'

'But all these people that are here this week to see the Mourn – I know they're not water-skiing or anything, but they'll need somewhere to stay, won't they?'

'This is just a flash in the pan. Once the papers and TV get bored of us, or a better story comes along, these people will move on too. Which is exactly what your uncle's worried about. He wants to keep people interested. He wants a proper tourist attraction, something to rival Loch Ness.' Bill sounded like he had a bad taste in his mouth. 'I was so proud of him for that book of his. He's never finished anything in his life before, and that's a real achievement – something I know I could never do. Your granddad would have been proud too. It was something for all of us. But Doug can't leave it there. He comes up with crazy schemes he hasn't got an inkling of how to follow through. He'd try and build a theme park and Hundredwaters rollercoaster given half the chance.'

'He wouldn't really, would he?'

Bill just grunted noncommittally.

'But you wouldn't let him, would you?'

'Neither will you, I hope. There may not be many of us dedicated Fearful left, but we see Mourn Home as a place of hope – a refuge. It's something time-honoured and important to us; something we can get a proper hold of in a world we all too often feel is speeding off the rails. Candy floss and cuddly toys in the shape of the Mourn; commemorative plates;

Mourn Stone keyrings – Doug's come up with them all. I feel sorry for Nessie, I really do. She's a cartoon character; a joke. The Mourn has the power to take all our lives any time it feels the whim. And I don't find that particularly funny.'

Tim didn't laugh either.

'I'm pleased you and Jenny have some of the same respect as your mother and me for what happens here. Because it's times like this when it gets to feeling like it's us against the world.' Strong words, but when he looked at Tim he smiled.

And Tim liked that thought. Standing side by side with his father against the crashing of waves, the blowing of storms, the tremor of earthquakes. It was a heck of a change from the kid who'd been desperate to escape, but right now that didn't feel like such a bad thing. Thoughts like this helped his troubling doubts fade further and further.

They stopped briefly for Bill to have a look at the building site at the edge of WetFun. He puffed his breath out in a heavy sigh. 'Bigger than I thought,' he said.

Foundations had already been laid and there had been more deliveries of materials since Tim had been here on Saturday. 'How long do you think it will take to build?' he asked.

'I'm not sure, to be honest. But I'm guessing he'll want it up and running by Easter. He's going to have to start filling it up as soon as the weather's any good.' He stroked his beard. 'Just a bit peculiar that no one was working today. I noticed when I was out on the lake, there were a couple of trucks delivering the breeze blocks and scaffolding, but not a bricklayer in sight.'

The shoreline was even emptier this evening than on Saturday morning, although Tim saw there was a boat moored at the near jetty that hadn't been there before. It was a large inflatable with an outboard motor, like a lifeboat, but with a low pod-like cockpit that looked just about big enough to shelter the driver. He was tempted to point it out to his father, but remembered just in time that he wasn't ever meant to have been here.

He followed Bill into the clubhouse and through to the bright bar. He'd heard that the earthquake had done several hundred pounds worth of damage, but even with the lingering smell of fresh paint no one would have been able to tell. Stones had been quick to make whatever repairs had been needed.

It was one big space where everybody was on display to everyone else, no little nooks or crannies to hide like in the Dows Bridges. It was a place to be seen. The fact that the walls were mostly glass made the goldfish bowl effect complete. There were big mirrors with coloured lights shining on them, splashing eye-achingly vibrant flares back into the room. The décor was mainly aspirational photos of speedboats and yachts, or glossy advertisements for flavoured vodkas and foreign beers. Tim didn't like it. It was trying too hard. And right now he reckoned it all seemed rather silly, seeing as he and Bill raised the total number of people in the room to six – and that included the owner and the young barman.

Vic Stones was sitting with the only two real customers at a table on the far side. He stood up, excusing himself,

241

and came straight over when he saw Tim and his father. He waddled around the tables, pushing chairs out of his path as he came.

'Bill, thanks for coming.' He shook Bill's hand hard, as though he was an old friend. 'And Tim? Good to meet you.' He shook Tim's hand too. He had a tough if slightly damp grip.

Vic Stones. For almost as long as he could remember this man had been the other side, the opposition, the *enemy*.

He was a large man; everything about him was obese, from the chunks of gold he wore on his fingers to the unlit cigar he had stuffed in the corner of his mouth. He pulled a chair out from the nearest table. 'Please, sit.' He wore a short-sleeved Hawaiian-style shirt, orange, untucked and voluminous. Beneath it he moved like a waterbed. 'What are you drinking?' A sharp blond goatee, sharper blue eyes.

Bill shook his head, then changed his mind. 'Actually, after the day I've had, a pint of Guinness would go down well.'

Stones nodded. 'I know the feeling. This week was the week my horoscope simply said, "Don't ask!"' He laughed wheezily at his own joke, then turned and gestured for his barman with the unlit cigar.

'Still trying to give up?' Bill asked.

'No longer trying – willpower's the thing. But I still like the taste of it on my tongue.' He ordered Bill's Guinness, a Coke for Tim and a rum and black for himself. Tim watched him carefully, knowing full well that he was the same age as his father, but thinking how desperate he was to appear younger.

Tim wasn't sure what he'd expected – not a fight, obviously – so far this seemed much more affable than he'd anticipated.

Stones shuffled in the chair to get his bulk comfortable, then cleared his throat as if to mark the opening of the conversation proper.

'They tell me they're having a tough time of it.' He gestured at the other two customers he'd been talking with. Tim recognized the two men now – scientists from the British Geological Survey who were staying at Mourn Home. 'They've been telling me that the quake's epicentre was underneath the lake bed somewhere,' Stones said. 'Which makes it difficult to do whatever it is they do. And what's worse is the police not wanting anyone in the water disturbing where they're trying to look. Seems like everybody's finding it tough to do their job these days.'

Bill simply nodded, letting Stones get to his point.

'And talking of the police, I see they've gone home empty-handed yet again. I doubt they can keep up the search for much longer. You've met the lad's parents? Nice couple; decent folk. You've got to feel for them, haven't you?'

'Yes,' Bill said. 'Yes, you do.'

'All they want is to be able to bury their son, say their goodbyes. I hope his body is found – for their sake.'

'Not for yours?'

Stones sniffed, rolled his fat cigar between his thumb and forefinger. 'I can't deny that the sooner I can get my boats back on the water the better it will be for me. But I'd like to see some of the pain taken away from those poor people. Losing a son is terrible enough – when it's a car accident, or cancer, or whatever the hell. But having someone claim he was eaten by a *monster*? That can only be a nasty twist of the knife. I'm sure they'd much rather believe it was an earthquake.'

Tim could feel a dangerous undercurrent of animosity now flowing between the two men. It had always been there, of course, but now the switch had been flipped.

'Nobody's saying it wasn't an earthquake, Vic.'

Stones shrugged his massive shoulders. 'True, I'll give you that. But you'd go so far as saying the Mourn actually caused the earthquake, no doubt?'

'It's a possibility.'

Stones made a kind of told-you-so gesture, an I-expected-nothing-less face.

The drinks arrived. Stones purposely waited for Bill to take a long swallow of his Guinness before raising his own glass and giving a hearty, 'Cheers!' Bill was immediately uncomfortable, knowing he'd been cornered to look ungenerous and petty, and mumbled an apology as he clinked glasses.

'So what're your plans to deal with this mess, Tim? I guess you'll be glad to knock your old man off the pedestal, won't you? Start getting things done your way? Not that people won't be sad to see you go, Bill. You'll be sorely missed by many, I'm sure.'

'I'm not dying, Vic.'

'Gracious, I do hope not. But Tim must be pleased to be getting his hands on the reins, eh?'

Tim couldn't help his eyes from darting to his father

then back again. 'Not really. I'll need Dad's help anyway.'

'Will you?' Stones affected a look of surprise. 'From what I hear you've got enough gumption to do things the way you want whether your dad likes it or not. So your mate Roddy tells me, anyway.'

'Roddy's not my *mate*.'

The fake surprise grew. Stones's sharp blue eyes widened. 'Oh, right, sorry. Didn't realize. You've fallen out, have you?' He spread his hands like an innocent man and changed the subject. 'But you, you're following in your father's footsteps, right? Tradition and all that. Can't knock that, can I? Very worthy. But what do you think? Do you reckon the police are going to find the body?'

Tim's eyes kept switching from Stones's face to his father's. Bill encouraged him to speak his mind by staying quiet. 'Not if the Mourn attacked him.'

'Right,' Stones nodded. 'Not if the Mourn attacked him.' He smooched his cigar. 'Is that what happened? Did the Mourn attack him, gobble him all up? That what happened, you say?'

'I suppose so.'

'You suppose so.' The way he repeated Tim's words made them sound weak. He looked out through the large plate-glass window. 'Tell me, Tim. You ever see it?'

The question surprised him. 'No,' he answered warily.

'A few people have this past week, though, haven't they? That nurse, and the little lad who was skipping school. It seems to be popping its head up all over the place. Would you like to see it, Tim?'

Tim wasn't sure he should answer.

'Seems unfair, doesn't it? Everyone else getting to see it, except you?'

Again Tim was looking at his father rather than at Stones – talking to his father, as if to convince *him*. 'I don't need to see it.'

Stones's eyes bored into him. 'Don't you?'

'No,' Tim said, shaking his head. But he got the feeling that Stones was looking so deep inside him he could see that this was a lie waiting to happen. It was like Stones had scratched at a scab and now the wound was beginning to bleed again. 'No,' he said again. Yet all of a sudden, he didn't believe himself either.

Bill said, 'I'm halfway down my pint, Vic, and I still don't know why you wanted to talk to us.'

Stones let his stare dig into Tim for a second or two longer. Tim looked down at his Coke.

'I've got a problem with today's headline,' the big man said at last. He had the tabloid rolled and tucked into the back pocket of his trousers. He spread it out on the table in front of them.

'I've seen it,' Bill said. 'And I'm not happy with it either. I'll have words with Doug about it; he spoke without my knowledge.'

'It's scaremongering, Bill. That's what it is.' He ran his large hand over the sheet to flatten the creases. '"The Mourn may kill again",' he read. 'I don't think I'm the only one in town who thinks you've gone too far this time.'

'I've said I'm going to talk to Doug—'

Stones interrupted him. 'They have a go at you as well, I see. Saying if it's your job to keep the lake safe, then where were you?' He sniffed. 'But there are a lot of people upset by it, so I've called a town meeting for tomorrow night. I'm inviting whoever's interested to come here tomorrow to talk about how we're going to handle your extravagant claims. And, I suppose, your family's position in this town in general. I wanted to talk to you today so I could warn you. I thought that was the fairest thing to do.'

'I don't need warning,' Bill said calmly enough, but his eyes were blazing.

'I thought you might want to hear what I'm going to say.'

Bill was silent.

'I'm a businessman,' Stones continued. 'Luckily my business is bringing pleasure to other people – I'm grateful for that. Through my business I'm also bringing money into this town. Who fills the market square in the summer? Who buys from the knick-knack shops? It's my customers. The people who want to hire my boats but fancy a daytrip into the town. And in case you forget, they are also who's been filling the rooms in your crumbling pile for the last few years. But that's going to change, of course, when my hotel's built.'

'It's going to be a while before it's built if your workmen keeping taking days off.'

Vic waved a hand, as if it was an irrelevance, but even Tim saw the flash of irritation in his eye. Bill caught it too.

'Is that what this is about?' he asked. He almost laughed,

slapped a hand down on the table. 'You've been stopped, haven't you? You've been caught out, for skipping proper procedures?'

'It *will* be built,' Vic said, his jaw and fist clenched. 'I admit it will take a little while longer than I would have liked, but don't you concern yourself, Bill, it will get built soon enough.'

Bill took a long, slow sip of his Guinness. 'I'll get the council to tie you up in as much red tape as I possibly can.'

'I'll look forward to the fight.'

Bill seemed a little more relaxed. 'So make your point, Vic.'

Stones rolled his cigar in his fingers, as if considering his words. 'I think this monster business is an embarrassment our town would rather forget. It makes us look like a bunch of medieval country bumpkins to the outside world. And have you ever thought of what kind of a polluted mess our lake must be? With centuries' worth of rotting animal bones lying on the bottom? Just think of all that filth flowing along the river Hurry and through the centre of our town. That dog's head this afternoon is proof of that.'

'Are you using us as practice for your speech tomorrow?' Bill asked. 'You do have a point, don't you?'

Stones locked eyes with him. 'Keep the house, Bill. I'm not going to try to evict you or your family. It's an ugly bloody thing but it is part of this town's heritage. Not just one family's, mind you, but the *whole town's*. Our parents and grandparents paid for it, didn't they? In *Monster Tax.* Turn it into a museum, that's what I say. Because that's where this nonsense should be – consigned for ever to the past.'

Bill took a gulp of his pint, motioned to Tim to finish his drink too because he was getting ready to leave.

But Tim was listening intently.

'You see, Bill, I don't think we have any need for a Mourner.' He winked at Tim. 'Sorry, lad, we only need a Mourner if there's a Mourn, and you're a bigger man than I if you believe such a creature exists.' He patted his belly, almost grinned.

Bill looked unmoved, but he was breathing heavily.

'I need proof, however. Funny that, don't you think? Ironic. I need to prove it doesn't exist, when for over three hundred years your lot have been quite happy to believe it does with no proof whatsoever.'

Bill pushed what was left of his pint aside; he wasn't even going to wait to finish it.

'So, out of my own pocket, I'm putting up the money for a scientific survey.' Stones watched both father's and son's faces closely. He preferred what he saw on Tim's so aimed most of his words at him. 'I'm sure you've seen the kind of thing at Loch Ness. I've had it at the back of my mind for a while, but Monday's events have given me fair justification, I think. And I want it done properly, by professionals.'

Tim looked over at the scientists from the BGS.

Stones sniffed, nodded. 'They know a few people, who know a few people. And a sonar survey of the lake bed will sure help them out in their research too, no doubt. They've got their own boat.'

Tim was sure he meant the inflatable. He looked at Bill, anxious about his reaction. But all his father did was push himself to his feet, ready to leave.

With an effort Stones was on his feet too. 'So we'll have definitive, scientific, once-and-for-all *proof*. Proof that there's no such thing as the Mourn.' He smiled happily. 'And then I can get my boats and customers back out on the water.'

Tim had stood up next to his father, but he wasn't ready to leave just yet. 'What if the scientists prove it *does* exist? They might find it down there.'

Stones smiled with the cigar between his teeth, his eyes glittering. 'I don't think either of us really believes they will, now, do we?'

Tim shied away from his look. But Bill stood firm. He asked calmly enough, 'You've said your piece?'

Stones sucked on his cigar as if thinking about it.

'Have you said your piece?' Bill repeated.

Stones nodded. 'For now. Yes.'

Bill reached behind his ear and made a show of putting his hearing aid back in. The fury rose red and patchy on Stones's cheeks. Tim would have laughed if he hadn't been in the middle. Bill put some money down on the table. 'For the drinks.'

'You'll have no argument left, Milmullen. Not when the scientists—'

'Oh, I make a point of not arguing with science,' Bill said. He and Tim were already halfway to the door. 'I learned a long time ago that it's far too stubborn.'

Revelations

Someone was leaving – there were two suitcases at the bottom of the stairs. Tim didn't see them until he'd almost fallen over them. His first thought was that his father was kicking the scientists out.

In the kitchen Anne and Jenny were clearing up after a busy breakfast and both were surprised to see him. 'I thought you'd already be around the lake,' Anne said.

'Why didn't you come down to help us?' Jenny wanted to know.

'Sorry. I slept in,' he lied. In fact he'd been awake since long before it got light, just lying there, thinking. 'I was up late planning my reading for tomorrow.' This was the truth, but he didn't add how unsuccessful another night with Old William's diary had been.

He was worried. Vic Stones had set off all kinds of thoughts in his head – like dominoes, each one triggered the next. It was impossible that Stones could have read his mind and known about his doubts and uncertainties, yet he'd managed to put his finger on them anyway. And it might be good news about his hotel being indefinitely delayed, but now Tim was wary of this scientific survey.

Because what if they couldn't find the Mourn? Would everybody have to stop believing?

For the umpteenth time that morning he forced everything to the back of his mind. *The nurse saw it*, he told himself. *And I saw the teeth marks in Marshal's head myself.* If he stuck to those two facts then he was sure he could convince himself to keep believing.

'Is your uncle up yet?' Anne asked.

'He went out ages ago.' Uncle Doug getting up was what had woken him. 'He didn't come home until after midnight then went again about sixish.'

'Your dad's still looking for him, that's all.'

'He was definitely around last night. He snores like a herd of buffalo.' He hoped this sounded like a good excuse for why he looked so tired. Having so little sleep this week made him feel like he was constantly trying to carry a soft but particularly heavy weight on his shoulders. He felt emotional and blurred and even filling the kettle for a cup of tea seemed beyond him this morning, as he managed to get more water down his front than anywhere else.

Anne tutted and took control, as mums do. Jenny raised her eyebrows in question, but he shook his head, not wanting to be interrogated in front of their mother. He sat down at the table and yawned like a cave.

'Looks like you could do with another couple of hours even now,' Anne said.

'Hmm.' He nodded. Then: 'Who's leaving? They left their suitcases at the bottom of the stairs. Is it the earthquake people?'

'Mr Spicer's decided to go home early,' Anne said. 'He says he doesn't like it around here now there's no peace and quiet, and I can't say I blame him.'

'He's not even staying for the Carving?'

'He seems very upset. There's a taxi coming to take him to the bus station.'

'He's gone a bit weird,' Jenny said. 'He *has*,' she defended herself against her mother's admonishing look.

'Maybe so, but we don't gossip about it in loud voices, do we?'

Jenny lowered her voice. 'He reckons everybody's lying about seeing the Mourn because they all say it looks different to what he saw. He told Dad he's not coming back until people admit he was the last true person to see it.'

Tim looked at his mother, but she was keeping a tactful silence. 'What about the earthquake people?' he asked. 'Has Dad kicked them out?'

'No,' Anne said.

'Is he going to?'

'No. I think it's Uncle Doug who wants them out now, but your dad won't have them treated any differently.'

Tim guessed Doug knew about their part in Stones's survey, but didn't understand why Bill had changed his mind. 'I thought it was Dad who was dead set against them being here in the first place.'

'He's just saying the opposite to Uncle Doug all the time,' Jenny said. 'All they do is argue nowadays.'

Anne plonked Tim's cup of tea down on the table a little too hard, slopping some dribbles over the side. 'Your father has never asked any of his guests to leave,' she said, then moved through into the guests' dining room. She had always been clever like that, Tim realized. She managed to tell the facts of the matter without giving away her own feelings.

The door hadn't even swung shut behind her before Jenny was leaning across the table.

'What happened at WetFun last night?' she whispered. 'Nobody's telling me anything.'

'Maybe Dad doesn't want anybody knowing.'

She tutted. 'Just tell me.'

He shrugged. 'Stones is organizing a hunt for the Mourn.'

'A *hunt*?'

'Like they do at Loch Ness – sonar, underwater cameras, all that kind of stuff.'

Jenny wasn't impressed. 'They won't find it.'

And this was exactly the thought that had been bothering him. 'What makes you think that?'

'Because it won't want to be found. It's kept hidden for all this time, it's not going to pop its head up and say "Hi, hello there" to someone like Vic Stones, is it?'

'Guess not.'

'Exactly.'

He drank his tea slowly. It was as though the two of them had both asked the same question, just managed to come up with completely different answers.

Anne chivvied him along when she came back through to the kitchen. 'Come on. Your father will be expecting you to be around the other side of the lake by now. He's been out there for at least an hour already.' And her words seemed to sum up so much for him – everything from his father's expectations to his own dedication.

He gulped down his tea and headed outside.

Bright sun; biting wind. He made his way across the driveway to the garage to fill his rucksack with feed. He noticed and tried to ignore the fact that there seemed to be even more 'ghouls and vultures' this morning. Lake Mou moved restlessly, looking agitated, almost as if it was unimpressed with all the attention. The police boats were there, further out towards the southern shore than they'd been before, but he couldn't see his father, and the *Bonnie Claire* was tied up at the feeding pier.

He heard raised voices from inside the garage and immediately recognized Bill and Uncle Doug arguing. Not particularly liking the sneak he seemed to be becoming these days, but too inquisitive not to listen in all the same, he lingered near the window. His first thought was that their argument would be because of the newspaper interview Doug had given, so was wholly unprepared for what he heard.

'It's not just irresponsible. It's bloody outrageous!'

'I'm trying to help, Bill. I don't understand why you can't see that.'

'How on earth did you expect me to react? Did you think I wouldn't know whether or not I'd put that dog's head in the feed sack. *I* was the unlucky bugger who had to cut the bloody thing in half in the first place.'

'I thought you'd understand what I was doing.'

'I do, Doug. I do. I understand you were trying to lie and cheat your way onto the bestseller lists by goading the papers with a couple of foolish pranks. I thought we'd stopped doing this kind of thing when we were kids.'

'No, Bill – no way. I'm not having you claim this is solely to do with my book sales. I'm trying to help the family out here, I—'

Tim was so wrapped up in his eavesdropping, and so taken aback by what he thought he was hearing about Uncle Doug and Marshal, that when someone tapped him on the shoulder he almost leaped out of his skin.

Sarah laughed, half catching him as he staggered backwards. 'Sorry. Didn't mean to make you jump.' She was wrapped up with gloves and scarf; her cheeks were a fresh, ruddy red from the cold.

Tim's cheeks had coloured as well, but because he was flustered, embarrassed. 'No, no, that's okay.' He gestured at the garage window and tried to laugh a little with her. 'You caught me spying and I thought you were my mum.'

'I don't blame you for not wanting to go inside.' She raised her eyebrows at the muffled but obviously aggressive swearing they could both hear. 'Is it your dad?'

'Yeah, and my Uncle Doug. I think he's been . . .' Although he wasn't sure how to put it, wasn't sure if he'd misinterpreted what he'd heard and jumped to conclusions.

'I need to talk to your dad, but I'm sure it can wait until later.'

Tim had lost track of the argument now; Sarah had distracted him. 'How come you're not at school?'

'I'm helping my dad organize things for tomorrow. It's weird; I've never seen him so nervous before. You know, he's really worried that you're not going to want him as your Underbearer. Apparently Cagey Brown has been telling everybody you're going to choose him instead. You do still want my dad though, don't you?'

'Well, yeah. I guess so.' The truth was, he hadn't really given it much consideration yet.

'I was thinking about what you were saying the other day, about wanting to go and see other places. I reckon if Dad was your Underbearer he'd be fine looking after things if we wanted to go away. I think he was always disappointed your dad never went on holiday more often – he never really got the chance to do his Underbearing stuff.'

Tim was half listening to her, half listening to what was going on in the garage. He nodded at her distractedly, heard the garage door open, slam closed a second later, then peeked round the corner to see his father stalking away towards the feeding pier and the *Bonnie Claire*.

'I have to talk to my uncle,' he said.

She followed him into the garage. It had been tidied up after the earthquake, tools put back on hooks, but there was still a large crack in the far concrete wall that would need mending. It ran from the ceiling to behind the large chest freezer. Doug was leaning back on the freezer, arms folded, staring at the floor. He was dressed in jeans and black leather jacket, which seemed to be *de rigueur* for most of the newspapermen Tim had seen this week too.

'Uncle Doug?'

He glanced up. 'Tim,' he said. 'How are you this morning?' His voice was completely flat and devoid of feeling. He sounded worn out. 'Oh, and Sarah. Sorry, love, didn't see you there for a second.'

'Is everything all right?' Tim asked.

'Everything being all right is what your dad and I seem to be disagreeing on at the moment.'

'I heard you talking about Marshal,' Tim said.

'Oh yes?' The name meant nothing to Doug.

'Mrs Kirkwooding's golden retriever.'

'Oh,' he said, and his expression instantly became guarded.

Tim moved further into the garage. 'What's happening? Did you put Marshal's head near the marker stone?'

Doug stood up straight. He pulled in a big breath, then let it out again – slowly – before answering. 'I did, yes. And although your dad won't believe me, I did it for the good of the family.'

Tim still wasn't sure if he was quite grasping all of this. 'Did you cut it up yourself?' The thought turned his belly, remembering the gory state of it.

Doug nodded. 'It wouldn't stand up to close examination – anybody with a magnifying glass and ten minutes of their time could probably work out the bite's not real teeth marks. But it was another way to keep the press interested in us. Your dad, however, was right. I didn't consider him knowing which bits of feed he put into the sacks.'

So the half of Marshal in the sack on Saturday had been the tail end; Doug had just dug the head out of the freezer.

Tim glanced at Sarah, needing her to share in his dumb-foundedness, and her face showed that she readily obliged.

'All I thought,' Doug continued, 'was that a dog's head would be far more dramatic for the papers to photograph than a hedgehog or crushed blackbird.'

The world felt worryingly unsteady beneath Tim. 'Is Dad going to tell the truth?'

'To be honest, I'm not sure. Do you think he should? Would you?'

Tim stood rooted to the spot. 'I . . . I don't know.'

Then he suddenly remembered something he'd overheard Bill saying about 'a *couple* of foolish pranks'. And at the same time cottoned on to something his uncle had said just a moment ago. 'Another way? You said, *Another way to keep the press interested.*'

Doug looked a little taken aback himself by Tim's real-ization. 'Did I?'

Tim's stomach felt hollow when he asked: 'Do you know the nurse from Manchester? Did you get her to make it up?'

Doug attempted a joke at first. 'When did you become Sherlock Holmes?' But maybe the look on Tim's face made him understand how difficult this actually was for his nephew. 'She's a friend, yes,' he admitted.

'So she didn't see *anything*? Did she? She lied. You asked her to lie.'

Doug stepped forward. 'Okay, Tim – so let's talk about this man to man, yes? You're sixteen tomorrow; let's talk about what you're going to do as the Mourner.'

'No, let's talk about you lying to everybody! Did you just make it all up? You couldn't have, could you?'

Doug admitted he had.

He'd almost been expecting it, but even so Tim was stunned into silence. He didn't know what to do, what to say – just stared at his uncle. At last he managed, 'But I believed her.' Even though what he really meant was that he'd forced himself to believe her. Then another thought: 'What about Gully? Did you—?'

'Of course not. No.' At least this Tim believed. 'Our problem was that everybody talked about the earthquake more than the Mourn. But I knew that if I could get just one person to see it, then more sightings would follow. The more attention something gets, the more people will want to be involved – that's the way of things. I was doing what I thought was best for everybody. I want the tradition to *survive*.'

Tim was angry. 'And it'll help sell your book too, won't it?'

Doug nodded, gave a loud sigh. 'Yes. Yes it will. But the greater payback's for the Fearful, and for *our family*. Your dad doesn't seem to see that – I don't know why not. But you must, surely. I only care about how many copies my book sells because that's more people who'll want to visit this place and keep giving their tourist pounds and pence to the *family*.'

'Dad wouldn't want it like this. It's not what he'd want.'

Doug snorted through his nose. 'And hasn't he made that abundantly clear! Look, Bill wants the family tradition to survive; he wants Mourn Home and the Mourner to have the same respect as they used to have. But money and celebrity *are* respect these days. And this is the only way to make money and keep the tradition alive.'

'But it's all a lie, isn't it?' He needed to lash out. There was a large cardboard box on the floor and he kicked it as hard as he could. 'It's just one big *lie*!'

'What do you mean?'

'Well, you obviously don't believe in the Mourn if you think you've got to do all this.' He searched his uncle's eyes, challenging him. '*Do* you believe?'

Doug considered the question for several full seconds. 'One day yes, one day no. But not completely since I was your age, I think.'

'Why not?'

'It started off with me being jealous of Bill, I suppose. I was a normal kid. How come my big brother always got all the attention? Nobody took any notice of me. So I just told myself I wasn't ever going to believe in it. Then as I got older I saw too many holes in the stories, and just didn't believe in *any* monsters any more.' He shrugged. 'And writing the bloody book didn't help. All that research just threw up more questions than it answered. But I've met plenty of sane people who are cleverer than me yet they still passionately believe in all kinds of crazy notions – and that makes me reconsider my ideas every single day.'

'And does my dad know?'

'I don't know what he thinks I feel these days. We don't talk about it. But I made sure he knew exactly how I felt when we were younger.'

'How do you mean?'

'We fought a lot about it. One day I was just that little bit too fed up with his sanctimonious claptrap and cracked him round the head with one of the oars from the *Bonnie Claire*.'

'He lost his hearing because of *you*?'

Doug nodded the tiniest amount. 'But whatever you may think of me, Tim, lad, I'm telling you honestly that what's happened this week wasn't only done for the sake of my book sales, okay?'

Tim didn't answer him – couldn't, not really. What did all this mean? How on earth was he supposed to sort his spinning head out now?

I've lost my proof, he thought.

He wanted to stay angry – because it was easy be angry. 'What do you want me to do? I don't know what to do any more. I don't know what you expect from me.'

Sarah was at his shoulder. Both he and Uncle Doug had forgotten she was there. 'Tim . . .'

He pushed her away. 'Everybody wants something from me. I just wanted to be like Dad. But I can't be, because it's all a lie. *I* really wanted to believe as much as *he* did.'

The earthquake had been the start of it. He'd thought he'd be able believe after that. But now he understood he'd just been one of the new Fearful, somebody who'd felt forced into believing. It had never been a choice. Even when he'd heard about the nurse and seen Marshal's head he'd had to keep reminding himself he believed, he'd had to bury his doubts. But now his doubts overwhelmed him. He was back at square one – as though this last week had never happened. He was as confused and lost as he'd been last Friday when Roddy had humiliated him in front of the whole school.

The anger drained, left him cold. There was an intense sadness in him too. He knew he would never again get to feel the same way with his father as he had done these last few days. He realized that now he would never be able to be what Bill wanted him to be, and he would for ever be a disappointment to him.

It was a painful realization. It broke his heart.

Doug looked surprised and concerned when Tim started crying. He took a step back and let Sarah put her arms around her boyfriend.

'Maybe I should leave the pair of you alone.' But he hesitated, perhaps wondering about Sarah's integrity – wanting to know whether she'd expose his fraudulence to the wider world. Eventually he said, 'Come find me if you need to talk. Okay, Tim? You too, Sarah. Any time.' Then with a small, uncomfortable cough he headed outside. Sunlight all too briefly lit up the garage's gloomy interior as he opened the door wide, then let it close again behind him.

All Sarah could do for Tim was hold him. 'Are you okay?'

'I don't know.' He thought he should still feel angry. He thought he should be fuming. But he just felt drained. He felt disappointed and defeated.

He noticed for the first time that the cardboard box he'd kicked had a flash of colour inside. When he pulled back the lid it was full of bunting and tangled strings of decorative flags. This was what would be strung around Mourn Home tomorrow, to celebrate his Carving. He showed it to Sarah, who smiled awkwardly.

He swallowed hard, brushed his tears aside. 'I can't do it,' he said.

'What do you mean?'

'I can't be the Mourner. You heard what my uncle said . . .'

'Maybe he's done the right thing.' She saw the argument rising in his eyes and carried on quickly. 'Maybe all he's done is help more people believe in the Mourn. And we need more people, don't we? If everyone who thinks like Vic Stones or Roddy Morgan had their way we wouldn't even have a Mourner, and there'd be no Feed. We have to have a Feed.'

'But the nurse and the dog's head were *lies*.'

'But like your uncle said, they were told for a good reason. Isn't making more people Fearful the best reason there is?'

He stared at the box full of bunting. 'I don't know.' He really hadn't expected Sarah to think like this. He was amazed at the aggressive nature of her own belief. If ever he'd felt the two of them were ill-matched as boyfriend and girlfriend, that feeling was strongest now.

'And what happened to Gully wasn't a lie, was it?' she said. 'You said you thought you'd actually summoned the Mourn.'

'I don't believe I summoned the Mourn because I don't believe there is a Mourn.' He prodded at the box with the toe of his trainers. 'I can't be the Mourner. I can't do it.'

Sarah was silent for a long time. When he looked at her he saw the way her eyes glistened with tears.

'Sarah, I—'

'Are you going to go away?'

He took a deep breath. 'I suppose I'm going to have to.'

'So we're finished, then, aren't we?'

He didn't answer, but their eyes met. She could read everything in his look. She stood very still, just wiped at her wet cheeks quickly. He stepped forward but she wouldn't accept his comfort like he'd accepted hers.

'Who's going to be the Mourner?' she asked.

Tim shrugged. 'Jenny?'

'Your dad would never let her. It's only men who are allowed to be the Mourner?'

'My dad will keep doing it then, I suppose. As long as he's able to anyway. I'm just scared what he's going to say.'

'You've left it a bit late to drop this bombshell,' she said with a strained smile.

'True. But it's not just about me. I'm scared *for* him – when Stones's survey proves there's no such thing as the Mourn.'

'Who says it will? Maybe you just want it to.'

He bowed his head, squeezed his eyes shut. When he looked at her again he said, 'I know you probably hate me right now, but whatever happens can you please not tell anyone until I've had the chance to talk to my dad first?'

She bit her lip, fighting her own tears. 'But you better tell him – you have to. I don't hate you now, but I promise

I will if you sneak off without saying anything. I'll hate you for ever if you run away.'

She walked past him to the door. The bright sunlight flooded in as she stepped outside, then seemed to evaporate as she swung the door shut again. He stayed staring at his feet. He knew she might have to hate him for ever.

Monster Boy III

It was a little before ten at night. There was decorative cloth draped over the Mourn Stone which would only be removed when Bill took a hammer and chisel to it at a little after ten the next morning. Colourful, if slightly damp, bunting hung around the garage and Mourn Home. Folding seats had been set out and filled the garden all the way down to the shore. There was even a special area just between Anne's flowerbeds for press and TV cameras, all organized by Uncle Doug. Everything was set. Everything had been arranged. But Tim had decided he wasn't going to be there.

He stood for a moment in the dark of the house's shadow and let the complete realization of what he was doing wash over him, in case he was going to change his mind. His bag seemed heavy even though it only had clothes and money stuffed inside, but his mind was made up. The last bus passed through the market place at 11.30, and although he hadn't really planned what he was going to do once he was on that bus, he knew it wouldn't stop unless he was there waiting for it.

Sarah would keep her promise; she would hate him for sneaking away in the dark. He doubted she'd be the only one. He'd resigned himself to his own cowardice by putting up barriers in his mind. Of course his feelings for his father were the hardest to ignore, the most painful – his betrayal the most difficult to reconcile.

Bill and Uncle Doug were still at Stones's meeting at WetFun. Bill hadn't wanted to go but Doug had managed to persuade him, because most of the Saturday morning regulars had said they were going. There seemed to be an uneasy peace between the two men at the moment – Bill probably undecided as to how things should be handled, wanting to get the Carving out of the way first, and then worry about it. Ideally for Tim the meeting would already be over and the water-sports club deserted, but he couldn't risk waiting any longer. Because before he went, there was something he needed to sort at WetFun. He'd just have to hope there would be enough noise from inside the clubhouse to cover what he was doing. And what he was doing, he believed, was for his father.

He didn't see how the tradition could prove itself. The scientists would trawl the lake back and forth, and like the police divers they would come up empty-handed. What would Bill do when the scientific data, the displays and read-outs and charts, all said that there was no creature anywhere in the Hundredwaters? No matter how much he played with his hearing aid he would not be able to avoid that definitive, black-and-white proof. It would snuff out what he held dearest, wouldn't it? It would be proof that his life had been lived mistakenly. It would prove his duty was a falsity.

Maybe it was guilt on Tim's behalf – he was the one who was sneaking away in the middle of the night after all – but he didn't want Bill to have to face such facts. He wanted his father to believe for ever, because Bill was the tradition, and the legend was Bill. Just because Tim couldn't believe, it didn't mean his father shouldn't. Tim wanted Bill to be able to believe for ever. Tim loved his father for everything that he was.

He stayed in the shadows a few moments more, making certain there was no one else around. As satisfied as he could be, if not quite satisfied enough, he hurried down the garden, having to thread his way between the lines of chairs, and out along the feeding pier. At the far end the *Bonnie Claire* bobbed gently on the deceptively peaceful lake. He swung his bag off his back, dug in the side pocket for the hammer and chisel he'd taken from the garage earlier and placed them in the bottom of the rowing boat. His bag, however, he left on the end of the pier, reasoning he had to return here anyway. He checked the lighted windows of the house behind him because Anne and Jenny were still up, but saw no one. Then he climbed into the boat, picked up the oars, and pointed himself in the direction of WetFun.

It was a clear night; no cloud to hide the moon or stars – or him. He had to force himself to row as quietly as he could, which forced him to row slowly. It was frustrating going. He kept dipping the oars gently, but his nerves got the better of him and he held his breath with every clumsy, audible splash. He cut straight across the lake, keeping well away from the shore, wary of the dark, silent tents even though he reckoned most people would be at the meeting.

It was an easier row than the last time he'd been out on the water, but it seemed to take him a long time to travel the short distance. He didn't row to the shore when he at last got close to WetFun, but carried on to the nearest jetty, and the boats that were moored there. He aimed for the outsized inflatable with its outboard motor and low cockpit – the boat Stones had boasted was to be used for the survey. The *Bonnie Claire* bumped gently against its tubular side and Tim tied up quickly before climbing aboard.

He forced himself to crouch down and silently wait – to watch for movement on the shore as well as calm his thumping heart. The clubhouse windows were misted over with the heat of so many damp bodies packed inside, and at the end of the jetty in the dark he felt sure he wouldn't be seen. There was a burst of muted applause and raised voices and now he didn't want the meeting to end, not yet. Just give him ten more minutes.

He didn't really know what he was looking for on the boat. There were a couple of metal boxes near the outboard motor, but they only contained life jackets. He investigated the tiny cockpit to discover it had a small hatchway door that was locked. It took him three fretfully loud but quick blows with the hammer and chisel to break in.

He hid behind the inflatable's high sides to wait again in case he'd been heard. When he was convinced he was safe, that he hadn't disturbed the meeting, he ducked inside the canopy shell. And here was what he'd been looking for.

Two laptops, one connected to a printer; instruments he guessed to be underwater microphones, or maybe even sound-wave transmitters – he didn't know, he was guessing. He did recognize a bulky underwater camera. This was the equipment the survey would use to prove the Mourn didn't exist, and therefore the equipment that would harm his father. The only thought in Tim's head was to destroy it.

Adrenaline made him rush, gave him confidence. He moved quickly now. Speed was what was important. He saw a flicker of movement out of the corner of his eye, but just thought it was the moonlight on the water.

He knew he couldn't start the motor – that was bound to bring someone running. But he had it all planned. He untied the inflatable from the jetty and re-tied its painter to the *Bonnie Claire*. Feeling his skin literally prickle with goose pimples he began to row out towards the centre of the lake. The inflatable tugged at the rope but moved surprisingly easily. He was going to sink it. Stones might bring more equipment and experts, he might have another boat they could use, but this one was going straight to the bottom where it could do no damage to his father's beliefs.

He pulled hard on the oars, facing the shore but checking over his shoulder that he was still pointed in the right direction. He was aiming right for the very heart of the lake, where it was as deep as one hundred waters. And he'd only managed seven or eight metres when he saw a shadow, movement, on the inflatable. There was someone on board.

'What do you think you're doing with our boat, Monster Boy?'

If it hadn't been for the adrenaline he was sure he would have stopped rowing, frozen up, probably dropped the oars into the water in shock. But his heart pounded hard enough to keep him going. Roddy Morgan shouted again. Tim knew he hadn't rowed far enough yet, not by a long way. He dug the oars in hard, trying to get as far from shore as he could.

He could see Roddy's black outline moving around on the inflatable. He pulled again and again at the oars with all his strength, gaining another few metres, then some more. Roddy was looking for something; his silhouette ducked in and out of the small canopy. There was a sudden flash that briefly, shockingly illuminated Tim in the rowing boat. Roddy shouted, too loud for Tim not to worry. Yet he pulled again on the oars. And again. Another camera flash lit him up for the whole world to see.

'Monster Boy!'

Tim let his arms sag; his muscles felt stretched. He glanced over his shoulder, knowing he wasn't as far out as he wanted to be, but realizing Roddy was not going to let him get any further. He slowly manoeuvred the *Bonnie Claire* back to one side of the inflatable.

There was a third blinding flash, but this time only centimetres from his face, dazzling him. His eyes watered with the brightness of it.

Roddy laughed. He loomed over the side of the boat. 'Just wanted proof it was you in case nobody believed me. You're in deep shit, Monster Freak.'

Tim blinked rapidly, desperate to clear his vision. The white spots quickly faded and he climbed back on board the inflatable, bracing himself for the fight of his life.

Roddy had the large underwater camera hanging around his neck. 'I saw you,' he said. 'I was in your garden – I was going to rip all your stupid decorations down. But when I saw you sneaking about I thought, Aye aye, what's he up to? And I followed you. You're a crap rower; I was at WetFun ages before you. I sneaked along the jetty and you kept looking right at me – you must have been blind not to see me.' He seemed especially pleased with himself.

Tim knew he'd not been looking for anyone actually on the dark jetty, though. He'd been looking beyond it to the shore and the clubhouse. He cursed himself for not being more aware, for being too hasty, too nervous.

'I had to run to get on board, but I've caught you now, haven't I, Monster Boy? What are you up to then? Doing a bit of monster hunting yourself?'

Tim didn't answer. He was panicking inside – he could feel the sharp fluttering in his chest – but there was no way he was going to admit it. He reached back into the *Bonnie Claire* for the hammer and chisel.

'I think you're running away,' Roddy said. 'I saw you had a bag full of clothes with you. I kicked it in off the pier, by the way. It was heading to the bottom last time I saw it.' He laughed – because he thought he was funny. He nodded at the tools in Tim's hands. 'I saw you breaking in too.' He spun on his heel and took a photo of the hatchway's smashed lock. 'You're up to your neck in shit, Monster Boy. You're crazier than even I thought you were.' It was a great big joke to him.

Tim glanced around, trying to gauge their distance from the shore. It still wasn't quite as far out as he'd have liked, but he had to do it now. He placed the sharp edge of the chisel against the inflatable's air-filled side and dug the sharply wedged point in.

Roddy was at last quiet. Probably confused more than anything. And Tim hammered the chisel with all his strength. But the blade just skittered away across the tough, rubbery material.

'What d'you think you're doing?' Roddy was shocked, but still confused.

Tim ignored him. He hadn't pierced the inflatable, but he could see he'd left a jagged scratch. Pushing the blade as hard as he could into the material, angling it sharper, he tried again.

There was a *pooff* and a rush of air.

'Hey! *Hey!*' Roddy wasn't impressed.

Tim knew that just one puncture wouldn't sink the boat. The tubular sides were made up of different cells, each filled with air. He guessed he might have to put a hole in them all to be completely sure.

But Roddy wasn't happy about it. He tried to grab the chisel out of Tim's hand. Tim shoved him back with all his strength, sending him sprawling on his backside. He had time to burst two more sections before Roddy was on him again, and by this time the inflatable was listing.

'What are you doing?' Roddy shouted. 'What d'you think you're doing, you mad bastard?' He snatched a mobile phone out of his pocket, but Tim knocked it flying out of his hand with one swing of the hammer. Roddy yelped, clutching at his battered fingers. He called Tim every name he could think of.

Tim ignored them all. He put another hole in the inflatable and with a rush of air the whole thing tipped precariously to one side.

Now Roddy was on him again; harder, quicker, fighting for the hammer and chisel. He hit Tim in the chest with his shoulder, slammed him backwards and down. Tim cracked his head against the outboard motor and the world fogged around him for a second. They tumbled together in the bottom of the boat, which heeled under them. Roddy cried out at the way the deck tilted unexpectedly. He staggered to his feet, trying to hold onto the side. Tim had lost the hammer but started gouging at the sides with the chisel, desperate to tear them open. It was all he could think about. *Sink it. Sink it!* The inflatable dipped so low on one side that water rushed over their feet. Roddy yelled; yelled for help. But by now they'd drifted a long way out from the shore.

The water was freezing cold. Tim realized the inflatable would never sink completely without all the separate cells being punctured, but he had to admit the boat was pretty much beyond repair. It slid away beneath his feet; water was filling up the pod-like cockpit behind him, twisting the inflatable over in a corkscrew motion as the still-inflated cells on one side tried to keep the whole thing afloat. He had to get to the *Bonnie Claire*, but he couldn't find the rope to pull it to him.

Roddy was trying to climb onto the inflatable's tubular side as it rolled underneath him. He splashed and kicked. Tim had to get on his knees in the water, feeling around for the rowing boat's painter; it was still tied to the inflatable – he didn't want the inflatable to pull the *Bonnie Claire* under. At last his numbed fingers found the rope. He yanked on it, but finally the deck of the inflatable went out from under him and he sprawled face first into the lake.

He gasped, the icy water stole his breath, but he wouldn't let go of the painter; he twisted it around his wrist. It was pitch-black even with his eyes open and the sounds from above were all but soaked up. He sank as he tried to kick, wasn't sure which way was up any more. As his mind spun he still had time to think that this was the first time he'd ever been in the Hundredwaters, and to realize he wasn't scared. At least, not of the lake itself, but because he wasn't an accomplished swimmer. He yanked down on the rope in his hands and managed to pull himself in the right direction. He'd never felt anything as intense as this cold, which was like a weight of ice forming around him. It made his legs and arms so heavy, so hard to move. He floundered, swallowed a black mouthful that made him choke. But broke the surface spluttering and kicking.

He hit his back against the *Bonnie Claire* and twisted in the dark, grabbing for it, almost tipping it. Forcing calm into his whole body, bullying his thoughts into ordering themselves, he hauled himself into the little boat.

Looking back towards WetFun he was amazed at how

far out they now were. And there was no one on the shore. No one to help them.

'Roddy!' he called. 'Roddy! Swim to me.'

Roddy was scrabbling at the slippery inflatable. 'I can't swim. *I can't fucking swim!*'

Tim took up the oars and tried to get as close to Roddy as he could, but the barely submerged inflatable blocked him. He couldn't get closer than a couple of metres, but that was still too far for Roddy.

Tim shivered violently. The freezing water was in his bones. 'You're going to have to try,' he called. He saw Roddy still had that bulky underwater camera around his neck and thought it must be dragging him down. 'Dump the camera and kick over to me.'

Roddy seemed to galvanize himself as the inflatable twisted almost completely over. He made a sort of leaping, pouncing movement but his feet slipped from under him and he splashed full length into the black water.

'Grab the oar. Get hold of the oar,' Tim shouted.

Roddy was flailing madly, his head all the way under. But by some miracle his fingers closed on the flat of the wooden blade and held on. Tim used all his strength to pull him up to the surface and drag him through the water to the rowing boat. Roddy was pale and spluttering.

'Grab the sides. Just don't tip me in.'

Roddy floundered.

'*Don't tip me in!*' Tim had to roll his weight back against the opposite gunwale or he was also going to be in the water once more.

Roddy scrabbled at the sides of the rowing boat and it lurched again. His hands and clutching fingers were everywhere at once, but he managed to get his head up. Without warning the camera around his neck flashed. A pop of light that the dark lake instantly gobbled up. Tim fell backwards. Roddy yelped and sank beneath the water again.

'Roddy! Roddy!' He held the oar over the side. The camera flashed again under the water. And again. Then Roddy burst up to the surface and managed to clamp his hands onto the *Bonnie Claire* with such a fierce grip Tim didn't think he'd ever let go. But what was more frightening was what Roddy was trying to say.

He spluttered and choked on the water. 'It bit me! It bit me!'

Tim wrestled him into the rowing boat.

Roddy had shocked tears in his eyes. 'It bit me!' The leg of his jeans was ripped and they could both see a deep gash and blood running down his shin.

Tim said, 'Let's just get to shore and get dry.' He was shuddering, his clothes feeling like they might freeze to him. He turned the little boat towards the feeding pier and rowed hard to help keep himself warm. He could see real terror in Roddy's eyes. His tears weren't from pain, but were hot from confusion, disbelief. 'You must have scraped it on the wood of the boat,' Tim said. 'You were kicking about a lot.'

Roddy watched the water, shivering, miserable, scared. 'I felt it bite me.'

Tim stayed quiet, just rowed. He kept checking over his

shoulder for Mourn Home, kept looking across at WetFun, but everything that had happened seemed to have gone unnoticed. It was amazing to him, because he'd been in the middle of it. He tried to look for the inflatable in the dark and thought he could see the silhouetted hump of the last couple of air cells that would not let it sink completely. But he knew the equipment would be ruined. Except for the camera Roddy had taken from around his neck and flung in the bottom of the boat.

Roddy was gripping his leg just above the wound with both hands, as if it would help the pain, or the confusion. Had he been attacked by the Mourn? Had he? Really?

They bumped against the feeding pier and Roddy was quick to leap out.

'Roddy. Wait.'

He didn't say a word, didn't even look back. He ran down the feeding pier. Tim was in two minds whether or not to give chase, but saw him run across the garden and head towards the town, not back to WetFun. Tim was in too much of a hurry of his own so let him go. But he realized Roddy had told the truth earlier, because his bag was nowhere to be seen. It had been thrown into the lake.

Tim climbed out of the rowing boat, but reached back for the underwater camera. He dropped it over the side into the lake as well, but not before taking out the roll of film and pushing it into his pocket.

The 13th Mourner

He still had time to get to the bus, but he needed dry clothes first. As he ran along the feeding pier he saw people emerging from the bright lights of WetFun and faintly heard their voices carry. He had to be quick before his dad came back. He sneaked into Mourn Home and was upstairs in his room before he remembered it wasn't just jeans and jumpers, but all his money had been in his bag as well.

He changed anyway, shoved his wet clothes under his bed. He was tempted to search his uncle's suitcase, but didn't think he could bring himself to be a thief on top of everything else he was being right now. He pulled more clothes from his wardrobe to fill a plastic carrier bag. Was he really going to leave home with just that? He kept checking the time. He had to move if he was going to get that bus.

Maybe Doug would understand if he took some money. Tim would pay him back the first opportunity he got. He dithered. He looked out of his window to see Bill and Doug at the water's edge by the foot of the feeding pier. Cursing himself he opened his uncle's suitcase and searched inside.

He rummaged under the clothes and in the side pockets. He found a cheque book but that was no good. He was beginning to panic. There were voices at the bottom of his stairs, then heavy footsteps coming up. He'd only just managed to get the suitcase closed and fastened again when Bill came in without knocking.

He was pale, tired. He noticed Tim's wet hair, but only said, 'Downstairs. We need to talk.'

It was probably to tell him about the meeting, Tim thought – hoped. He followed his father down to the kitchen. Roddy wouldn't have grassed him up – there hadn't really been enough time and he'd not gone in the direction of WetFun. He wondered if he'd ever find it funny that Roddy was now the one who believed. It was probably something Roddy would want to keep to himself for a long time yet.

Anne and Jenny were sitting at the table, both in their dressing gowns. Doug hovered near the back door, still in his coat. Tim was about to say hi, but then he saw his open bag, wet and dripping, on the tabletop.

'What's going on, Tim?' Bill asked. Not angry – not quite, not yet. 'I fished this out of the lake by the feeding pier not two minutes ago.'

Tim hung his head, stayed quiet. Roddy had thrown it in, but all it had done was drift ashore. He couldn't believe he'd not looked harder for it. But then he hadn't been thinking straight; he'd been in a rush, and freezing cold.

'Tim?' Anne asked.

But he shook his head.

Bill pulled soaking T-shirts and socks out of the bag. 'I want to know what's going on.'

Anne said, 'Sit down, Bill. You're making everyone nervous.' But her husband ignored her. She turned back to her son. 'You need to tell us what's going on, Tim.'

'Is it because of Sarah?' Jenny asked.

'No,' Tim said.

But Bill rounded on his daughter. 'What's that?'

Jenny gave Tim an apologetic look, as if she wished she hadn't said anything now. 'They've split up,' she said. 'They broke up earlier this morning.'

'What's that got to do with anything?' Bill growled. 'There are more important things in the world than that sort of thing.'

'Bill, please,' Anne said. 'Will you sit down and talk about this in a way that—'

'No, Anne, I won't. I've just had to spend over two hours with Vic Stones and his imbecilic cronies talking at me like *I'm* the idiot, then I come home to find my son's clothes are packed into his bag and washed up on the shore. I want to know what's going on.'

Tim stared at his hands. Cold water ran from his hair down the back of his neck.

When the telephone rang, everyone jumped.

Anne stood up, but Bill said, 'I'll get it.' Even so he let it ring three times, four, while he stared at Tim. At last he went out to the hall to answer it. The kitchen stayed silent, although Bill's voice was too indistinct through the wall to hear anything.

'You're going to have to tell us something,' Anne said to Tim.

He looked at his watch. He was never going to get that bus, so what did it matter? And with that admission he felt exhaustion flood through him.

'I agree with your father that we need to know what's been going on,' Anne said. 'I don't think there's anybody in this house who isn't concerned about you. We've all seen you've been worrying a lot recently. You know, this may be your last chance to get those worries off your chest.'

He knew she wanted to help, wasn't offering him an escape route exactly, but perhaps a way to open up. And he dearly wished it was that simple. But maybe his mum just thought it was nerves; a touch of anxiety because of the Carving, butterflies about his first public reading. He wondered if she knew how deep his misgivings ran.

The door slammed back on its hinges as Bill shouldered his way into the room again. 'What do you know about Stones's boat?' He leaned over the table towards Tim, his clenched fists on the scarred wooden surface. 'The survey boat. Do you know anything about it?'

Uncle Doug and Anne exchanged confused looks. 'What boat?' Anne said.

Bill breathed heavily through his nose. 'The survey people had a boat with a couple of thousand pounds worth of equipment on it, and it's been sunk in the lake. They thought it had just come free of its mooring, but it's been purposely wrecked.' He forced Tim to meet his eye. '*What* is going on?'

It was well beyond the point of Tim not being able to tell the truth now. He felt overwhelmed with weariness and he gave himself up to whatever consequences would follow. 'I did it for you,' he said.

'What? What did you do for me?'

'I sank the boat so they couldn't do their survey.'

The silence in the room lasted for only the briefest moment before everyone's voices erupted at once.

Tim carried on talking – they could listen if they wanted to. 'I was scared the scientists would prove the Mourn was all just a story. I thought if I sank their boat and wrecked their equipment they might not be able to do the survey. I didn't want people to think Dad was crazy any more. I didn't want that.'

Bill's voice was the loudest, so he won. 'What on earth are you telling me? Are you stupid? Look at me. *Look* at me! What were you thinking?'

Tim shook his head; couldn't explain.

'How do you think this makes you look as the new Mourner? That's going to look bloody marvellous at the next town meeting Stones decides to hold, isn't it? The thirteenth Mourner is a bloody thief and vandal!'

'I did it for you.'

'Don't be so bloody ridiculous.'

He looked at his mum and Jenny and Uncle Doug, but none of them seemed to be able to help him.

Bill paced like a grizzly bear. 'And what do you think the police are going to say? We can't have a Carving if the new Mourner's got himself banged up in jail, can we?' He smashed his fist down on the table. 'Are you *stupid*?' He didn't seem to be able to contain himself and had to storm from the room.

The rest of them seemed to suck in a fresh, much-needed breath of air when he'd gone. His furious presence had seemed to starve the kitchen of oxygen while he'd been there.

'What were you thinking, Tim?' Anne asked. Her anger wasn't as strong as the worry, the shock.

'I did it for Dad,' was all he could say. 'Dad believes, and I want him to always believe – because it's who he is, it makes him my dad.'

'Do you really think he would care what that absurd survey of Vic Stones's will show? He will believe until the day he dies, no matter what. *That's* what makes him the person he is.'

Bill strode back into the room. He dropped something down onto the table in front of Tim. It was Old William's diary. 'Show me your reading,' he said. Then when Tim didn't move he flipped the book open and pushed it towards him. 'Come on. I want to see which reading you've chosen for your Carving.'

'I haven't chosen one.'

Bill's face flamed red behind his beard, even though it seemed to be the answer he was expecting. 'I'm sick and tired of your—' He slammed his fist down next to the diary, banging it loud enough to wake not just their guests but the whole of Moutonby. 'This is a duty carried by better men than you for many years. Men that have made this house proud. I just can't seem to get it through to you how important you are going to be to this town. You don't *care* for the tradition. You don't *care* that lives depend on you.'

Tim was rocked back in his seat by his father's anger. 'I do care,' he said. 'I do. And I've tried to talk to you about how I feel, but you won't listen. You just keep shoving that book at me, over and over again.' He looked at his sister for help; she knew. But she was just as shocked as he was. Her face was white, eyes wide. And when he turned to Uncle Doug the man was staring down at the tabletop, not meeting anybody's eyes.

Anne tried to put a hand on her husband's arm but he shook her off.

'This book is what makes us a family. And if you don't care about this family then you are no son of mine.'

Tim stared at him, feeling sick inside. He couldn't have stopped the tears even if he'd tried.

Bill brought his angry face close to Tim's. '*Do you think—*?'

'Are you blind as well as deaf?' At last Uncle Doug came to the rescue. 'Can't you see the boy doesn't *want* to be the Mourner?'

Bill's rage was as free-flowing as Tim's tears. He turned it quickly on his brother.

Uncle Doug was unperturbed. 'Open your eyes – the boy's the same as me. He doesn't believe in the bloody thing.'

Bill looked as though he was being attacked from all sides.

Very quietly Jenny said, 'He told me he didn't.'

Bill actually staggered on his feet. He didn't know who to shout at, who to aim his anger at. He sat down suddenly on the nearest chair. The anger was still there, but it had been popped like an over-inflated balloon.

'I was running away because I don't believe in the Mourn,' Tim managed in a whisper. 'I'm sorry, Dad. I'm really sorry.'

Anne was next to him. 'Tim, please, think about what you're saying.'

He was shaking his head. 'I don't believe in it. I've tried to – I wanted to be like Dad. But I don't.' He wasn't sure if he could explain this to others out loud; he'd found it difficult enough for himself inside his head.

Anne had her arm around his shoulder, but she was looking at her husband. 'Bill . . .'

'Of course he believes.' He sounded a little calmer, but the veins in his forehead throbbed. 'He's my son. His Carving is tomorrow. He has to believe because he's the next Mourner.'

'You can't force him to do anything, Bill,' Doug said.

'*He is the Mourner!*' Bill exploded again. 'He has been since the day he was born.'

Tim was shaking his head; the tears ran and ran. 'I don't want to be.'

Bill tried to force Old William's diary on him. 'Read it! *Read* it! As my son, you *are* the Mourner.'

Anne took the book and came in between them. 'We are going to have to talk about this sensibly, when we've all calmed down a little, yes?' She handed the diary to Jenny, then took Tim's shoulders to make him stand. 'Let's talk this through.'

Bill strode to the opposite end of the table as if staying close to his son caused him pain. 'You are the new Mourner. There is no way around it. Your responsibility is not just to us but to all the Mourners who've gone before you.'

Tim was clutching at straws. 'Jenny believes. Let her be the Mourner.'

'Don't be ridiculous! *Read the book*. Only you can be the Mourner.'

Again Tim looked around the room for help. His eyes met Jenny's, and she held his gaze.

'I'm the Mourner now, am I?' he asked.

His mother took his arm, worried he'd make things worse.

Bill only scoffed at the question.

'So as Mourner, I get to choose my Underbearer. That's the way it goes, isn't it? Yes?' He swiped at his tears. All eyes where on him. 'And I don't want Mr Gregory. I choose Jenny. Jenny is my Underbearer.'

Bill gripped the back of a chair. 'Tim . . .' he warned.

Tim stood up slowly. 'Yes, I'll be your Mourner, and I'll have my name carved into the stone tomorrow morning, if that's what you want. But I'm not staying here. I don't want to be here.' He reached out and took the handles of his bag. 'Jenny is my Underbearer, and when I leave home tomorrow it will be her job to take over my duties.' He waited for somebody to say something, but nobody seemed to know what to say. So he left them to dwell on their own silences and went upstairs.

The Carving

Tim was sitting on the end of the feeding pier in his best suit, his feet dangling over the side. Behind him on the shore there was quite a crowd gathering for his Carving – old and new Fearful alike. In his hands he was holding a small, rolled, black cylinder. He turned it over and around between his fingers. It was the film from the underwater camera Roddy had been messing with last night.

Earlier he'd had two separate visitors to his room, both asking the same question. First had been his mother.

'Are you sure you're doing the right thing? None of us want you to leave home,' she said.

'Dad says he can't bear to be around me.'

'He needs time, that's all. Time to cool off.'

'Maybe he'll cool off quicker if I'm in London with Uncle Doug.'

Anne hadn't looked happy. 'Just so long as you know we'll miss you. And I'll look forward to the day you come home again, as our Mourner.' She saw him open his mouth to speak. 'Just let me believe you'll come home again. I'm your mother, don't forget.'

He nodded, held back the tears because it was obvious

that once he started she would too. 'You don't hate me, do you?' He knew it was a childish thing to ask, but he needed someone to reassure him in the most basic way.

'Never, never think that,' she'd said.

Tim stared at the film in his hands. She'd also told him she'd persuaded Bill to keep what the family knew about the survey boat to within the family, but that could only happen if Roddy Morgan also stayed quiet. Tim reckoned Roddy very probably would.

He remembered the flash going off three times when Roddy was in the water last night. Three pictures had been taken while he'd claimed he was being attacked by the Mourn.

Jenny had been his second visitor. She'd knocked, come into his room without asking and sat next to him on his bed.

'Are you sure?' she'd asked.

Then when he'd nodded: 'Thank you.'

There was nothing Bill could do about it. Old William had written himself that the Underbearer would take on the duties of the Mourner if for some reason the Mourner wasn't around. Richard's wife had been his Underbearer, back in 1834, so there was even a precedent for women taking the role. And Tim wasn't planning on being around much at all any more. He didn't know what he wanted from the world just yet, but he didn't think he was going to find it in Moutonby or Lake Mou.

Jenny had said, 'Your name will still be on the stone, you know.'

'It's just ticking the right boxes, though, isn't it?' he'd

told her. 'Keeping the Fearful happy by doing what the tradition says. Give them a couple of months and they'll all know you were the one who was meant to be the Mourner anyway. We both tried to summon the Mourn – maybe they'll come to believe you actually did. Especially if that's what they want to believe.'

'It's not going to solve all our problems. There will still be a WetFun hotel some day, probably another survey too.'

Tim had shrugged. 'Don't even get me started about what's going to happen if I ever have a son . . .'

They'd laughed. These would be bridges they crossed in time. For now, Tim was doing what he felt was right – for everyone.

She'd hugged him and whispered, 'Happy birthday.'

'Happy birthday,' he'd said.

He heard Uncle Doug's footsteps on the planks behind him. He knew it was time. He'd have his Carving, watch as his father engraved his name into the Mourn Stone. Then he'd announce Jenny as his Underbearer, and get ready to leave.

He stood up and brushed himself down. He looked out at the police boats still searching for Gully's body. This was the last day they were going to look – and nobody was hopeful. Tim considered the tube of film in his hand one last time. Maybe this had been what they were looking for; it might give them a few answers anyway. Those three photos could be duds – worthless shots of empty, black water, taken accidentally by Roddy as he'd panicked. Or they could show a picture of the Mourn as it had attacked him: definitive proof.

He slipped it into his pocket.

Uncle Doug was at his shoulder. 'Ready?' he asked. 'A few people are getting antsy.'

'Your publishers, or the TV people?'

'More like Mike and Sylvie. They've cancelled two flights already this week.'

Tim smiled. Then asked: 'And my dad?'

'I think he just wants to get it over with now.'

Tim knew how he felt. The cameras and reporters still made him nervous but he needed his father to know he was willing to have his picture beamed around the world, his face in all the newspapers, because he wasn't ashamed of what his family did. That wasn't the reason he was leaving.

'Has he spoken to you at all this morning?' Tim asked.

'Only to say he wants us to leave as soon as the Carving is over. He doesn't want me speaking to the Fearful; he says he'll tell them about my friend the nurse – and the dog's head palaver – when I'm already long gone.' Doug pushed his hands into his trouser pockets, rocked on his heels. 'Which I can't help feeling is probably for the best.'

'But you got what you wanted: loads of publicity for your book.'

'For my book, yes. Let's hope I also got what I wanted for the family, eh? Time will tell, I suppose.'

They stood for a moment, staring out at the lake and the valley. Tim knew he'd see this view again, he just wasn't sure when.

'It's beautiful, isn't it?' Doug said. 'A fine place to grow up.'

'Yes.' But Tim's eyes were on the water again, his gaze drifting back and forth over the restless waves.

Doug was watching him. 'You can spend the rest of your life looking if you're not careful.'

Tim didn't doubt that for a second. He saw flickers and shadows, but nothing solid.

Doug sighed. 'You know, a wise man once said, "For those who want to believe, no proof is needed. But for those who can't believe, no evidence is enough."'

Tim thought about it. He guessed he probably agreed.

He turned to follow his uncle back along the pier. But before he did he took the roll of film out of his pocket again. He'd stopped searching, he'd made his decision. His decision was not to believe.

He dropped the film into the water.

As they walked together towards the shore he asked, 'What you just told me – who was the wise man who said it?'

Uncle Doug smiled. 'Ah, well. That'd be me. It's the last line of my book.'

Creepers

Keith Gray

Derwent Drive was known as the Speed Creep. A continual chain of Dashes into the Blind. If we could make it to the end . . . we'd be the best.

We'd all heard the story about the Creeper who dropped Blind into a garden, only to discover he was standing in a dog pound. It was also the longest creep around here: twenty-five houses all in a row, no bends, no kinks. And no Creeper had ever done the lot. But Jamie and I reckoned we could do it. Jamie was the best Creeper around. He was the best buddy you could have. And he was mine.

**SHORTLISTED FOR THE GUARDIAN
CHILDREN'S FICTION AWARD**

RED FOX DEFINITIONS
978 0 099 47564 4 (from January 2007)
0 099 47564 2

Malarkey

Keith Gray

John Malarkey is the wrong person in the wrong place at the wrong time. Up to his neck in it and on the run, he's still trying to figure out why. All he knows is that Brook High is no place for a conscience, the teachers don't run this school, and he's only got twenty-four hours to prove his innocence.

PRAISE FOR MALARKEY – SHORTLISTED FOR THE GUARDIAN CHILDREN'S FICTION AWARD

'Funny, hurtful, pulsing . . . foul and grim yet warm and moral' Kevin Crossley-Holland

'Edgy . . . emotionally honest and passionate' Julia Eccleshare

' . . . grabbing the reader by the scruff of the neck . . . Tough, tender and true' *Guardian*

RED FOX DEFINITIONS

978 0 09 943944 8 (from January 2007)

0 09 943944 1

Keith Gray

'I know a place you can go'

It's a secret place hidden among the run-down buildings of the derelict dockyards. A community of young people have gathered in an old warehouse to get away from a world they don't fit in to. Through separate but interweaving narratives *Warehouse* tells the stories of three of the community's members. There's Robbie who is running away from his violent older brother; Amy, who has had her rucksack stolen and is too proud to ask her smothering family for help; and then there's Lem, an ex-drug-addict whose perceived role as leader by the other young people is too much for him to cope with.

'Keith Gray's exploration of an invisible sub-culture hits you so hard it almost hurts. It has the power and realism to grip the reader and lead you into a dark, underground world of emotional outcasts'
Damian Kelleher

RED FOX DEFINITIONS
978 0 09 941425 4 (from January 2007)
0 09 941425 2